HOLLER
Of THE
FIREFLIES

ALSO BY DAVID BARCLAY MOORE

THE STARS BENEATH OUR FEET
CARRIMEBAC, THE TOWN THAT WALKED

HOLLER
OF THE
FIREFLIES

DAVID BARCLAY MOORE

ALFRED A. KNOPF

NEW YORK

THIS IS A BORZOI BOOK PUBLISHED BY ALFRED A. KNOPF

Knopf, Borzoi Books, and the colophon are registered trademarks
of Penguin Random House LLC.

Visit us on the Web! rhcbooks.com

Educators and librarians, for a variety of teaching tools, visit us at RHTeachersLibrarians.com

Library of Congress Cataloging-in-Publication Data is available upon request.
ISBN 978-1-5247-0128-4 (trade) — ISBN 978-1-5247-0129-1 (lib. bdg.) —
ISBN 978-1-5247-0130-7 (ebook)

The text of this book is set in 11.7-point Horley Old Style MT Pro.
Interior design by Jen Valero

Printed in the United States of America
1st Printing
First Edition

For my BFF, Etefia Umana Sr.,

the Akbar to my Jeff

The roots of education are bitter, but the fruit is sweet.

-ARISTOTLE

1

MOMS HAD WARNED ME I'd get deep in trouble one day. I shoulda believed her. Today was *that* day.

I hadn't really wanted to ditch my family and ride to West Virginia. At least not until after William Dexter got stretched out on our concrete block in Brooklyn. After that happened, everything changed.

Now the bald dude with the scar kept glancing back at me from the front row of my bus. The expression on his face said he wanted to carve me up like a turkey on Thanksgiving.

I got tense and reached for my right eyelid. I always did that when I got anxious. Rubbing it, I sank down in my seat and stared out my bus window to avoid Bald Dude's insane googly gaze.

Outside on the highway, I read a sign: WELCOME TO WEST VIRGINIA: WILD AND WONDERFUL.

Some comedian had spray-painted over it: DON'T DRINK THE WATER!

They had so many trees down here. I couldn't see not one tall apartment building nowhere. Out the window, there were only green hills and sleepy trees.

For the gazillionth time since I climbed on a different bus this morning at Port Authority, I wished I hadn't left home. I missed Brooklyn already. I missed Daddy and Poppa. And even though that noisy argument me and my moms had had made me eager to leave, I actually missed her and Shireen too.

After a while, the big gray bus slowed down and rolled into a parking lot in front of an old gas station that was locked-up dark. The folding door at the front of the bus squeaked open.

"Horsewhip Hollow!" the driver yelled back.

I had arrived, finally. I stood up to exit and, of course, crazy Bald Dude with the scar stepped off right in front of me. This man, made a' muscle and fat, musta been at least two feet taller than me. I was twelve years old, but short for my age, like my daddy.

Bald Dude's skin was pale and red in spots, not smooth and cocoa brown like mine. His looked like it'd been sunburnt too many times.

The only hair he had was some brown stuff on his chin. I think it mighta been called a goatee. I was probably wrong about the name.

I did know he was built like a pro wrestler.

A beast.

"Here you go, sonny."

The driver handed me my blue suitcase and red duffel bag out on the hot parking lot. He smiled at me and then glared at crazy Bald Dude.

"I don't feel right leaving him here with you," the driver told him.

"Gimme my bag, old man," angry Bald Dude grunted. He glared at me, sideways.

"Get it yourself, boy," the driver told him.

Bald Dude sighed and reached into the luggage area on the side of the bus to snatch out an old camo duffel and a big ice cooler. I watched him check inside the cooler. Packed in the ice there were dozens of bags of Brooklyn Starr Franks. The Beast shut the lid and grunted at the bus driver like he'd expected to find some of them missing.

I glanced around the lot. Just one parked car. And that car looked empty.

In a minute, this bus was about to leave me alone here, a million miles from home, with a lunatic white man who for sure wanted to delete me.

My phone had zero bars.

I swallowed real hard.

"Dalton Spratt," the driver said to Bald Dude, pointing at him. "The operator before told me all about the commotion this morning. I'm leaving you two boys here alone. If I should hear about any more hijinks involving this young'un and you, you will wish your daddy never met your mama. Understand?"

Bald Dude Dalton frowned at him, spat onto the cracked

gray parking lot and strolled over to the grass to sit down on a curb in the shade.

"Mr. Spratt!" the driver shouted at him. "I don't chew my cabbage *twice,* yuh hear? So, listen up: If any harm befalls this here boy, the local authorities will find you and you'll be in a world a' hurt!"

Dalton just grunted again.

That did not make me feel no better.

I wiped my forehead. The sun was *beaming* down here in West Virginia. *Soooo* hot. I missed the bus's AC already, as weak as it had been.

The bus driver saluted me and took off.

Now it was just me and Dalton.

I glanced around the lot again, frowned at the empty car sitting across the way and decided to plop down under another shade tree, far away from Dalton.

There didn't seem to be nothing or nobody around. I didn't understand. I drained my water bottle and stared into the distance, at all of those mountains.

I felt like I had landed on an alien world.

Maybe I had.

Bezzzzzzzzzzzzzz!

Some fly buzzed. Their tiny wings beat and make that noise.

Black and green, it settled on my hand. I watched this bug and thought of Poppa George. He compared people to flies: irritating and distracting.

"Boy," Dalton called out, "don't you know the Lord hates a snitch?"

Now here *he* went buzzing.

I glanced over. Dalton stared toward the mountains. Then he jerked his head at me.

"Cockeyed little pig," he called out.

My eye stared crossways, but I wasn't that fat.

"You gonna make me use my fists," he said.

Dalton spat again, and stood, stretching on the way up. I clenched onto my luggage harder and glanced around again. No place to run. Only this dusty parking lot and an empty highway and train tracks.

Deserted.

I covered my bad eye with my hand and scrunched my face. I heard Dalton crack his back.

I was gonna die here.

Dalton delivered a nasty grin and stomped toward me.

I never shoulda left Brooklyn. Back home was still safer than out here in West Virginia.

2

JUST YESTERDAY, I HAD BEEN safe back home in Bushwick.

Brooklyn.

New York City.

Well, *kinda* safe.

Me, my father, my mother and my little sis had got caught up in a street fight. It was nuts. In the twelve years I been alive, I had never seen nothing like that.

It all went down on Knickerbocker Avenue in Bushwick, right in front of the police station there. An army of us had shown up to protest that the police had shot an unarmed Black man on my family's block.

He lived in the Bushwick Houses projects, a few streets over. His name: William Dexter. And the police had killed him for resisting arrest.

The week before that, the cops had busted down the door of some old Spanish lady in Hope Gardens and gave her a heart attack, she had been so agitated. The NYPD had accidentally thought her home belonged to a crook. The police broke into the wrong apartment on the wrong floor and almost scared her to death.

The old lady was laid up in the hospital now, and folks in the hood were hot because of her and how they did William Dexter.

The angriest had to have been my moms. She got me and the rest of my family out there two nights ago, protesting police brutality.

That demonstration had started off quiet enough.

We all held candles in front of the police station.

We sang.

After that, some local minister spoke and preached and then let some of Dexter's family speak. They tried to get Dexter's widow to say words, but she couldn't.

She didn't cry at all; just stood there, like a zombie.

I felt so sorry for her.

And then, somebody started screaming on these cops who had tried to enter the police station through some barricades. One of the protesters—this dude named Cappy— shoved one of the cops and took him down on the sidewalk, jujitsu-style.

All these other cops piled onto them two, trying to drag Cappy off of the first cop. Two more protesters jumped into the jumble, tangling with the police. Our neighbor Antonio was in the mix. One of the cops nearby drew her gun and that was when most of the crowd bolted.

Like, a *wave* of black and brown and white bodies crashed into me. They forced my sister Shireen into my chest. I felt my mother's long fingernails dig into my arm and heard my father curse.

"Niecey!" he yelled. "Over here!"

"Charles!" she shouted at him. "Get the kids!"

Ma's nails felt like they dug a hole in my arm. She pulled me toward her, and I grabbed on to my little sister. The crowd running away from the wrestling and the gun had started to lift me off my feet.

$x = 0$

"Mommy!" Shireen yelled.

"Javari!" Daddy shouted at me. "Hold on to your sister!"

I tried, but it was hard.

I felt like my arm was about to get torn away. My mother huddled around me and Shireen until Daddy pushed his way to us, and we all fell onto the ground beside a parked ConEd truck.

Ma let go of my arm and squashed Shireen and me closer. My father sat on the asphalt and cursed again.

Shireen was about to say something when we all heard a voice over a loudspeaker: "Disperse! Everyone, leave this area! This is now a police-controlled active scene! Everyone, clear out! You will be arrested!"

3

MY MOMS'S NAILS HAD CUT into my arm, but not as deep as I thought. I had told her she needed to cut her nails closer. But she never listened to me. Maybe 'cause I never listen to her.

Rubbing my arm, I walked along Knickerbocker Av', behind the rest of my family. It was hot and I was tired. The pavement was still warm even though it was night.

In the street, my mother and Shireen led the way, followed by Daddy and me. We all walked slow, dazed and crumpled from everything that had just happened.

I stepped onto the sidewalk. Let them walk in the street.

Just then, this white dude came out of one of those new rich apartment buildings. It was night, but he wore sunglasses and a long pink T-shirt almost like a dress. He sat this tiny little dog down on the sidewalk and tapped his foot, waiting.

I walked right by him.

Neither one of us met eyes and we didn't say nothing. Instead, I stooped to pet his dog.

Bushwick was still the same from when I was a kid, but also different. Basically, white people had moved in now. It didn't used to be like that.

Was the Shwick still even for plain ol' regular folks?

Brick.

Concrete.

Red.

Brown.

Gray.

A lot of the places where families like mine lived were two- or three-story town houses. And a lot lived in old apartment buildings. Some of these were small. Others were seven stories tall.

We had some projects too, or public housing. Those were taller.

We also had more graffiti here than other parts of BK. I always liked to see graffiti or bright murals painted around . . . storefronts . . . the sides of buildings. . . .

Grafs were beautiful.

Plus, they told stories. I liked being reminded of things that happened in and that only belonged to my pocket hood.

Bushwick wasn't more than maybe three square miles, but it felt bigger. People around here acted like they were super-sized dinners, though we were mostly regular meals. Something about these blocks that swelled your head.

I wanted to do different.

Back on the street, out of nowhere, my mother shouted

out a curse word. I didn't know who she was talking to. We all ignored her and kept walking.

Like I said, I wanted to do different.

I never missed a day of school and I loved mathematics and the sciences. In those I got all Es and a G sometimes. I sucked at English but succeeded in anything STEM.

Science.

Technology.

Engineering.

Mathematics.

"The problem is," Ma started again, "cops think they can do any friggin' thing they want."

My father shook his head like he couldn't believe it either. Shireen stared straight-on.

In school it was easy for me to picture numbers and equations in my brain. They were real and sturdy. In mathematics you could graph any equation or inequality with a good solid pencil and some paper.

$$-(-a) = a$$

I was great with inequalities and equations. Language arts and reading for me were less set: harder to grasp.

A cop car nearby flashed its lights, sirens. Tore off in the other direction.

I figured one day I would start my own development company. I had already learned some code. I loved to design too.

We were almost back home.

I was glad.

Still angry about William Dexter and how the protest ended, my mother continued to shout, "That brotha was walking down our own block—like we are now—and cops just shot him! For nothing! Shot him dead for nothing."

I watched her brush her long braids out of her face.

"What's to stop them cops from rolling up on us right now and shooting us all dead?" Ma asked. She jerked toward Daddy for an answer.

"No sense in getting worked up now," he said without looking at her.

"Who's to stop 'em, Charles?" she asked him again.

I spoke: "If the cops were to roll up on us right now, and asked me to stop, I know I would do what they say."

Moms froze in the middle of the street.

"Ain't that logical?" I added. "I mean, why'd Dexter run?"

William Dexter had resisted arrest, I knew. The cops had stopped him to grill him, and he jetted. They said that when they caught him, he tried to pick their gun, so they shot him.

$x = x$

My mother's eyes glared at me. "You think those pigs use logic, Javari?" she yelled. "These white folks care more about their freakin' *dogs* than they do about you!"

"Calm down, Deniece," Daddy told her.

"Mommy, please calm down," Shireen said.

"All cops ain't white, Ma," I said. "The Black ones shoot Black people too."

She shook her head at me. "Did you see what they did to that man in Ohio? He laid facedown on the floor, and they still shot him."

"Terrible." Daddy shook his head. "They don't see us as human."

"Why would you shoot another human being who was facedown on the concrete?" Ma asked. "No decent human being would do that. I'm disappointed my own son don't know no better."

"Deniece . . . ," Daddy said.

"What did I tell you, Charles?" she said, sticking her key into the front door of our crib. "This comes from him spending too much time around George. Makes me feel like we raised the wrong son."

Here we go again. I felt a knot tighten inside my chest.

Nobody said nothing else until we'd climbed the two flights of stairs to our apartment. On our door somebody had taped some papers. Ma stood there, staring at them.

"Charles?" she said to my father, who snatched off the papers and read them to himself.

I could see written at the top of one page: NEW YORK LEASE TERMINATION LETTER.

My father quickly folded them up before I could read any more.

$x = -1$

4

SINCE BEFORE I WAS BORN, our family had lived in the third-floor apartment of our three-story town house in Bushwick. It's just me, Ma, Daddy, my doofus sister Shireen and Poppa George.

Four bedrooms.

Now, my poppa can't leave his room.

He used to stay here together with my grandmother when she lived, and he was a porter on the trains for Amtrak. But my grandmother died before I was born, so I didn't know her.

I did know my grandfolks raised my father here. After my grandmother died and Daddy went off to college, Poppa George stayed.

My grandfather told me our neighborhood used to be all German and Sicilian way back in the day, before the Black and Puerto Rican people moved in. Most of the time I had lived in Bushwick, my neighbors had been brown and Black.

But they started to complain when these new whites came.

The old Blacks and browns said that after the new whites moved in, our rents shot up. And that was pushing us poor ones out.

Today, the new whites, I think, had more *interesting* lives than me and my family. It looked like they did more *interesting* things.

This one white lady who now lives on our block told me she was a writer. She wrote books and they were in the library and in real bookstores. Nobody in my family had ever done nothing like that.

My father worked at a hardware store and my mother was a home health aide. They both had regular jobs. Like I said, Poppa George used to be a train porter, but nowadays he just laid up in his bedroom.

He had bad lungs.

Ma says, the older and sicker Poppa gets, the more mean he is.

I don't know. . . .

I love him. He's my granddaddy.

And he's smart.

I kept thinking about that letter on the door. . . .

After coming home from the protest, I kicked off my sneakers inside my bedroom. I stared at the empty blue suitcase on my bed and sighed.

I had put off packing till the last minute, thinking my

trip might get canceled. . . . I wondered if Poppa was still awake.

Without knocking (I never banged on my poppa's door), I twisted the doorknob and stepped into Poppa George's bedroom. Eyes shut, he sat in his chair beside his radio, listening to some old tunes.

I knew from experience this music was John Coltrane, a dead jazz musician that my grandfather loved. Poppa vibed with jazz like young ballas do with hip-hop.

Clark Terry, I knew because of him.

Ms. Ella Fitzgerald?

A dude named Monk.

Everybody Poppa George loved was dead or old.

Except me.

I knew Poppa loved me. I wasn't sure if he loved my father, as much as they argued all the time. Poppa George called Daddy irresponsible. He was still mad about my father dropping out of college, not finishing his degree. Poppa always criticized Daddy's job at the hardware store, saying he could do better in life for us.

I sunk down on his bed, staring at him. It always smelled in his bedroom. Like pee. It bothered me when I was little, but I got used to it.

Next to the radio on his dresser sat a bunch of old photos in frames. My daddy when he was my age. My parents on their wedding day. Me in diapers.

My favorite was the one of my grandparents when they were young.

Real young.

My grandmama was beautiful. In the picture, they're at Coney Island, sitting in the sand, smiling and happy.

Frowning, Poppa finally opened his eyes. He switched off his radio, which meant he was ready to talk. My granddaddy never spoke when his jazz played. Considered talking over jazz disrespectful.

That's another thing I learned from him.

"Well?" Poppa George said.

I shrugged my shoulders.

He went on, "I was concerned. They said on the news a riot broke out at the police station?"

I nodded. "Nuts."

He stared at me. His eyes were all clouded over like somebody had poured milk into them. However Poppa stared at you, he seemed mad.

And he probably was mad at you because he was always mad at everybody and mad about everything. Because of this, my mother did her best to avoid spending her free time around him. But every day she had to empty his toilet, clean up after him and cook his food before going to her real job.

My folks and Poppa George just didn't think the same.

He asked, "Did your mama instigate the riot?"

I laughed. "Poppa, no! She didn't start nothing!"

I could tell he suspected I was making up a story. "That doofus father of yours lets her flap her gums too much. Now, your grandmama, she was a *lady*."

"It was these dudes," I told him. "I think Cappy and

that dude Tonio. They jumped some cops, and everything exploded." I laid back on his bed.

"Ig'nant Negroes," I heard Poppa say. "Always starting something they can't finish."

The way Poppa talked about other Black people, you would sometimes think that he wasn't Black himself. Another reason Ma couldn't stand to be around him.

I sat up. "It wasn't just Blacks," I said. "There were whites there too. The new white folks that live around here now. They was as angry as anybody."

"They *were* as angry," he said, correcting me. He always did that, even though I knew he'd only graduated from middle school.

I knew how to speak good English. I just didn't feel like speaking it all the time.

Poppa George tried to talk some more but coughed. After he calmed down, he leaned forward and told me, "You think living amongst all these new white folks makes *you* something?"

I frowned at him.

He said, "Every day you come home, come up here and tell me about all these fancy crackers moving into our neighborhood."

"No, I don't. . . ."

"You're nothing to them, Javari. They ain't your friends. You're gifted at math, boy. That is how you'll get ahead in this world. Focus on your gift."

5

"YO, I'M TELLING YOU, 'Von, they just did *not* care,"
I said again. "They just started piling on top of that cop.
Right in front of the police station and the other cops!"

I switched my phone to my other shoulder and tried to
make room for another T-shirt inside my duffel bag.

"They all wound up in a big ball on the ground," I said
into my phone. "And the female cop pulled her gun, and
everybody started running. Nuts! I'm pretty sure Cappy
and his crew set it off."

I tried zipping up my bag. The zipper got stuck. I listened to Ke'Von for a second.

"No," I answered. "We got into the argument after that.
Said she thought they'd done a bad job raising me. Just because I ask questions, I guess."

I yanked the zipper backward and then forward. The
bag closed. I sat down on my bed.

"Well, that ain't what I meant," I said into the phone.
"I'm just asking, if you know that cops like to shoot dudes,
why are you even gonna *try* to give them problems?"

19

Somebody knocked on my bedroom door.

"Right?" I said. "Just do what they say," and then I shouted, "Come in!"

Daddy stepped inside and slapped hands with me. For a while, he stood there beside me in my bedroom, listening to my phone convo with Ke'Von, until he suddenly yoinked my phone.

"Bye, Ke'Von!" Daddy yelled into the phone, and then held it up to my face. "Say *adios* to your *amigo*," he told me.

"What?" I said.

"He'll rap when he's back from camp," Daddy said into the phone, and hung up. He tossed the phone onto my bed and sat down across from me in a chair. Daddy pointed for me to sit.

I did.

"You ready?" he asked.

I shrugged.

"Nervous?" he asked.

I shrugged again. "I'm cool."

Daddy just nodded, staring at me. I felt weird.

I went on, "I had been worried about West Virginia, but *now* I'm really looking forward to leaving here."

He chuckled. "You and your mother. Fight like gang rivals. Crips and Bloods."

"I'm serious, Daddy. She always on me. Why she be on me so much?"

My father stood up and stroked his beard. This year, he'd started growing gray hairs in it. I rolled up another undershirt and stuffed it in my blue suitcase while he paced around.

"Your mother's just worried, Jay," he said. "You know how it is out there. She's afraid you might wind up like William Dexter. Or the rest of 'em . . ."

"Yeah."

"You smart. Smarter than me or your mother. Probably Shireen too, but don't tell her that."

I looked down.

"You always was different," he said. "And quiet. A gentle boy."

"Shy," I said.

"Yeah," he said. "Yeah, you were." He stepped up to me, then went on, "Sometimes I wonder if you feel you're good enough, you know, like maybe you put yourself down."

"I *don't*."

"You ain't still self-conscious of your eye, is you?" he asked.

Without thinking, my hand went up to cover my right eye. I pulled my hand away as soon as I realized. In my mind, I could see my own eye, looking away crooked to one side.

Daddy said, "When I was older than you and I went away to college, I remember feeling that way—not good enough. I used to feel like the dimmest lightbulb in the box."

"You the sharpest man I know, Daddy," I said.

He smiled. "Not according to your gramps. He says I'm a doofus."

"Poppa thinks that about *everybody*," I said.

"I work with my *hands*, Jay," he said. "I want you to work with your *mind*." He brushed my right eyelid with his finger. His hands always felt rough. "Do better than me," he said.

"I will," I said. "It's just camp."

"It's an *opportunity*, Javari. Remember, you a black diamond, son. *Rare. Strong.*"

"Sometimes," I said, "I don't like meeting new people."

He grinned. "I know."

The rocking back and forth made me feel like a baby in a crib.

At first, every time I fell asleep, Ma would tell me to wake up. And if I didn't, she'd poke my ribs until I did. She stopped doing this after I heard my father tell her to stop.

She never appreciated me sleeping on the subway. Said that people would rob you or do something worse. Said it would get me deep in trouble one day.

But this early morning, I didn't care if I fell asleep there. I'd just gone to bed when I had to wake up a couple hours later. I had my mother and father sitting beside me in this subway car. If they let somebody murder me, they were bad parents.

Ma was still steamed at what I'd said the night before,

after the stampede, I could tell. I didn't care no more. Pretty soon I'd be rid of her.

Well, for at least fourteen days.

Since they both thought I was 'sleep, Ma and Daddy chatted about those lease papers somebody stuck to our door. Our lease let us stay in the apartment we rented, our home.

Turns out, my parents owed our landlord a dumpster full of money for old rent. The landlord was suing us and wanted to throw us out on the streets.

"You know what that's about," Daddy said.

"Yeah," Ma said.

"All these rich folks moving onto the block, he knows he can collect higher rent from new tenants. . . . Wanna ask Mel?"

"*Never*. We'll come up with the money somehow, baby. We *got* to."

Hearing this, I tried to drift back to sleep but couldn't. I kept thinking about how worried their voices sounded. And that made *me* worried.

Even though she'd still been acting mad, I could now tell Ma was getting into her feelings.

She reached down and tugged on the money belt she had duct-taped around my waist back in Bushwick. My mother had taped together the buckle of a fanny pack. I guess to make it harder for somebody to snatch it off of my dead body after they'd slayed me for my hidden stash of cash inside.

With the buckle taped up, I had to wriggle the whole fanny pack down my waist and thighs like underwear or something just to get it off. I didn't know where Ma got her ideas sometimes.

We had a whole other big argument about me not wanting to wear it until she said that if I didn't wear it, she would cancel my trip. So, I did what she said.

"Javari?" she said. "You listening to me?"

"Yes," I lied. I didn't know what she had just been talking about.

Daddy looked up at the ceiling of the garage. We all stood inside the Port Authority Bus Terminal in Manhattan. He was looking at its ceiling so intense, like an architect trying to figure out what the blueprints looked like.

The bus driver had started up my bus's engine. Passengers were getting on. I wanted to make sure I got a good seat. It would be a long ride.

"Well, you look like you were staring off into space . . . ," Moms told me.

"*Deniece,*" Daddy said, still studying the ceiling.

I covered my funny eye for a minute, like I always do when somebody says I'm staring.

Ma pulled my hand down and got up in my face. "Remember to call us from Pittsburgh after you switch buses," she said. "That's crucial. Remember, you change buses in Pittsburgh and again in Morgantown."

I nodded, more than ready to hop on this bus and leave my troubles behind.

"Don't worry, *Mama!*" the bus driver shouted, and slapped her shoulder.

She pulled away; Ma sometimes had the same problems I had, dealing with people.

"I'll remind him where to switch," the bus driver said. "We'll take care of Junior."

Ma smiled all weak at the driver. She hugged me tight and whispered something into my hair, but I couldn't hear what she said. Daddy bumped my fist goodbye and I jumped on the bus.

"Don't you sleep on that bus!" Ma yelled after me. "Watch yourself, Javari!"

From up high inside the tall gray bus, I watched my two parents standing inside Port Authority Bus Terminal get smaller and smaller until we turned a corner. I looked at my Brokelyn Wireless phone.

5:33 a.m.

Inside the bus station, it was so dark. Outside it was sunny already, I knew. Too early to be awake on summer break.

I yawned.

I sat back in my seat and suddenly wondered if maybe I had just done something very wrong. It had been my uncle's idea to apply to the summer STEM camp at Appalachian

Ridge Christian College. Back then, I didn't expect to get in, but I did. And then everybody got excited, so I felt like I had to go along.

Daddy said I could have fun doing mathematics and science and coding. And that part sounded good. But now, now, it all seemed like a bad idea.

I didn't even like meeting new people. Not really. It took me a long time to get used to anybody. I wondered if the driver would let me off before we left this bus station. . . .

But then, the bus rolled out of the dark and into the bright morning sunlight. I squinted. The world looked clear.

No doubt.

I covered my tired eyes from the brightness.

I felt them hang heavy. . . .

It was dark.

And then this loudness woke me out of a dream.

It was sunny.

Somebody was shouting. Somebody *else* was yelling. Waking up in my bus seat, I suddenly knew that all the noise was about me.

"Aw, get outta here!" some man shouted from the seat behind me. "What did you see, you blind ol' dog!"

"I seen enough!" another man shouted back. Then, he started shaking me. "Kid! Kid! Wake up! Wake up! You getting robbed!"

6

"SHUT YOUR MOUTH!" the man behind me yelled at the one who told me I was getting ganked.

"What's all the ruckus back there?" the bus driver asked over a speaker, and then I felt the bus slow down and turn off the highway. I glanced outside and only saw green bushes and trees in the sunlight.

I wiped my eyes. The bus had stopped.

"Whahappened?" I asked the man who'd warned me.

This dude sucked his teeth, stood up and stomped toward the front of the bus. He stood there awhile yapping at the driver.

I turned around to see the other angry dude, glaring at me. He was a swole-looking white man with a bald head and one of them goatees, or whatever. And a scar across his forehead. He looked really pissed.

The bus driver made it back to us, with the first man standing behind him.

"What's all this ruckus about?" the driver asked Bald Dude with the scar.

"*Really?*" Bald Dude said. "All this over a backpack?" He grinned and looked away.

"There it is!" the first guy shouted. He pointed to the floor beside my seat. I looked down and saw my backpack there. The zipper was open.

"The kid's backpack fell off his lap," Bald Dude said. "I picked it up for him."

"Picked it up?" the guy who snitched shouted. "Ha!" He looked at the bus driver. "Baldy was a-going through the pocket! Ha!"

The bus driver stared at Bald Dude, then at me. "What happened?" he asked me. I felt Bald Dude's eyes burn the back of my bean.

"When I fell asleep, my backpack was in my lap," I told the driver. "When I woke up to them shouting—I don't know how it got—" I picked it up and looked inside. "I think everything's here."

The bus driver's eyes went back and forth between me and Bald Dude until he finally made him switch seats with this lady in the front of the bus. At first, Bald Dude complained, but the driver told him it was either that or: "I kin leave you by this mall outside Pittsburgh, if you'd prefer that."

Bald Dude huffed and changed seats, giving me the stank eye the whole time. I sighed, feeling more at peace with him apart from me. I checked my backpack again, to make sure, and felt my money belt, then caught something fly by outside my window.

A horse.

A pretty brown one, running behind a fence beside the highway. The bus left it behind, but I could see another tan-speckled horse just standing there on the other side of another fence.

I wondered if that was the brown one's girlfriend. Soon it was gone too. Now I could see all kinds of new stuff out my window. We had really come a long way.

There were green trees and wide fields. Every now and then I spotted a house, like a big farmhouse, out sitting all alone in the middle of these open green-and-gold fields.

Just then, I smelled something awful. A stink spread throughout the whole bus. I gagged, hiding my nose in my T-shirt.

This Mexican lady sitting across the aisle giggled at me. I scrunched up my face at her. "Did somebody use the bathroom in here?" I asked her.

"Bathroom?" she asked. "Ah, no . . . *el zorillo*," she said, pointing out her window. "*Eh.* Somebody run over the *skunk* outside."

Oh, man.

Skunks really did smell like skunks!

That funk stuck around for miles.

2:04 p.m.

My phone had no bars.

After eating a hamburger at the bus stop in Morgan-town, West Virginia, I had tried again to use my phone to call Daddy, but I couldn't get any signal. Probably the fault of my jacked-up phone company.

Brokelyn Wireless.

It was crazy cheap, so they probably didn't provide a signal outside of the big cities. When we transferred buses in Pittsburgh was the last time I had a good signal.

I was far away from NYC now. I still had at least three more hours of travel to go.

Waiting for my next bus transfer to roll up, I wandered the stop.

I found this shop that sold the biggest, greasiest dough-nuts I had ever seen. It took me a few minutes to squeeze the dollars out of my homemade money belt, duct-taped around my waist.

I was embarrassed for taking so long. The cashier and other customers behind me in line didn't say anything, though. One of them waiting was Bald Dude from the bus.

He'd seen me dig in my belt for cash.

I ignored him and walked around the bus stop some more. I was glad I'd be changing buses again and leave that bum behind. I didn't like how he was eyeballing me.

Biting into my doughnut, I continued to stroll, but there really wasn't anything to see besides a crowd of people wait-ing. I did find a pretty stray dog wandering around there, begging. She looked miserable. Something about strays always got in my heart. I fed the skinny dog most of my doughnut and patted her head.

If I coulda taken her on my bus, I would have.

At last, my third bus of the day arrived at the stop. Final time I had to change. This new bus would take me to camp.

Before I could climb on, I saw Bald Dude leaning against a pole, chewing some gum. He eyed me eating the last of my doughnut.

"That's the *last* thing you need," he said to me, and grinned.

This rat-face was talking about my weight. He spat out his gum. It almost tagged my kicks.

I stopped. "Yo, you better watch where you spit!" I told him.

"You talking to me, Crook Eye? I cain't tell which way you looking, slaunchwise."

"Trash spitting out trash," I told him, and climbed up into the new bus.

Just before we left the bus stop, Bald Dude tripped up the steps into my bus. I leaned my head back against my seat and groaned. He started toward the back, toward me.

Someone else climbed on the bus in the front. It was my old bus driver, from the previous route. He leaned over and buzzed into the ear of the new driver, who jumped up and told Bald Dude to sit in the front, behind him.

This time, Bald Dude didn't even say nothing. He just did like he was told.

I sighed and tried to chill.

$(3\ ^4/_7 - 1\ ^1/_2) \div (2\ ^3/_8 + 2\ ^1/_4) = ?$

After a few of those, I felt more calm.

I dug into my backpack and reread the letter that Dr. Hunter, the lady at Appalachian Ridge Christian College, had sent. The instructions pointed out that my final stop was Horsewhip Hollow, West Virginia.

After that, no more bus drivers to watch out for me. And it was my luck that Bald Dude's final bus stop was the same as mine.

Which was how I fell into my current circumstance.

Me and Dalton the Bald Dude alone on a parking lot with him coming to put his hands on me.

7

5:35 P.M.

Still no phone bars.

Sitting solo in this dusty, hot parking lot with crazy ol' bald-headed, scarred-up Dalton Spratt was not the beginning of a fun summer of STEM. And he was not the kinda education I'd been hoping for in the middle of West Virginia.

How did I let my dumb uncle trick me into coming to Horsewhip Hollow?

I glanced around.

Dalton kept pacing back and forth on the gray parking lot. He wiped his dome of skin and scowled up at the sun.

As bad as cops could be to Blacks, I prayed that any cop would show up now. I'd settle for any plain ol' security guard.

Dalton stopped a few feet in front of me under my shade tree.

I jumped up to defend myself.

He was way taller and looked a hundred times stronger. My eyes darted around the empty lot again, but still didn't see nothing. Dalton had stood himself between me and the empty car.

I knew I didn't have a chance fighting him, but that didn't matter. Where I'm from, we don't go down easy.

"Now, tell me agin, boy," he spoke down to me, grinning. "Why shouldn't I stomp you within an inch of your life for lyin' on me?"

"I didn't lie on you! That other dude got you in trouble."

"You and him together."

I shook my head. "I didn't say nothing. I was 'sleep!"

He nodded. "Well, you best get ready to nod off agin. I'm 'bout to put you back to sleep. . . ." Dalton snickered hard at this. "But first, why don't you hand over that scratch you got hid in your drawers."

"Huh?"

"You heard me," he said, taking another step. "You embarrassed me on that bus. I figure you owe me. Fair's fair. How much cash you got in that fanny pack?"

He grinned. I stood my ground.

2 × 5 = 10 knuckles

"I am sorry, boy," Dalton said all low. "I'm about to rob you and don't even know your name. . . ."

He snickered.

"*Javari?*"

Somebody else had called out my name. Dalton stopped snickering.

Standing on the curb, I leaned over sideways to peek

around Dalton's beer belly. I saw another white man walking toward me from that parked car. This one had all of his hair and was grinning at me, friendly. He was dressed in khakis and a white polo shirt.

"You *must* be Javari Harris," he said again, smiling wider. "I'm with Uncle Billy's General Stores. Welcome to Horsewhip Holler!"

"*Yeah,*" I mumbled.

Dalton looked confused. This new guy had just magically appeared. Eyeballing Dalton, I snatched up my bags and started marching toward the Uncle Billy's dude.

"I'm Wendell Davis," the man said, shaking my hand. "One of your camp's corporate *Nephews.*" He grabbed my suitcase and we headed toward the parked car.

"Where were you?" I asked.

Wendell nodded toward his ride. "I dozed off in the back seat, listening to my tunes." He wore earbuds. "I'm sure sorry."

"I was getting bothered. . . ."

"I am *so* sorry, Javari," Wendell said. "This heat got me licked!" He turned to glance back at Dalton, who scowled. "Everything okay?" Wendell asked me.

"It is now," I said.

Wendell popped the trunk of his car. "Who's that tater?" he asked.

"Nobody," I said, climbing into the passenger seat.

"Looks like he wants to take a swarp at us."

As Wendell's car pulled out of the parking lot to head up into the mountains, I looked back over my shoulder and saw Dalton under the shade tree with his cooler.

He jammed his finger at me.

Wendell drove us up a hilly road, pointed toward those grayish-blue mountains I'd seen from the bus stop in the valley.

"Blue Ridge Mountains," he said, nodding out the window. "Elevation, pert' near seven thousand feet."

" 'Pert' near'?" I asked.

"Yeah!" Wendell agreed. "Thereabouts."

Huh? I was crazy confused.

Anyway, the tops of the Blue Ridge Mountains did look kinda blue. Hydrocarbons in the air, breathed out by all these trees, I'd read, formed the bluish color.

One of the hills in the distance was missing its top. Like somebody had just scooped off its head, leaving it ugly and bald, like that Dalton.

Wendell said that was mountaintop mining, used to collect coal. Anthracite, he said.

I knew mined coal was used for fuel. And to warm homes.

He linked his phone to his car speakers. Some country music jerked on, whining. Sounding a little like jazz. Wendell smiled, tapping his finger on his steering wheel.

"Where we're headed ain't too far up the mountain,"

he said. "This here road, Foggy Gully, takes us right through Old Town, and then farther up Mount Tackett is your camp. Bet round here's sure different than what you used to, huh?"

I nodded. The scenery here was pretty. It had already started to relax me after all that pressure with Dalton.

"Brooklyn, right?" Wendell asked.

"Yup." I hoped we wouldn't have to talk much. I didn't know him like that.

Wendell shouted, "We love those hot dogs from there! We have to buy 'em online. They don't sell 'em round here."

"Bushwick Starr Franks?"

"Yeah! That's it. Me and my girlfriend love them things. Hot dogs are big in these parts."

The drive got steeper.

"And pepperoni rolls," he added.

We turned a corner on the road, and I looked over a low stone wall, into the valley. It looked like a whole mile drop! Way far below were grassy little hills and a tiny river too, hiding beside some train tracks.

A few clouds were making shadows on the hills in the valley. Tons of bright green trees everywhere. Everything was lit up by the sun.

"We don't have Uncle Billy's stores where I'm from," I told Wendell. "They're illegal in New York."

He chuckled. "Javari, Uncle Billy's General Stores ain't illegal. New York City just don't want the competition we bring. It's a great family-run discount department store chain, wholesome values . . . founded decades ago right here in Appalachia."

I had read up on Appalachia. It was a large part of America that ran through the southern mountains into the Northeast. Every place I read said it was full of mountain people called hillbillies.

Hillbillies were supposed to be poor like my family was. I shook my head. This place didn't look poor. I knew poor.

Me and my family were on SNAP. In New York, that meant we got help from the government to buy groceries. My parents worked a lot—a whole lot—but sometimes, that still wasn't enough.

The eviction paper hung on our door was new, though. The fact that even Daddy seemed bothered was what scared me. He never let nothing bother him unless it was serious.

So, I figured we really might get set out on the streets.

Where I grew up, a lot of people lived on the streets and others were so broke they actually lived *under* the streets, in tunnels beneath the subways.

We passed by a small yellow house built into the side of the mountain.

"You from here?" I asked Wendell.

"Horsewhip Holler?" He frowned. "Shucks, naw! I live in Charlotte. North Carolina? Nowadays, Uncle Billy's is only in Horsewhip for the STEM camp every summer. Uncle Billy's owns Appalachian Ridge Christian College. Or ARCC for short."

ARCC was the college holding my STEM camp. I

didn't know that a business like Uncle Billy's could own a whole school.

"Horsewhip *loves* us," Wendell told me. "Right here is the oldest part of town, Javari. In effect, the original Uncle Billy's General Store is that little old building yonder. We don't use it no more; it's just for show. Like a museum."

The original store sat on one side of a tiny town square. The house closest to it had a red, white and blue flag hanging on its front porch.

It wasn't an American flag, but kinda looked like the flag from England. It was red with a big blue X in the middle with little white stars on it. I knew I'd seen it before. . . .

An old white man and woman sat on the house's porch, staring. When they saw me looking, they bobbed their heads at me.

"Oh, *nooo* . . . ," Wendell let out, gasping. He parked the car in front of the shop and leapt out. "Not agin," he said before his car door shut.

I wasn't sure if I should get out too. I peeked through the car's front windshield but couldn't see why he was upset. This first Uncle Billy's store looked like some tiny, closed shop with some gang tags spray-painted on it.

I hopped out of the car.

Wendell was standing there, snapping pictures of the store with his phone. His mouth hung open.

"Howdy, Wendell!" the old man shouted from his porch.

"Howdy, Fred! Miss Dorothy!" Wendell yelled back.

"They gotcha agin!" old Fred shouted.

"Yeah," Wendell said. "Yes, they did."

"Fred and me woke up this morning and it was splattered afresh!" Miss Dorothy shouted.

Chick-chick, Wendell's phone went, taking pictures.

Wendell was actually taking pictures of the spray-painted graffiti, I realized. These grafs hadn't always decorated the store.

"Don't suppose you-all saw nothing?" he asked them.

"Naw, we ain't seen nothing," old Fred said. "They come at dark, usually."

Chick-chick, Wendell's phone went on. "Splattered afresh," he repeated to himself. "Wait till I tell Larry. He won't believe this mess."

Chick-chick.

When I got closer, I could see it wasn't gang tags. In neon colors, somebody had spray-painted: SAVE THE HOLLER!! and UNCLE BILLY BRIBES POLITISHUNS!!

Somebody couldn't spell.

"What's a holler?" I asked Nephew Wendell.

"It's a hollow," he answered. "What hillbillies call the valleys in between hills?"

"So, a hillbilly painted this," I said.

He didn't answer.

"You know who did it?" I asked Wendell. He stared at me like I was foolish.

"No, Javari. If we knew who's doing this, they'd be locked up at the sheriff."

Chick-chick.

"Somebody doesn't like us," he said under his breath. Scrolling through his pix, Wendell bit his bottom lip.

"I thought everybody loved Uncle Billy's," I said.

Wendell squinted at me. "You should probably get back in the car." He returned to his pix. I turned to walk to the car and heard: *Sploitch!*

I lurched back around and saw Wendell's face was red.

And I don't mean he was blushing.

I mean that his face was now the real color red. Red drizzled down from his eyes and onto his nose and cheeks.

8

WENDELL'S FACE DRIPPED.

Blood? I thought.

Wait, *whahappened?*

"Ah!" he yelled. "My eyes! What! Oh, oh . . ."

Somebody else laughed.

I glanced around. It came from the woods. Sounded like a man's evil chuckles. Wendell had bent over, wiping his face with a handkerchief.

"You hurt?" I asked him. "You okay?"

He shook his head and blinked his eyes. He frowned into his red-stained handkerchief.

"Paint," he said. "Some huckleberry shot red paint in my face." He stared at me and looked nuts.

I busted out laughing.

"This ain't funny," he said. "Not funny at all!"

"Sorry," I told Wendell.

Fred and Miss Dorothy across the street covered their mouths, snickering. We heard more laughter from the bushes. It echoed. It was hard to tell exactly where the laughs were coming from.

Very spooky.

Wendell turned to scrutinize the woods, and this time I saw it happen.

Sploitch!

"Hey!" Wendell yelled, grabbing the back of his head, now covered in bright white paint. "Hey!"

We both ducked down in front of his car's front grille.

I tried to decide if I should make a dash for the car door. I shaded my eyes, just in case more paint went flying. The car's license plate sat right in my face. It read: WILD, WONDERFUL WEST VIRGINIA.

You ain't kidding, I thought.

Puh-plotch!

Another paint explosion, blue, burst on the hood. I felt some of the spray tickle my forehead.

"Y'all best hightail it!" Fred shouted at us.

"Shake it!" yelled Miss Dorothy.

Wendell grabbed my arm. His red-smeared face looked terrified. Like one of those dudes crouching on the battle-field in a war game.

"Javari," he said. "Make a run for the door. Now!"

We both sprang up and bolted around the car. Wendell jumped inside the driver's side, but my door was locked.

"Open the door, man!" I shouted. "Open the door!"

I could see him in there, fumbling with switches. I

glanced around the woods and heard that crazy laugh again, and then I heard the car lock click.

I scrambled inside.

We both sat there quiet for a minute, Wendell rubbing his eyes.

Puh-plotch!

This paint hit the middle of his windshield and convinced Wendell to start his engine and peel off. He flipped on the windshield wipers, but they only smeared the paint around more.

We zoomed away. About a mile up this Mount Tackett, Wendell stopped to clean off his windshield with some rags he had in his trunk.

The whole time he was muttering and cursing.

Some cat had been out there in the bushes shooting paintballs at us. Well, mostly at Wendell and at Uncle Billy's store. I had been standing out there, wide in the open, and didn't get tagged once.

After we continued our drive farther up the mountain, Wendell shot me an angry glance like he was wondering why I hadn't got all painted up like him and his car.

Sure, Wendell covered in paint was funny, but that deep bass laugh from the woods spooked me.

And then, I remembered.

That red flag with the big blue X on that porch?

It was the *Confederate* flag. It was racist. The flag the slave states flew during the Civil War, years ago.

But there it was today, right here in Horsewhip Hollow.

*   *   *

I pushed my eyes toward the hills again. Something about all these trees made me calmer, and I needed chill.

The high peaks out there reminded me of blue-black giants lying down on their sides, taking naps. The ridges almost looked out of place, they were so real. Built out of something not from this planet.

Hyperreal.

Whatever else that was happening in my world—the bullies, the naggy parents, just regular people being nasty, shootings, evictions, strangers being strange—these mountains made me not get stuck in any of that.

At least for a little while.

They were awesome.

Not like how everybody always says stuff is awesome, but really, really awesome.

I watched Wendell's pale hand knock again on the wooden door. Waiting, he stared down at the hallway rug.

"They splattered my shoes too," he mumbled.

Glancing down to the other end of the hallway, I noticed that everything was tan here. Tan walls, tan ceiling, tan carpet. It made you feel relaxed, but at the same time . . .

We heard the door unlock.

A small tan boy cracked it and looked out at us. He didn't say anything, just stared.

"Um, *Veer*?" Wendell said to him.

"Yes," the kid said, quiet.

"We haven't met yet, Veer. I'm Wendell Davis, one of Uncle Billy's Associate Nephews." Wendell put his hand on my shoulder, pushing me toward the door. "And this is your roommate, Javari Harris."

Veer looked me up and down, then told Wendell, "I don't think I have one. Are you sure?"

Wendell gave a fake chuckle. "Veer, everybody gets a roommate at camp."

Veer frowned at Wendell. "What happened to your face?" he asked.

Wendell fake-chuckled again, rubbing his cheek, trying to get off more red paint. He led me into the college dorm room and sat my suitcase on the bottom bunk bed.

"I'm gonna use y'all's bathroom for a sec," he told us. "You fellers get acquainted." He rushed toward the hallway. "You'll be living together for fourteen days!"

The door shut. Veer just stood there, staring at me. I stared back. This was why I hated meeting new people.

"You from India?" I asked.

"Naperville," he answered.

I glanced around. Our room wasn't that big. There was a bunk, two beds stacked over one another. A desk and bookshelf on each side of the room.

A small table.

Two closets full of cases of bottled water.

"My parents were born in Asansol," Veer told me. "*That's* in India."

The new roommate was still staring at me like he was reading a Google search. Did I mention I *hated* meeting new people?

$a^2 + b^2 = ?$

Finally, Veer turned away. "I took the lower bunk," he said, "but you can have it, if you want. You're way . . . bigger." He plopped down at a laptop and started playing some computer game. Stuffed in earbuds.

I tossed my duffel bag onto the top bunk and stared out our single window. Part of the view was blocked by a tall tree. The window was shut. It was actually chilly in our dorm room. I looked around but didn't see any AC.

Outside, I could see the yard and footpath we took to get to this dormitory building. Past the footpath was the parking lot and, behind that, some big building with a tower on top that looked just like the kinds of college buildings you saw in movies.

This place was different than I thought it would be. I'd never been somewhere like this before. I did feel scared, but also excited.

Being here was really . . . new.

Ba-knock, ba-knock!

I opened our door for Wendell. He'd got rid of most of the paint on his face. There were a few splotches behind his ears. His face now had a pink glow.

"This ain't coming off till I get home and scrub," he

said. "Javari, this is Rich, your RA." Wendell pointed his thumb over his shoulder.

A skinny young white guy with dark brown dreadlocks strolled in behind Wendell. He slapped my hand like he was Black.

"RA stands for resident assistant," Wendell told me. "In college, they're like live-in hall monitors. You need anything, you come to this dude right here at the end of your hall."

Rich the RA handed me a small cardboard box and a big envelope with *TAY-2B* on it. "I brought you dinner."

I peeked inside the box. Two huge sandwiches, potato chips, a drink and muffins.

"You just missed supper in the dining hall," Rich said. "I knew you'd be hungry."

"Thanks," I said.

"Our sit-down meals are real savory," Rich added. "Dining hall's right next door. Y'all's john and common lounge are down the hall here. Let's see . . . Oh! Lights-out at nine. But I ain't too strict about that one."

He winked.

"And like I done told Veer," Rich said, "do *not* under any circumstances drink any water from the tap. That's what all this bottled water's for." He tossed me a set of keys. "There's more info in that packet."

There were some stickers and two maps inside the envelope and other junk. Plus a letter from that same lady, Dr. Geraldine Hunter, that had been sending me stuff. And a schedule for every day of the camp.

"Anything else you need?" Rich asked. "You and your roomie Veer here can help each other out."

"I need to call my moms, let her know I got here," I said.

"Oh, yeah. Listen, after you chow your grub, I'll walk you over to one of our communications rooms," Rich answered. "Any types of phone calls, video calls you need, you can make from one of them. Our Wi-Fi here sucks 'cause of the mountains."

"Cool."

Rich said, "Red Man here tells me you're from the Big Apple!"

Wendell was rubbing behind his ears. Veer didn't look up from his game.

"I been to New York once," Rich said. "Freshman year, spring break. It was so cool. We went to a jazz club and a reggae concert in Central Park. You listen to reggae, bro?"

I frowned. "I don't like it." I hated reggae.

"What? Yo, I have some *bad* reggae playlists. Don't I, Wendy?"

Wendell started, "Well . . ."

Rich said to me, "We'll chill, vibe to some reggae and you tell me how you run the streets in New York. *A'ight?*"

He held up his hand for a high five. I *hated* high fives. Just then, Veer screamed and jumped out of his chair.

"Level twenty-five!" he yelled. His laptop read: YOU HAVE NOW ENTERED LEVEL 25 KILL ZONE!

Veer bobbed up and down on his tiptoes. "Yes! I am un-beatable!" he shouted at the ceiling. "Unbeatable!"

9

AT 7:00 A.M. SATURDAY MORNING, about two dozen kids from my dormitory met for breakfast in the college's small dining hall, which was in a separate building next door. Veer and me left our room together, but the minute we two strolled into the eating area, he shot off without a word.

It looked like he had already met some other boys here. He didn't ask me along to eat with them. I sighed, plucked up a food tray and ate by myself, looking through a big window at the foggy yard outside.

It was loud in here from the chatting all around me. I read my schedule. There were assemblies every morning, then classes or a field trip, then lunch, then more classes or a field trip. Then time in something called the Brain Cells . . .

My waffles and eggs were delicious, though. And that orange juice they had was some of the best juice I ever tasted. Even their milk tasted better.

After breakfast, two Uncle Billy's guides walked us to the other side of the main yard for the opening assembly.

From what I could tell, most of ARCC's buildings sat along this one big green "yard" that looked like a long park. It was crisscrossed with footpaths and flower beds sprinkled all over.

At one end of the yard was that tall tower building. And on the opposite end of the yard, I could see what looked like the white steeple of a church. A giant black cross covered half its front.

Sitting between those two buildings was a huge fountain. When me and my group of camp kids got near it, a spray of cool mist floated down on our faces.

I shivered.

It was *so* foggy.

ARCC sat on a mountain and was *surrounded* by mountains. The weather was chillier up here than down in the valley. And the air felt more damp. I yanked down my baseball cap tighter around my head.

Niece Verity and Niece Nickie, our Uncle Billy's guides, led us past the huge fountain. They were both young ladies who grinned nonstop, but when we passed that fountain, I heard Niece Verity whisper, "Nic, here's where I saw that *thing* last night. I was all alone in the fog. Its *face*, girl . . . hideous. Like a nightmare."

Scared to death, Nickie glared at the fountain. When the two Nieces caught me near them, their fake smiles suddenly snapped back.

Was she talking about some animal?

I shrugged and checked my Brokelyn Wireless phone.

No bars! No signal!

Rich blamed the mountains.

But maybe it was just my useless phone.

My group of campers cut down a path. Me and this other kid were the only Black ones I could see. A few Asians. There was one girl who looked like *maybe* she was Spanish.

I didn't know.

The other Black dude was tall and good-looking, like some TV star. With a green-dyed Afro puff on top of his head, he wore a LA Lakers jersey. I was wearing my Brooklyn Nets throwback my uncle gave me.

We wore ours different, though. He was built like an athlete. Walked with a super-straight back. I caught myself slouching, and suddenly straightened up.

"You work out?" I asked him all of a sudden. I surprised myself. My entire body felt hot.

The kid seemed surprised too. "Calisthenics," he answered.

"Me and my daddy sometimes do that in the park," I lied. My father hated working out and so did I.

The expression on Afro-Puff's face said he knew I was lying.

"My old man is a Marine," Afro-Puff said. "I play football and b-ball too. As long as I keep straight As."

"Cool." I struggled to keep up. His legs were long and mine weren't very.

He frowned at me. "What happened to your eye?"

Like a reflex, I almost covered it. But I stopped before I did.

I said, "I was born with it. When I was little, I wore an eye patch to fix it, but that didn't work."

There was an operation that could fix it, but my folks told me they couldn't afford it.

"*Hmph . . .*" was all Afro-Puff said.

Niece Nickie shouted at us, "To the right, *Futureneers*, you'll see ARCC's new engineering center. When classes begin this fall, it will offer programs leading to both a bachelor and a master of science!"

Afro-Puff snapped a pic.

"Yo, it's very *vanilla shake* up in here," I said to him, grinning like a clown. "We niggas need to stick together this summer." I giggled. I never knew what to say.

His eyes widened. They darted around to see if anybody listened. "Man, we don't use the N-word," he said.

"*We?*"

"My family."

"Well, *my* family does. Some days, it's every other word out our mouth," I joked.

Dude stared at me like I was talking another language. "Where you from?" he asked.

"Brooklyn. Bushwick. You know it?"

"We left New York years ago," he told me. "After my mom died. Pardon me, *Brooklyn*."

I guess I knew what *not* to say. Afro-Puff swung his long

legs even faster and left me behind. He glared at his phone like he had something important to read.

He had bars, I saw.

$J \neq AP$

Finally, Niece Nickie pointed toward the largest building that sat near the end of the main yard. "This is our auditorium, y'all," Nickie told my group. "We're all meeting here every morning for assembly—"

"Wooo!" Niece Verity shouted.

"Before you break out into your chosen sections," Nickie went on, "or head out for field trips."

The auditorium was huge. "How many kids are there?" I asked.

"Seventy-nine campers from middle schools all over America!" Nickie shouted.

My stomach felt sick just thinking about meeting all of them. Especially with how bad my Afro-Puff convo just went. Real cool dudes never liked me, it seemed like.

I covered my funny eye.

This huge auditorium with red seats held mostly white kids, mostly boys. One of them rocked a wheelchair. There were also Asians and kids who looked Mideastern.

I did see a tiny crew of Black and brown kids sitting near the front of the room. Afro-Puff was there, giggling about something with Veer, who had ditched me again.

Now I stood alone, like a dummy.

I tried to get Veer and Afro-Puff's attention, but they acted like they didn't see me. Afro-Puff was probably no good anyway. Poppa George said you always gotta watch Black folks.

There were too many people here.

I took a soft red seat and started turning over equations in my head, so I wouldn't have to talk.

J

$J + a$

$J + 2a$

$J + 3a$

$J + 4a$

$J + 5a$

"Glorious morning, *Futureneers!*"

This short and round Black woman had shouted over a stage microphone.

She said, "On behalf of Uncle Billy's General Stores and Appalachian Ridge Christian College, I welcome you to our annual Futureneers STEM Camp!"

Wendell and some other khaki-and-polo adults clapped.

The lady went on, "I am Dr. Geraldine Hunter, chair of the Computer Science Department here at ARCC and director of your camp. For the next fourteen fun-filled days here, you will build rockets, race boats, explore nature and learn code! Plus, for the first time, we are featuring an exciting new virtual reality experience for you!"

Kids sat up in their seats for that.

"And, also for the first time, we will host a contest with

cash and prizes!" The kids started to chatter, but Dr. Hunter held up her hand. "Nephew Tom?" One of Uncle Billy's khaki workers ripped off a tarp in the middle of the stage.

The room gasped.

Underneath the tarp was an old-school pirate treasure chest. This one was made out of wood but painted to look gold.

Dr. Hunter shouted, "You'll all form teams and work on a project of your choosing! The group who impresses our judges the most wins this Lost ARCC of STEM chest! Brimming with goodies and cash! Only *one* group of Futureneers will be triumphant! Blast those brain cells!"

That prize money sure blew up *my* head.

My family needed it.

Do or die.

10

AFTER ASSEMBLY, US CAMPERS HAD an hour free before we left for our first field trip. I decided to go roam around ARCC to relax. Being caged in that auditorium with all of those strangers had really worked my nerves.

Walking across the college's grass almost felt like walking across the carpet in my uncle's fancy living room. Soft green carpet. I bent down to touch the grass to be sure it was real.

The auditorium was next to that church I saw earlier.

Dr. Hunter had called it Brigwood Chapel and invited us all to Sunday services there. It was optional, so I knew I wouldn't go.

Me and my folks used to go to church in Bed-Stuy when Shireen was little, but we stopped. I don't know why we stopped.

Just kinda fell off.

I hiked along the big rectangle space of lawn.

On one side ran a tall chain link fence covered in green ivy. It was hard seeing through the links, but there was something over there. Like some shadow moved along with me. Following on the other side.

I stepped closer to the fence to get a better view. As soon as I got close, I heard something rustle.

Was that a squirrel?

Or a bird?

It rustled some more. It seemed big.

Who knew what they had running around here in the country.

Not a bear . . .

I pressed my nose against the fence, trying to see. It looked woodsy over there, out of control. If it wasn't for this fence, all that drama on the other side might break through.

Wildment.

Just then, something big moved again out of the corner of my eye. Twigs cracked. I kept along the fence until I came to an enormous trimmed bush. There was a gap behind it.

Soon I squeezed between the back of that bush and the chain links. I could see into the woods way better from back here. Just on the other side, in the weeds, I saw something, red, lying on the ground.

I squinted. It looked like a wet marble.

Or a sticky, red eyeball?

This bush totally hid me from the rest of the lawn. And it also hid a hole in the fence. Large enough for me to crawl through.

So I *did*.

I didn't think there were no bears near here. And, really, I *had* to know what that red, sticky thing was.

This other side of the fence was as wild as it had looked before. Dark and shady and even chillier than the campus I'd just left. Dead, wet leaves covered the ground here like black oatmeal.

I plucked up the slick little red ball I'd seen. Leaves and dirt clung onto one side. I squeezed it. Out oozed red goo.

Paint again.

Another noise nearby made me dive back through the hole, back to the college. I'd dropped the leaky red ball where I'd found it.

Back behind the bush, I yanked off some leaves and used them to wipe my hands clean of paint. I crawled out from behind the plants and stood staring down at the smear of red still on my hand. I heard a noise.

"Pissshhh!"

I glanced up.

This husky young white dude stood there. He wore a tan uniform like a cop's. Bald with one of them goatees.

I guessed that was a look in West Virginia.

"Pissshhh!" his walkie-talkie squawked again.

This dude looked at me hostile. "Where'd you come from?" he snapped.

"Brooklyn," I said.

He narrowed his eyes. "You that stranger what's been prowling around?" He put a hand on a nightstick attached to his belt.

"Stranger?" I repeated. "I came for camp, man."

"I'm with the campus security," he said. "Gonna ask you to turn around and put your hands on your head."

"What?"

"I said, turn around and put your hands on your head."

What was this mess?

The badge on his uniform said: E. STURGILL, ARCC SECURITY.

I felt like I was back in Brooklyn, being stopped on the sidewalk by the cops. His hand tightened around his nightstick. I did what he said. Behind me, I felt his hands pat me down from my shoulders to my hips to my butt and to my legs.

He didn't find nothing.

"Turn around, please," Security said. "What's your name?"

"Javari."

"Javari what?"

"Harris."

He asked somebody over his walkie-talkie if my name was on the camp list. I didn't like this dude.

"Look, man—" I started.

"Pissshhh!" his walkie-talkie squawked. *"Javari Harris, New York City. On the list for Taylor, sure enough. Over!"*

"Roger that! Over!" Security shouted into his walkie.

"Javari Harris, you are on the list. You the boy from New York City."

"I told you that."

He said, "I apologize for the confusion. Your dormitory is Taylor Hall. Right up yonder."

"I know where it is," I said, starting to walk toward my dorm. I stared down at my hands. They were red, dirty and now sweaty.

Thanks to him.

"I didn't know who you was, creeping around like that!" I heard him call to the back of my head. "Strange stuff's been going down."

I kept walking. But I felt like his weren't the only eyes watching me go.

11

THiS FiRST DAY WE ALL took a field trip to Charlotte, North Carolina. The bus ride took forever. I'd thought I was done with buses for a while.

Charlotte the city disappointed me. The downtown wasn't anything like Midtown in New York. You couldn't really compare them.

First, we visited Uncle Billy's. Or really, the main headquarters for Uncle Billy's General Stores. We found out Uncle Billy himself was way long dead.

This trip was basically them showing off their boring offices and warehouse. Then we went to a baseball game in Uptown Charlotte. And after that they actually gave us a mini-STEM camp right on the diamond.

Nephew Tom introduced one of our camp instructors, Molly Ferguson. Ms. Ferguson wore a blue tracksuit and could really toss a baseball. Her and Afro-Puff played catch on the field before her STEM lesson.

Watching Afro-Puff try to show off, I tripped over something.

It was the edge of a boy's wheelchair. He had brown hair and light brown eyes, and he wasn't that big, but when he saw that I'd tripped over his chair, he sat up tall. Before I could say anything, the kid shouted, "You blind? Heads up!"

What'd he just say?

He had almost made me fall. I shouted back, "Check yourself, you little—"

"Futureneers!" Ms. Ferguson yelled at our crowd.

Glaring at that boy, I moved away into the herd.

"How many of y'all like baseball?" Ms. Ferguson called out. More campers than I woulda thought lifted their hands. "Not bad!" she shouted. "How many love STEM? *Better!* Well, I love 'em both! I'll show you why!"

Ms. Ferguson cut the red laces holding the outside of the baseball together. Next, she gripped some pliers and began peeling away this yarn, or string, under the baseball's leather cover. That yarn was wrapped around and around. Finally, she used a small knife and showed us a hard center beneath the string.

"What we got here?" Ms. Ferguson asked this girl who'd come to camp in a white church dress.

"I don't know," Church Dress replied. "Plastic?"

"Good answer!" Ms. Ferguson shouted. "But *wrong!*"

"Is it cardboard inside?" a boy with bright blue rubber bands in his braces asked.

"Cardboard?" the wheelchair boy echoed. Everybody laughed. His chair was fancy, like it was built for speed. *"Cardboard?"* he repeated in disbelief.

Blue Braces blushed. Ferguson told him, "I'll give you a hint: you've got some in your mouth."

"Metal?" Blue Braces asked.

This one Asian girl standing between us muttered, "Meathead," at him. He glared at her.

Afro-Puff called out to Ms. Ferguson, "Rubber, ma'am!" A couple of boys near him snickered.

"Right answer, Lester! These little rubber suckers are in every baseball you've ever thrown! And inside the rubber, at the very core, is cork."

I musta been squinting hard at the rubber center. That same Asian girl leaned into me and said, "You're a frowner."

"I ain't frowning," I told her.

"I been watching you," she said, shrugged and walked away.

Strange girl.

I think I remembered Strange Girl from the dining hall.

We dissected more baseballs and Ms. Ferguson said how the rubber and cork inside made the balls soar through the air when they were hit. Then, three of the baseball players strutted back onto the diamond, just wearing regular clothes. One wore a giant silver cross around his neck. Two of them were pitchers. They talked to us about staying in school and never giving up until we reached our dreams.

They took turns throwing baseballs back and forth between the campers. I thought one of the players might throw me a ball, but he changed his mind and tossed it to Strange Girl.

Jake, the tallest pitcher, held up his ball and told us, "This is what y'all want, right here. The ol' four-seam grip. Your index and middle fingers should lay across the red horseshoe seams. See?"

We all gripped the baseballs we had.

"Your thumb goes under the bottom one," Jake said, showing us.

"What difference does it make," asked Strange Girl, "how you hold it?"

"Good question, young lady," said Jake. "So, gripping it like we showed gives you the best grip over the horseshoe so when you throw, your ball flies true."

"Max backward rotation," the other pitcher added.

The pitchers told us that the balls' stitching also controls how they soar through the air. Those little stitches make a tiny air bubble around the ball that can make it fly faster. That, plus the angle of a pitch and how it spins, can make it a curveball, slider, screwball . . .

Facts I'd never even known.

Jake tossed his ball up in the air and caught it. "Basic aerodynamics," he said, winked and grinned.

We all practiced throwing using the different grips. I could get a good spin going. But of course Afro-Puff's was better.

After the lesson, the Nieces and Nephews served us a

pretty good picnic of hamburgers, hot dogs and salad right on the baseball field. I ate so much, it made me sleepy before they told us to climb back on our bus again.

On the long ride back to ARCC, I fell asleep.

That night, Nephew Wendell woke me when we'd stopped in front of my dorm building. By then, I was so tired I coulda stayed asleep right there in the back of that bus.

Everybody else had left him and me behind. It was late and deserted. Mountain fog had rolled in.

Walking me to Taylor Hall, Wendell suddenly stopped halfway across the lawn. He gasped and hooked my arm. Squinting into the shadows, he screamed so loud, unexpected, I almost shot out of my socks.

"Oh! Oh, my . . . Lord!" he yelled. "What *is* that!"

By the time I looked where he was pointing, all I saw was a bunch of bushes move in the fog. Whatever Wendell saw had gone.

"What'd you see?" I asked.

He caught his breath. "Well, I thought it was a big man at first," he said, eyes wide. *"But that face* . . . like something out of a horror— And it had this enormous, huge back, like a buffalo's. And barefoot! It didn't look human."

I focused my eyes on where he'd seen this thing.

Wendell shook. "It was cutting straight at us before I hollered. It's gone now."

"You say it wasn't *human*?" I asked.

"Not like any human I ever saw. That face . . ."

A monster. Like Verity and Nickie was talking about this morning. I caught a shiver.

"Let's get you inside," he said. "Come on. I gotta tell Larry. *Lord!*"

I was real wide-awake now, no surprise.

12

"FUTURENEERS!" DR. HUNTER ANNOUNCED, a little pissed. "This will only work if there's *no* drama. We *will* make this fun! Four campers per group, everyone! Pick your batch of four!"

Glaring at us, she marched back and forth across the stage of the auditorium gripping her mic. Her expression said she was undecided about whether it was smart to let us pick our own teams for the competition.

I glanced around for my roommate, Veer.

He had partnered up with a group of boys on the other side of the room. One of them was Lester the Afro-Puff. The other was that buster in the silver wheelchair.

The fourth member of their crew was that other white boy, Blue Braces—the one who'd thought baseballs were made from cardboard. He had jet-black hair like a mop, with eyes that matched his braces' bands.

I hated this.

I sat in one of the soft red chairs by myself. I didn't really know nobody. I sunk down farther into my seat, trying to disappear.

"Javari!" Nephew Wendell shouted.

I hoped he wasn't gonna bring up that creepy whatever-it-was from last night. That gave me nightmares for nothing.

When Wendell told Rich the RA what he'd seen, Rich thought Wendell had been dreaming. And when ARCC security asked me about it this morning, I had to tell them all I'd seen was some bushes wiggling at me in the fog.

Who knew what it really was.

But the way that same security guard that hassled me before got so interested, it seemed to me like he knew something. He took it more serious than anybody else here, except for Wendell.

Wendell sidestepped into my row. "Need a group?"

"Uh . . ."

"What about over here?" Wendell said to me.

I turned to where he pointed. It was at Strange Girl, the one who'd told me I frowned too much yesterday, and at a blond-haired white girl. The blonde had a sad expression on her face.

Wendell said to me, "Everybody else is took." He waved to the two girls. "Oh, Miss Whitt! You too, honey! You girls meet Javari from New York City? He's nice. Come on."

They glanced at each other and sidestepped down the row to where I sat.

Wendell leaned into Strange Girl. "I'm sorry, honey. What is your name agin? I'm so pitiful with foreign—"

"*Tuyet,*" she said.

"That's right!" said Wendell. "*Tu-yet*. So musical-sounding."

"*Twit?*" I asked her.

She looked annoyed.

"Oh no!" Wendell said to me and the blonde. "Tuyet is no twit! Her name only *sounds* like 'twit.'"

"Got it," I said.

Like this whole thing'd made her tired, Tuyet added, "It means 'snow.'"

"*Pretty,*" Wendell sang. He looked at me and the white girl again. "Right?"

We nodded.

"So, Tuyet Nguyen and Javari Harris," he said. "This very smart, talented, lovely young lady is Miss Rebecca Whitt!"

"I know," said Tuyet. "She's my roommate."

"Hey," Rebecca mumbled at me. "Everybody calls me Becca."

Wendell smiled bigger and glanced toward the stage. "I think Doc Hunter's 'bout to start. You three cool with forming up? Javari's real nice."

Around the room, all the other campers had made their four. Me, Tuyet and Becca were the only ones left. To me, we seemed like the rejects.

"That's fine," Tuyet said, crossing her arms.

"Sure," said Becca. She made a funny face at the carpet.

"Yeah," I agreed. "It's cool."

Dr. Hunter spoke up from the stage, "You all have your groups? Marvelous! Just what I love to see from our Futureneers—no drama! So! Each crew will develop an exciting STEM project to present at the end of camp. The winning project gets Uncle Billy's Lost ARCC of STEM treasure chest of tech wonders and cash!"

The room buzzed.

"Blast your brain cells, Futureneers!" Hunter shouted. "Next up, we'd like to—"

Booooruppp! Booooruppp!

An alarm had gone off, shattering everybody's ears. I covered mine with my hands.

Booooruppp! Booooruppp!

"That, I believe, is our *fire* alarm, everyone!" Dr. Hunter announced. "Nieces and Nephews, please escort your—! OH!"

All of the water sprinklers in the auditorium had switched on and rain flooded down in waves from the room's ceiling. Now everybody really started screaming and running for the exits.

Booooruppp! Booooruppp!

Nuts!

Outdoors, on the other side of the auditorium's glass doors, soaked campers were laughing and hollering in the sun.

I shook my head and wrung water out of my New York Mets jersey.

I didn't even know how Tuyet and Becca had just disappeared. I thought they were right behind me.

Some other girls helped the wheelchair kid in Veer's group dry off his chair with paper towels. I overheard his name was Jerry and those girls really fussed over his chair. I knew stainless steel wouldn't rust. I could tell Jerry hoped those dumb girls didn't know that.

Somebody inside shut off the alarm. Niece Verity came around, saying it had been a false alarm.

A prank.

Some knucklehead had lit some newspapers on fire in a metal trash can to set off the alarm.

What a bum!

As I wrung out more water from my Mets jersey, I noticed somebody in the distance, across the sunny yard, running away. I couldn't tell who it was.

They were a shadow.

And looked barefoot.

Whoever that was, they could *really* jet!

Soon they disappeared behind a line of trees all the way on the other side of the yard.

Strange.

13

THE REST OF OUR FIRST DAY of STEM classes, after we had all dried off, was a lot less dramatic. We all chose three sessions when we signed up for camp, and the ones that me and my uncle Mel had picked seemed to be good ones.

We had decided on Automata (that one sounded cool), Sharing Nature and Coding for Better Lives. The last one, I still didn't understand what it was supposed to be even after taking the first class.

I'd really wanted Robot Wars, but that session filled up. My Coding for Better Lives class was taught by this kooky Chinese guy.

Wang Yong.

At first, he seemed very serious, but then all of a sudden, he would grin out of nowhere and say crazy stuff. He had us all laughing, and I liked him.

Plus, we got tablets to use during that session.

Ms. Ferguson, from the baseball field trip before, turned out to be our instructor for Sharing Nature. This teacher and class I'd been the most worried about. It *seemed* cool, but I hoped it wouldn't get too boring.

The other campers at our first sessions were as quiet as I was. Most of them. This one boy named Scotty never shut up. To be truthful, I was too stressed to speak much, having to meet all these new people.

In addition to the lessons, every day they had some group activity or field trip. Later this week was a visit to a potato farm, which kinda sounded dumb. The fact the Nieces and Nephews kept calling it a Trip to the Tater Plot made it sound even dumber.

I was *hoping* for field trips, because I was curious to see what the real people who lived in Horsewhip Hollow were like—those *hillbillies*. Wendell didn't seem to think much of the folks around here. But *he* seemed kinda crazy to *me*, so . . .

Our next instructor strolled into our classroom and waved, excited, at the twelve campers in my group. We all sat in a small brick school building near the church.

"Welcome, kiddos," he said. "Hungry for some STEM?"

Dude pulled out a bag of celery sticks and started to munch on them. He offered me some. I shook my head at the green stalks.

"Stem?" the instructor repeated, offering celery to this Asian boy in the front. "Get it? These here are actual *stems*. You guys not into science comedy? Naw? Okay."

A few of us snickered.

He smiled, leaned against the desk in the front of the

classroom. His name was Ethan Cunningham. Our Automata instructor this summer.

A young guy, Mr. Cunningham had sandy hair and was average height. He had green eyes and looked like he worked out. Not what I thought of when I thought of a scientist.

But that's what he claimed.

He'd asked all us kids to call him by his *first* name. That was what he preferred. "It's just more *light*," he'd said. "I'm antihierarchy."

This morning, Ethan opened the cabinet behind his desk. Inside were cardboard boxes overfilled with metal rods, springs, smaller boxes, an old circuit board, all sorts of tools, a wooden duck, screws, small cans of paint, buttons, two rusty hooks, cables, ribbon and a Rubik's Cube that had all its sides painted black.

Ethan carefully selected one cardboard box in particular and dropped it on his desk. "Okay, then!" he said. "Who in this stuffy room is ready to blow the roof off?"

We sat still.

"Um. That was *not* rhetorical," Ethan said. "And this is not Mindreading 101. I require a show of hands."

Our hands shot up.

"Swell, kiddos!" Ethan shouted.

He grabbed something made out of metal gears and plastic wires and blades from the box and wound up a big crank on it. The thing whirred and spun and flew into the air, launched by the set of small propellers.

It didn't stop climbing until it hit the ceiling.

14

THAT NIGHT, AFTER LIGHTS-OUT, I laid in my top bunk, eyes wide open.

Worrying.

The cricket noise outside our window was thumping!

Plus, Veer snored crazy loud.

And I couldn't even listen to any of my music because my phone got no signal up here.

I sat up.

Back in Bushwick, I had my own bedroom. I didn't have to fight to fall asleep because of some little boy "sawing logs," like Poppa George would say. Veer's racket was driving me nuts.

Plus, it had only just got dark.

I slid down to the floor of our dorm room and peeked out the window. On either side of the tree there, I could see over the main yard. A nice view. I wondered if I'd still have a room when I got back to BK.

The additive inverse of a is −a.

Sleep was hopeless now. I cracked our door.

The fluorescent hallway lights were still shining bright and buzzing. Down the hall, near the stairwell, I could hear reggae music and loud talk coming from Rich the RA's room.

Before lights-out, Rich had taken me and Veer aside and mumbled for us to be careful. "Doc Hunter don't want us getting you kids in conniptions over nothing, but, just so you know, be extra careful around campus, okay?"

Veer and me had nodded.

"We got a *creeper*," Rich whispered.

Whatever, I wanted out.

It was too early to go to bed. But it'd be impossible for me to sneak past Rich's open door if I was going to make it outside. I shut our dorm room door and made a face at Veer, who slept and snored even louder.

I stood at our window for another minute, studying the tree that sat just opposite. It was so close, I could reach out and touch it.

I opened our window.

The tree's bark was smooth and slick from rain. Just stretching out toward it felt risky. Like the tree dared me.

I closed my eyes in the dark, concentrating on the trunk. It almost felt like it hummed, like I could feel the tree sap pump. That was the sound of my heart, I recognized.

This Appalachian tree talked to me. Told me to jump.

Wildment.

So, I went.

The next minute, I crawled in the wet tree branches, in

the dark, making my way one hand and foot and hand and foot at a time toward the dirt below. I stopped for a quick minute to peek into the girls' window. They had the floor beneath ours.

But the room under mine was pitch-black and dead quiet.

No snorers in there. I felt jealous.

Now, I neared the bottom of the tree. I hadn't thought about how I'd make it down this last bit. The big branches had ended. All rough trunk down to the ground.

I dangled from the lowest branch, wondered if I was doing the smartest thing, and then finally let myself fall several feet to the ground.

I landed funny. Stumbled over what I thought was a tree root and bumped my knee against something hard.

I cursed and got scared because I'd been too loud. I was sure I'd get caught.

And how would I climb back up this tree?

I was so short.

In the dark, I felt for some nubs on the trunk. There had been branches there before somebody sawed them off. I hoped I could use the knots for my feet to climb back up again.

I decided I'd worry about that later.

Right then, I took off.

* * *

Outside on campus felt way cooler than inside Taylor Hall. The grass was damp from showers and mist.

The crickets were way louder out here. Not at all like the cicadas you heard sometimes back home. These little bugs had *bass,* their woofers and subwoofers cranked up!

I strolled across the main yard in the dark, wearing my T-shirt, my New York Mets pajama bottoms and tan house slippers. I picked up a few rocks and tossed them into the dark bushes.

Wendell and his crazy imagination. He'd said he wasn't a hillbilly, but I wondered. Pretty soon I'd plopped down in the moon shadows on the steps of the enormous ARCC Administration Building. The one with the tower on top.

"Pissshhh!"

I jerked around. Where'd that come from?

"Pissshhh! I cain't wait for his new EP to drop. Over!"

The sounds were coming from nearby, I realized. I raised up and stared out. There was a dark stairwell nearby, leading, I guessed, to some basement beneath the huge building.

Footsteps were coming toward me. I ducked down into the stairwell and peeked out to watch that same security guard who hassled me before walk down the path.

Rich the RA had told me his name was Elrod. Rich called it one of those "shameless hillbilly" names.

"Pissshhh!" Elrod's walkie-talkie squawked again. "Breaker, breaker. Elrod, what's your twenty? Over!"

I watched the security guard stroll up the building's steps in the dark. He was working overtime, I figured.

Maybe he was always on duty?

I shook my head. A nuisance, I thought.

"Pissshhh!" went his walkie-talkie. He spoke into it, "I'm at Whitt Hall, Larry. Over!"

"Roger that. Pissshhh!" his walkie-talkie answered.

Elrod had stopped a few feet from where I'd just been sitting seconds before. He couldn't see me now, though. I wondered if he'd heard me. I sank back deeper into the stairwell.

Behind me, I heard a rustle.

Rat, I thought. I swallowed hard. I was hiding with the rats. I shouldn't have snuck out. I hoped I could climb back up that tree in the dark.

I crept up the steps and squinted out. Elrod still stood there, smoking on something. I gulped, walking backward, deeper into the stairwell. I *really* didn't wanna be found out by him again.

Walking down and backward, I stepped on something squooshy.

It grunted.

Before I could turn around, something damp and rough clamped down over my mouth. I tried to scream but couldn't. I got punched in my ribs.

I stood still there, scared in the dark stairwell.

Soon I heard Elrod's footsteps as he walked off into the distance toward another part of the campus. Only now, I was wishing he'd come back and save me from whatever buffalo-backed beast-monster was down in this stairwell with their dirty paw squeezed over my mouth.

After Elrod was long gone, whatever was holding me let go.

I swung around. Darkness. I stumbled away.

"Wait!" somebody whispered.

And then, a boy's face popped out from the darkness. Lit up by a flashlight, I realized.

I cursed, turning to run.

"No, man!" the boy whispered. "Wait!" He stepped closer into the moonlight, so I could see him better.

He was older than me. Spoke with a deeper voice.

A Black boy too, but light-skinned, kinda gold, with brown freckles on his face and hazel-colored eyes. He was also a skyscraper and "big-boned," like Poppa would say.

The boy stared at me, then stared out at the yard, then back to me.

"The perimeter ain't secure," he said. He looked me up and down. "Don't make me pop ya. Set."

"What?" I said.

"I know you," he mumbled, nodding all slow. He stared a minute, then, pointing his forehead at me, he said, *"Cricket."*

15

CRICKETS SINGING AROUND HIM, he moved along with a bulky black duffel bag slung around his back. No shoes on his bare feet.

And he was strong-looking. Like he wrestled bears.

One of the first things this Cricket had told me was that he was thirteen. A year older than me.

The two of us snuck across the main yard, sticking to the shadows. I squinted at Cricket in the dark. I wasn't so sure that he was only thirteen. He coulda been lying.

I started to speak but he shushed me again. He gave me an expression like I was the bonkers one. Maybe I was . . .

Why else would I follow him out of the stairwell, creeping around the ARCC campus at night? We both might get shot, some cop thinking we're trying to steal.

It was late now.

I shoulda been in bed.

I knew I shouldn't be out here, following Cricket. I didn't know anything about him but his name. And that he was a Black boy with freckles.

But these folks around here, I felt, were *interesting*. There was something familiar about how they acted and sounded but also real different. It was hard for me to solve their "equation," which made me curiouser.

Now Cricket made me real curious. Plus, I'd always thought Black boys with freckles were cool. I didn't have any.

We hid behind a tall tree near the fence. He dropped his bag beside the tree. His duffel looked heavy. After he put on a pair of sneakers, Cricket peeked out from behind the tree, checking for anybody.

"Elrod's gone," I told him. "He passed us."

Cricket nodded. "That's my enemy. Me and him . . ." He mashed his two beefy fists together and stared down at my Mets pj's. "I didn't think they let Blacks in their camp."

I frowned.

"You one of Uncle Billy's *Negroes*?" he asked, and giggled.

I cursed again. "What the hell are you doing, sneaking around here at night?" I glanced at his duffel bag. "What else is in there?"

He stepped in front of it. "You the police?"

"Cricket?" I sniffed and spat. "What's your real name? You don't go here. I ain't seen you at assembly."

"Holy spit!" he said. "I wouldn't go to their rotten camp if they paid me!"

"You live around here? What's your *real* name?"

"You know, you ask questions like a sheriff. Maybe you

is one of them. I *thought* you might be okay. That's why I didn't spray you full-on with my paint gun."

"That was you?" I asked. "Shooting paintballs at us?"

He let out a deep, spooky laugh. Same as the one we heard that day.

"If I'd *wanted* to hit you, I *woulda,*" Cricket said. "That other dude—Uncle Billy's *Nephew*—he had it coming. I sure scared him the other night too. When you boys got off that bus?"

"That was you too?"

"A' course."

"But Wendell said he saw something like a half-man, half-animal! With a huge hump for a back."

"Barefoot?"

I nodded.

Cricket said, "I'm big and camouflaged. Had my duffel bag hiked up on my shoulders. I kin look ferocious when I want."

He walked stooped, head turned toward the ground, but his eyes turned up. Made him appear devilish.

Then Cricket showed me a rubber Halloween mask he had in his bag. The Beast from *Beauty and the Beast*. I couldn't believe this dude.

I laughed out loud at his disguise.

The kid looked hurt for a minute, then he grinned at me. He musta realized how goofy he looked.

"You might be okay," Cricket said. He stared at me for a while. "I'll show you something cool."

Cricket leaned his heavy shoulder against the rusty door again and the whole thing moved. The pushed door made so much noise—groaning—that it made me nervous. If Elrod had been on patrol upstairs, he woulda heard for sure.

My tour guide wasn't fazed.

We stepped inside the dark room. It was wet and drippy. A few thick pipes ran upward. Water leaked from the walls, ceiling, all over.

I could tell by the smile that spread on Cricket's face that being in here made him happy. He turned to glance at me. I really didn't know what to think.

My house slippers were soggy.

We were under the fountain in the center of the main yard. He'd led me down through a hidden door beside it and into this little room full of pipes and dark metal—where you could see how the mechanics actually worked.

The fountain's heart. The part, buried deep, that you can't see.

"How'd you get keys to open the door?" I asked him. "You work here or something?"

"You kiddin'?" He snorted. "You couldn't *pay* me to work for ARCC!"

I walked over toward a rusty pipe and squinted at it with the beam from one of Cricket's flashlights. The pipe disappeared into a big metal box, sunk into a hole in the ground full of water.

Some kinda well?

I wasn't sure, but I thought the box might be a motor, or pump, made to suck the water upward into the fountain. This box was attached to these metal pipes that branched into the ceiling, like tree limbs.

"This is kinda cool," I said. "A secret world, man."

"We better hat-up and go." Cricket glanced at an old military watch. "He'll be back around this side soon. I got him memorized."

He winked and grinned.

We crawled through the small door that led out of the fountain room. I slipped and almost fell.

Cricket snickered. "You're funny."

"What?"

He jerked his head and stuck out his hand. We shook. His grip squished mine.

"I'm Javari."

"That's weird."

"Yeah, like Cricket ain't."

He smirked. I felt strange.

Then Cricket said, "I gotta go. Maybe sometime I'll show you the *real* Horsewhip Holler. Sure ain't this camp. See you round."

I woke up sleepy.

I barely remembered climbing back up the tree outside

my dorm building and crawling back into bed. Turned out, those tree knots made good places to step up on.

Veer was already out of bed. I guessed washing up. He'd slept right through everything.

Had I dreamt meeting Cricket?

Was he real?

I sat up and stared down at the floor.

My tan house slippers were crazy dirty, stuck all over with puckered mud and a couple of twigs. There were dried, muddy footprints too, trailing back toward the open window.

I yawned, hopped down from my top bunk and cleaned up the mess.

16

WALKING OVER TO THE DINING HALL with Veer, I had yawned at least three or four times. He stared at me the fifth time but didn't say nothing.

In the shower that morning, I'd stood there letting the water spray over me (weird yellow water, smelled like eggs) as I wondered if Veer remembered me climbing through our window last night.

If he did, he wasn't gonna let me know.

When we got to the dining hall for breakfast, Veer veered off again to join his new group. Standing in line, I scanned all the food they had to offer: granola bars, fruit, yogurt, juices, all kinds of doughnuts. . . . They even baked these special *bluecherry* muffins—blueberries and cherries!

I got scrambled eggs, bacon and oatmeal and sat down at a small table beside Tuyet and Becca. I didn't know any other Futureneers like that. My two teammates didn't seem to notice me until I let out another monster yawn.

"Late night?" Tuyet asked.

I shrugged.

Tuyet told us she was Vietnamese American, born and raised in Houston. Her long black hair swung as she turned from me to Becca. It ran down her back to her butt.

Tuyet grinned when she caught me watching her hair.

This one was kinda chill.

Becca, though, was a local girl from North Carolina. She was taller than me and built funny like an ostrich. Becca had a pretty face, but it didn't seem like she liked to smile.

Least not at me.

Anyway, Tuyet had called me a frowner, so I guess Becca and me had that in common. I scooted my chair closer to the table and accidentally bumped Becca, who all of a sudden tensed. Like she didn't like being touched. Me and Tuyet exchanged looks.

"I think we got the worst dorm," Tuyet said, swirling her cereal like she was suspicious of it. "You see the other dorms? They're much bigger."

Becca shook her head. "Taylor is small, but it's the newest and the nicest one. It was built for the older students when college is open."

How did she know so much about ARCC?

"*Maybe*," said Tuyet. "I just thought our room would be bigger." Unsatisfied, she spooned some cereal into her mouth. "My uncle's old shed's got more space to it."

"Talkin' with all that food in your mouth," Becca said to Tuyet, who rolled her eyes.

"One thing, though: I don't like our RA," Becca added.

"Becca, this is like the millionth time you said that," said Tuyet. "And we've only been here three days. Leslie's cool."

She shook her head. "That gal says stuff un-Christian."

"Like?" I asked.

Becca glared at me and paused. "You expect *me* to repeat it? It's the sorta stuff my folks would not approve of. That's *enough*."

"Mr. Wallace Rachpaul and Mr. Kofi Diallo are two very special young men," Dr. Hunter announced at morning assembly. "At the ages of seventeen and eighteen—only a few years older than most of you—they have designed an exciting virtual reality game that transports the player into a whole new world."

You could tell Dr. Hunter felt exhilarated.

I leaned my skull back against the headrest of my chair. One seat away, Becca was almost asleep. Tuyet stared at a fingernail.

The auditorium was mostly dried out today, but you could still smell moisture in here from that stupid sprinkler prank. I just realized that Cricket probably had something to do with that.

"Futureneers!" Dr. Hunter went on. "Please join me in welcoming Mr. Rachpaul and Mr. Diallo to our stage as very special guests of our third annual STEM Camp!"

She clapped.

Uncle Billy's Nieces and Nephews around the room clapped.

Only a few of the Futureneers clapped until Hunter glared at us. Then, it got louder in the auditorium.

These two Black teenage boys walked onto the stage. They smiled and waved and kinda slinked toward two stools beside Hunter.

One of them, Wallace, was tall with a huge Afro. His partner, Kofi, was shorter, but thicker like a football line-man.

I could tell right away by how they were dressed and even by how they walked that they were from New York. There's a certain way and style about how we do.

These dudes were surprised by the size of the crowd. Looking uncomfortable, they plopped down on the stools.

I noticed the taller one, Wallace, had a little scar on one side of his face. You couldn't see it unless you sat on this side of him. The scar shined a bit when he shifted his head away.

Hunter chatted about the new VR game they'd designed, *Flexus: Meet the Maestro.* "Boys, how'd this come about?" she asked.

"Oh, *Flexus* is Lolly's baby," the one named Kofi said.

Wallace grinned. "Well, the baby's not born yet." He beamed at us with really white, perfect teeth. I got jealous of his smile. Wallace said, "You kids out there get to assist with our baby's birth!"

They wanted us to test it for them. See how real people responded to their game, outside their lab.

Kofi added, "Lolly here came up with the idea when *he* was a kid."

"Well—" Wallace started.

"Now, Kofi," Hunter interrupted. "What is this you call your partner?"

Kofi snickered while Wallace rolled his eyes.

"Lolly," Wallace told her. "It's a nickname my brother gave me when I was little. He couldn't pronounce my name, Wallace, so it came out like Lolly."

"Oh, my!" Hunter shouted. "You're just as cute as a sack of puppies!"

He laughed.

"Can I call you Lolly?"

"Please don't," he said, laughing some more.

"So, *Wallace*, who inspires you?" Hunter asked.

"My mother, mostly," he answered. "And my girlfriend."

Some kids in the audience squealed.

"And," Wallace went on, "I study histories of Black artists and engineers for inspiration too. Lately, I've been reading about Wilson Nero, the tech guy."

"I knew Willie!" Hunter said.

"I *read*," said Wallace.

"Stunning."

They went on talking about how the boys got started in coding and building apps. Their VR game evolved out of some LEGO world Wallace had built when he was twelve.

If they could do something like that, as young as they were, I wondered what I could do myself.

After the talk, the Futureneers mobbed the stage.

"Ooo! Ooo!" one girl yelled. "I have a question! I have a question!"

"Go ahead," Wallace told her.

She looked embarrassed, but spoke, "How'd you get your scar?"

Wallace rubbed his spot. It seemed old.

"Um, what kind of question is that?" Hunter asked the girl. "STEM questions only, please." Hunter told Wallace, "Rude little campers!"

"It's okay," he said to the girl. "But how I got this is a *loooooong* story. Some other time."

"Okay, rude little campers!" said Hunter. "No more drama!"

"Thanks again for helping us improve *Flexus*," Kofi said to us. "Letting us test this on you. Your feedback'll go a long way."

"Yeah. Your reactions will mean a lot. We put so much love into making our game," said Wallace, "but we need to know if real players love it too."

Beneath the auditorium was a monster-sized room full of cubicles—these were the Brain Cells. The STEM camp had set up stations for all of us to test the *Flexus* game. There were enough VR headsets and game systems for five groups of campers to compete at a time. And we could play during free time!

Tuyet, Becca and me had picked the name Fractal Dactyls for our group. Turned out, me and Tuyet both liked fractals. Becca said she didn't care.

Each crew got a run-through of *Flexus* and were shown how to set up our virtual avatars on our separate video monitors. All the groups flipped through a selection of different faces, body armor and weapons to see what was available. You could also make your avatars talk inside the game by using the tiny mic in your helmet.

The Fractal Dactyls settled on one with a bright blue battle suit with gold trim. Our guy was eight feet tall with enormous smashing fists. I had to fight with Becca and Tuyet just to make him a dude. They wanted to make our guy a woman, but I got them to change.

"We can always redo him later," I told them, even though I knew we couldn't.

Over the next couple weeks, our groups would compete to make it through the game to some place called Maestro Island. If you got your avatar there, past a bundle of obstacles and the other avatars, your group won the game.

But there was no prize for that.

Right away, I saw problems with my own group working together as a team. Tuyet seemed like she always thought her way was the best way. And Becca didn't seem like she had no way at all.

I hated working with other people. I was better on my own.

I'd snapped on one of their VR helmets and hand controls and was still figuring how to move our avatar around the 3-D enviro when the designer, Wallace Rachpaul, strolled by our cubicle.

"You designed your avatar already?" he asked. "Good. What's your name?"

"Javari."

"Cool to meet you, Javari," Wallace said. We slapped hands.

Later, he said he could tell from my accent that I was from New York. He called over his partner, Kofi. Both of them were from Harlem.

"A'ight, man," Kofi told me.

"Let's see what you got," I heard Wallace say.

In my helmet I couldn't see them or Tuyet and Becca, who stood around me in the VR cubicle. There was a video screen where they could watch the game without goggles. The only thing I could see now in my goggles was an outer-space alien landscape.

In the sky, floating above me, were the words:

FLEXUS: MEET THE MAESTRO
BY ST. NICK STUDIOS, INC.

So cool.

"Walk straight ahead, under the floating credits," I heard Wallace say. "That's the boring stuff. The real adventure starts straight ahead."

"Toward the horizon?" I asked.

"Yup," Kofi said.

"In our game, you always walk east, toward the horizon," Wallace said. "That's where your destination is."

In the game, I walked a long ways. It was the scenery of another planet. A giant red moon was in the sky, which was purplish black.

All of a sudden, a huge alien insect flew at me and landed on my arm. I held up the bug. It was about the size of a pigeon, with bulging green eyes and sharp spikes all over.

"Is this bug cool?" I asked.

"Depends," Wallace said.

"What it look like?" Kofi asked.

Before I could answer, Wallace said, "Use your judgment, Jay. The rules of our game are a little different. In the real world, most people fear them, but I think loads of ugly things are . . . misjudged."

In the game, I reached out to pet the nasty bug. It let out a soft *zizz*ing noise. That sound mixed with the howl of the wind in this place, the rush of air in some sandy desert.

"We gonna move on to help the next group," I heard Kofi say. "Keep exploring, Jay."

"Yeah, good luck, man," Wallace told me. "You got this." I felt him slap my back and heard them walk away.

I nodded, stretching out my VR arms in front of me. The bug flew off. As I watched it fly away, it dropped something out of its scaly butt.

Like doo-doo.

I frowned.

Where the doo-doo landed, I noticed, it glowed.

I made our avatar scoot forward in the sand. I stopped it a few feet away and stared down. There were these glowing gold nuggets there.

Shining.

I reached down and grabbed at them and they disappeared. Just then, a blinking note flashed in the sky above me:

DRAGMOR PELLETS ADDED TO YOUR SURVIVAL KIT. MAY THEY BRING YOU LONG LIFE! TO ACCESS THEM LATER, HOLD DOWN YOUR RIGHT AND LEFT "D" BUTTONS SIMULTANEOUSLY.

"Tuyet! Becca!" I called out. "I think I just found treasure."

"Oh!" I heard Becca say.

"That was fast," I heard Tuyet say.

"Yeah," I said. "It's a bunch of alien bug crap."

"Eww!"

I laughed. "It glittered like gold!"

Somebody sighed.

"I ain't sure I'm gonna like this reality," I heard Becca say.

17

MY MOTHER GLARED at the video camera.

"Javari, what do you mean, 'monster'?" she asked me.

"I didn't see it. But Wendell did."

During lunch I was chilling inside one of the ARCC communications rooms where we could call home. On a big video screen, I clearly saw Ma, Daddy and Shireen sitting on the couch in our TV room back in Bushwick.

I leaned back against the soft leather headrest in my chair. We had some time before the next camper's turn for a call.

Daddy said, "This Wendell sounds like a joke."

"Yup," I said. "But I also heard these two other counselors talk about seeing the 'monster' too. Creeping around late at night."

"Nuts," Daddy said, shaking his head.

I laughed. I couldn't wait to tell them who the creeper really was.

Shireen said, "Javari gonna get ate up by a monster!"

Ma glared at her and at me and then at Daddy.

"I'm sure it's nothing," Daddy told her. "You know those, what you call 'em, hillbillies down there. Colorful people. Wild imaginations in the hills . . ."

Ma nodded. "That is what worries me. Maybe *too* wild." She stared into the camera again. "Javari, what about this bald man? The one who attacked you on the bus?"

Daddy laughed. "Wait. Hold up. He didn't attack the boy."

I hadn't really told them everything that had happened between me and Dalton Spratt on the bus and in that parking lot. How he was about to put his hands on me.

I didn't want to worry my folks too bad. I was about to tell Ma that the "monster" around here was really a thirteen-year-old Black boy terrorizing these white folks.

I knew she would find that funny.

"Ma—" I started.

"Javari, soon as you hang up off this call, I want you to tell your camp director about this bald man. Okay? He sounds threatening. You got me worried now. . . ."

"Niecey, take it slow." Daddy rubbed her shoulder.

Shireen shouted, grinning, "That bald man gonna stomp on your bones after that monster's done!" She fell into Daddy's lap, giggling.

"Shireen!" Ma shouted.

Maybe I told them too much. I decided to leave Cricket out of our video chat. He might make it worse.

"Lemme speak to Poppa George," I said.

"He's resting," Ma said. "And you spend too much time with him as it is."

"But—"

"Javari, don't press me now," she warned. "You 'bout to get on my last nerve with all this."

"You wanted him to go," said Daddy.

"That stupid Melvin talked me into it," Ma answered. "I didn't know it was gonna be like this."

"Jay is fine. Ain't you, Jay?"

"I'm fine, Ma. For real."

She glared at me. I could tell she was about to say something crazy.

"Time's up," I lied real quick. "Counselor's here."

"Well, let me—" Ma started.

"Adios, Shwick!" I yelled.

"Don't get ate!" Shireen shouted before I ended our call.

"Almost there!" Ms. Ferguson called back to the rest of us. Her voice wasn't deep, but it wasn't light either.

And she had a short haircut like a dude's. Every time I'd seen her, she wore that same blue tracksuit with no makeup at all. And she liked to slap my back so hard it stung.

I tucked my rolled-up rubber mat under my arm and stepped faster after her. I was breathing heavy. A few of the other campers in our group were having trouble walking up this mountain too. I don't think most of us ever got this much exercise.

Plus, it was the last session of the day and I was beat. Ms. Ferguson was hard keeping up with!

Our instructor finally reached the top, stopped and spun around toward us. When I got there, out of breath, there was a wide light blue sky behind her. This was probably the best view of the mountains that I'd seen so far.

"Here!" Ferguson shouted at us kids in her class.

"Wow!" this white boy named Travis called out. What he said was how we all felt looking at this sight.

"God's Eye Point," Ms. Ferguson said.

"Huh?" a white girl said.

"That's the name of this mountaintop, Elizabeth," Ferguson answered.

"God's Eye!" Elizabeth shouted, like she just got it.

"Yes! Beautiful, ain't it? How the Lord sees our world. But I didn't bring you way up here just for this lofty vista. We are here this evening to *listen* to God's world too."

"Relax, Javari."

My eyes still shut, I felt Ms. Ferguson tap the top of my head. It felt funny. Her footsteps on the dirt drifted away.

"Travis, stay centered," I heard her say.

I almost started to laugh. I felt this was sort of dumb. She brought us ten kids all the way here in a bus and led us way up this mountain to see the view. Then, she made us sit on our mats on the ground and shut our eyes.

What good was this when we couldn't even see the view anymore?

Couldn't even see the world?

This was how she "shared nature," I guess.

"You all hear our world talking to you?" Ferguson asked us. "The wind, leaves bristling, the *trees* around us, talking?"

Huh?

It took me a while, but I began to understand what she meant. The other night, I felt that tree outside my window say something to me. Telling me to jump into its limbs.

Not like a loud voice.

But a soft one.

"Keep listening," Ms. Ferguson went on. "Hear, even, the birds . . ."

"I hear lots of birds," somebody said.

"Yes," Ferguson said. "The birds. Birdcalls. What kind do we hear?"

Shree-shree! Shree-shree! Shurah-shurah-shurah!

"I heard one!" I shouted.

"Me too!" said somebody else.

Shree-shree! Shree-shree! Shurah-shurah-shurah! the bird called again.

"That bird's been singing this whole time," some girl said, irritated. "Y'all just noticed!"

Ferguson said, "Ms. Archer's tuned in. Some of the most beautiful things, we take for granted every day."

Shree-shree! Shree-shree! Shurah-shurah-shurah!

"That was a warbler," she went on. "A *Connecticut* warbler, I reckon."

"Connecticut?" Elizabeth yelled. "He sure flew a long way!"

Everybody laughed.

Ferguson said, "And he *is* a he. Male warblers make birdcalls all day long, trying to attract lady birds. Though it's hard to tell the difference between the males and females. They look almost the same."

Somebody snickered. I wondered if Ms. Ferguson was a kind of human warbler.

Shree-shree! Shree-shree! Shurah-shurah-shurah!

"That little songbird uses his *syrinx* to make music," said Ferguson. "His voice box. Soon we're gonna grow some voice boxes of our own down in the Brain Cells."

"*Ewww!*"

"Not *real* ones," Ferguson said. "Fake voice boxes on the computers. So we can learn how songbirds like the warbler use notes and tones to sing and share their truth. Real beauty."

That sounded cool.

She said, "But for now, let's listen a little more, eyes closed, and discover how many other types of birdcalls we can pick out. Okay?"

I leaned back onto my mat.

Listening.

Shree-shree! Shree-shree! Shurah-shurah-shurah!

Ha-kaa! Ha-kaa!

Pur-tweel-pur! Pur-tweel-pur!

All this junk had been going on all around me and I hadn't even noticed. Maybe I needed to spend more time listening.

18

OR MAYBE I LISTENED too much already.

I couldn't sleep.

Again.

Those crickets with their subwoofers were back. Plus, it was too chilly in our dorm room tonight. And I couldn't stop thinking.

About *Flexus*. It was a pretty cool game.

Wallace and Kofi'd left that afternoon. Dr. Hunter said their next stop was Texas to talk to other kids about designing games.

I wanted our group to get to Maestro Island first! But whoever won the game then would only get to brag.

The real prize was in that ARCC treasure chest that Dr. Hunter had shown us. Whichever group won the final project contest won the ARCC prizes and money.

Funds.

I rolled over onto my side.

I wondered exactly how much money was in that chest. I bet it had to be enough to get us caught up on our rent.

It must be nice to be rich.

I wondered if Wallace and Kofi were.

Even after they'd left, all we could talk about was their game. In Coding for Better Lives, out on the yard between the buildings, the instructor, Mr. Wang, told us we were *obsessed* with the *Flexus* game. He said, "You all—*everybody*—think about using code to build games. That's *boring*!"

We snickered.

"I'm sorry." Mr. Wang jumped in my face. "Boring!" he shouted. He strutted over to the boy sitting across from me. "Don't be boring," Wang said to him, like he was begging.

We laughed louder. He was trying to make us laugh.

"*Eh?*" Mr. Wang said, grinning. "Just because everybody else codes dumb games does not mean you have to. *Eh?* Plenty other great things you can design using code. That's what we begin to learn now."

I knew you could use coding for lots. Like designing hardware, buildings and even art. Not just games.

"You may even use code to create environmental and political apps!" Wang added.

I bet building games made more money, though.

During this session, me and the rest of the Fractal Dactyls sat in a circle on the grass. We spoke about Wallace and Kofi's VR while we were quizzed about different lines of code on our tablets' tutorials.

But instead of *Flexus*, these girls just wanted to talk

about the boys themselves. Tuyet thought Wallace was cute and that his scar made him "mysterious."

Becca said she hated the scar. Thought it was ugly.

"Focus!" Mr. Wang shouted at us before he pranced over to Blue Braces. He always needed help.

"I'm not good at math," Blue Braces complained to Wang, who leaned over and whispered to him, "You do not need to be a whiz. But you do need to use your brain. Think before you answer."

My tablet read: *What is crucial to reverse a string of code?*

    A) Change the state of the string object

    B) Know your coding language

    C) Reverse all of the string's integers

    D) All of the above

I thought and picked B.

Correct.

These questions weren't even that hard.

"Sorry, but that boy Wallace is a thug," Becca mumbled to me and Tuyet. She stared at her tablet.

Stupid.

Tuyet nodded. "But Wallace does have beautiful eyes." She sat her chin on her hand and gazed at a cloud, like she was staring into dude's pupils.

"You see his big Afro?" Becca said.

I was confused. I turned to Becca, who tried to type out

a string of code on her tablet. She got it all wrong. And the questions were so easy.

"What's wrong with his Afro?" I asked. "You afraid of his hair? They ain't thugs, dummy."

"*Mmm-hmm,*" she said.

"I guess you think *I'm* a baby gangsta?" I asked her.

Becca turned to me, like she was trying to peer into my soul.

"Javari," Tuyet said. "You know nothing about boys."

What was Tuyet talking about? I *was* a boy!

"He probably got that scar gangbanging in Harlem," said Becca.

"Gangbanging?" I asked.

Becca nodded. "You can just tell with some boys."

"You think some boys just look more *naturally* like thugs," Tuyet asked her. "*Darker*-skinned boys?"

"That is not what I said, girl," Becca answered. She looked down at her tablet, made a face and asked me, "Why *does* your skin do that so much?"

"Do *what*?" I asked.

"You know, get *sooo* puffy after it's scarred?"

Tuyet spoke up, "They're called *keloids.* Just swelled-up tissue."

"It's *weird,*" Becca said. "Don't look human."

I frowned at her. That girl sure was ignorant, I thought. Becca's string of code needed reversing.

That was earlier. Now it was night.

Still couldn't sleep.

I'd been lying in bed, thinking, for what seemed like hours when I started hearing this one stupid songbird over and over again outside.

Ha-kaa! Ha-kaa! the dumb thing went. Over and over.

I peeked down at Veer, who was snoozing. Sleeping on his stomach, so he wasn't snoring too loud.

Ha-kaa!

I hopped down and poked my head out the window. I wanted to strangle that bird. I decided to shut our window and was smacked in the face. It was wet, slimy, smelly.

Gross.

I hopped back and heard laughter outside. I recognized that laugh. It had been one of the first noises I'd heard on my ride into Horsewhip.

I shook my head.

19

IN THE DARK, I DROPPED from the tree to the ground just below my window. Again, I had on my Mets pj bottoms with my T-shirt. But this time I'd laced up my sneaks instead of wearing slippers.

I glanced around the yard. It was empty in the misty air.

Except against one tree, my eyes started to make out a giant leaning there. The giant was wearing a rubber Beast mask.

I frowned, bent to pick up the dirty rag I'd tossed down from my window and walked over toward him. I beamed the rag right at his head, but he ducked fast.

"Missed!" Cricket called. He pulled off his mask. "But I snagged you square in the forehead!" He laughed.

"Not funny, man." I rubbed my forehead.

"It was hysterical."

I didn't think it was. "Still creeping around? How'd you know where I stay?"

"Always interrogatin'," he complained. In the dark, I

could see that black duffel bag lopped over his back. "What *you* doing?"

"What you mean, what I'm doing, man?" I laughed. "I'm '*sleep*. We all are. At least, I *was* until you woke me," I lied, "crying like an ignorant *bird*."

He said nothing. Just tilted his head at me, then turned, started to stomp away, barefoot. He got more and more hard to see in the dark.

My heart thumped faster.

"Bird!" Cricket called over his shoulder. "You coming?"

I squatted down and squeezed through that hole in the fence behind the bushes. It was the same hole I'd squeezed through my second day here when I found the paintball.

Cricket said he'd seen me that day. He'd been hiding on the other side of the fence and watched Elrod yell at me, search me and tell me to go back to my dorm.

"That rent-a-cop's a racist knothead," Cricket said. "I bet he don't harass those white kids the way he done you."

I agreed and had just about scrambled through the hole again when I heard the back of my T-shirt rip.

I cursed.

Cricket snickered in the dark.

I hated messing up my undershirts. I didn't have that many of them with me here in West Virginia. This one had doubled as a pajama top.

Safe on the other side of the fence, officially off campus grounds, I stood up and reached around to feel the rip in my favorite tee.

"You mad 'cause you messed up your shirt?" Cricket asked. He spun me around. "It ain't bad, Bird. Easy to sew."

"Why you call me Bird?" I asked.

He shrugged. "You come when I bird-called, didn't ya?"

"You think you're cool," I told him.

"Naw, I sure don't. *You* think I'm cool, my man. That's why you done crawled through that hole after me." He giggled.

I didn't know what to say.

"Let's float," said Cricket. "Rent-a-cop's due back yonder."

He marched off down a leafy hill. I followed.

"What's your name besides Cricket?" I asked. "You know, your *real* name."

"I don't know you like that, Bird," he said to me. "I ain't sure you ain't a-working for *them*."

I sucked my teeth. Cricket stopped all of a sudden on the hill to face me, eye to eye. He squinted.

"*They* had slaves, you know," he said. "Black slaves that caught other slaves when they run off."

"Who? What?"

"I read that. You might be like one of them traitor-slaves. You cain't trust everybody."

He continued marching down the hill. I stood where I was.

"Um, I think I'm heading back, man," I said. I glanced around in the dark.

Which way *was* back to the college anyhow?

I got nervous.

"You wanna know the *real* Horsewhip?" he asked. "Or you just wanna see the slick and pretty Horsewhip them Uncle Billy's opossums show you?"

I did wanna see more. But also . . . "It's late and I don't know where you going, man. Ya heard?" I said.

"Suit yourself!" he called back through the trees. He kept on.

I gazed around again, realized I had made an idiotic choice, but still continued after him.

At the bottom of the hill was Cricket's bike. Not a regular bicycle, but like a red and rusty Honda dirt bike, not even as nice as the ones like we ride back home.

His was *way* older.

He had it hid behind the entrance sign that read: APPALACHIAN RIDGE CHRISTIAN COLLEGE. "RIGHTEOUSNESS GUARDS HIM WHOSE WAY IS BLAMELESS." PROV. 13:6.

"Cool bike," I told him.

"I call her Miss Daisy," he said. "Like that old racist flick? She's beat-up but gets the job done."

Cricket clapped his Honda dirt bike into neutral and held down the clutch. It hummed after three taps to the kick starter. I was surprised at how quiet it sounded. Not like Ke'Von's bike back in Bushwick.

I hopped on the back of Miss Daisy.

We zoomed off.

The old road here was bumpy. I had trouble holding on. Still, it was the most fun I had since coming here.

We kept on zooming down steep Foggy Gully Road. It was rough and the air felt wet against my face. Smelled like dirt.

Peeking ahead at the road below, I watched the spot of brightness made by Miss Daisy's one headlight. It was so dark, that was almost all you could see.

Rocks and then broken pavement running in front of us.

After flying down hills and around corners, we reached a tight curve, rolled past that little park there and screeched to a stop in the middle of Old Town. The back tire slid around, kicking up rocks. Cricket shut down his bike and jumped off.

I swung my feet onto the gravel. My butt was sore from all them bumps.

"She's fast," I told him. "Needs shocks."

Cricket didn't speak but started to hunt through his duffel. He pulled out a can of yellow spray paint and left his bag beside his bike.

This boy had lots of stuff stuffed in that duffel. I could see: granola bars, fruit, cans of soda, tiny boxes of cereal. All of it I recognized from the dining hall at ARCC.

Cricket was a thief.

At that moment, I felt like I knew totally who he really was. Like I suddenly knew the type of character he might be . . . But again, I didn't even know his real name.

His paint gun also stuck out of his bag.

I crouched down beside a large rock, stretched my thighs and watched him start to spray-paint the outside of the original Uncle Billy's store. Yeah, the same one where me and Wendell had got paintballed the other day.

Uncle Billy's had already scrubbed it clean.

But now Cricket painted more words onto the side of the building. I just crouched there, watching what he was writing and keeping an eye out for old Fred and Miss Dorothy next door.

This would for sure be the last time I hung out with this dude, I thought.

"There!" Cricket stood back to consider what he had sprayed. I walked over to stand beside him.

His work said: HORSEWHIP NEEDS CLEAN WATER. At least he spelled his message right this time.

"Yo. I noticed the other day you misspelled the word 'politicians,'" I said. "You spray-painted it: P-O-L-I-T-I-S-H-U-N-S."

"I know how I spelled it. I added the 'SHUN' part to warn folks away from them."

Oh.

Cricket dropped down onto the big rock. "That's called

artistic license," he said. "You should know better, future genius."

He went through the haul in his bag and offered me a granola bar. But I copped a bluecherry muffin instead. I knew those were the best.

I took a bite. Cricket cracked open a Coke and offered me a sip.

"Pop?"

I shook my head. He swigged and looked me in the eye again.

"I think that's cool, your funky eye," Cricket said.

First time I heard that!

"So . . . ," I started, "you, like, *really* hate Uncle Billy's, huh?"

He nodded. "Cain't stand them mangy buttholes."

"Why so much?" I asked. "New York don't like 'em either."

He nodded again, swigged more Coke. "They're smart then in New York if they hate Uncle Billy's." He dug around his bag again. "Uncle Billy's . . . they *take* but don't give. Least not to us hill people."

I ate the rest of my muffin, thinking on this.

"We ain't even got clean drinking water," Cricket went on.

"Why?"

"Mining," he said. "All the mining in our hills spoils our water bad."

I felt sorry for Horsewhip Hollow. Though it wasn't

Uncle Billy's fault, at least they could get these people bottled water, like they did with us campers. Be good neighbors.

"I squeeze through ARCC's fence, sneak onto their school to slip off with some food, bottled water, whatever else I kin get," Cricket said. "It makes a difference. But they know about me now. That security guard is on the watch."

"Elrod," I said. "He's a freak."

"He's a mangy butthole, I told ya."

I laughed. Cricket laughed.

"You sound *stupid,* Cricket."

"I know . . . ," he admitted. "That morning that rent-a-cop caught you by the fence, I heard you say you from New York."

"Oh, yeah?" I said. "You knew facts about me before we even met."

"Yup . . . my *real* name is Alcott Washington. Factual. I love fountains, especially when they're lit up at night and full of waterspouts. Oh, another quintessential fact about me is I sometimes run barefoot for stealth."

He wiggled his dirty toes.

I almost laughed at him but held it in. He was real. I didn't wanna hurt his feelings.

"You set off that fire alarm," I said. "I got soaked."

Cricket plucked his shoes from his bag and started lacing them up.

"I saw you after," I went on. "Sprinting across the yard. Was that you? I couldn't see. Sun was too bright."

"That sun *was* blazing yesterday. Ooo-whee! Another thing: I burn easy 'cause of my light skin." Cricket stretched and inspected his elbow. I started to ask a question, but he said, "I rode this here bike since I was ten and nobody bothers me 'cause I look so old."

"It's cool."

"Sure it is." He stood up. "I'll take you back up the mountain. I give you permission to use my secret gateway to leave your anus-infested camp. Just don't let nobody catch you. Come on."

20

"GOD IS ALL ABOUT US, everywhere we look."

A galaxy of stars flashed in our eyes. Ocean waves crashed on a sandy beach. A forest of tall trees, letting sun rays break through.

Somebody held up their hand to block out the sun. The screen zoomed in to reveal a gazillion veins running through their palm.

"Is our Creator the greatest scientist who ever existed? Do we all live in God's great laboratory?"

The voice of this narrator was putting me to sleep. For morning assembly, the video playing on the jumbo screen was called: *Is God in Fractals?*

I knew that fractals were like repeating patterns in nature. Like how the veins in one leaf are tiny versions of the limbs of trees or even the whole shape of a tree.

Or how water ripples resemble the rings of the planet Saturn in outer space.

Fractals were crazy interesting.

This video tried to be interesting but had ended up dumb. I was sure God knew all about science, but whoever made this video didn't.

I glanced around the dark auditorium. I wasn't the only camper having trouble focusing. Lester the Afro-Puff was nodding off.

I yawned loud.

Becca stared at me a minute, then went back to the video.

I rubbed my elbow. It was sore and bruised from me climbing back into my dorm window last night. And I hardly got any sleep, running around with that Cricket.

But still, it had been wild. Cricket was dangerous but also fun. I didn't think I'd ever met any kid like him.

I took a gulp from my bottle of water. I wondered if I should save some water bottles for Cricket. Since the faucet water around here was so stank.

I had to be careful about him, I thought. I took another sip, and just then, Tuyet leaned over to whisper to me and Becca.

"Y'all," Tuyet mumbled, "I'm worried. I think the other groups already chose their final project. We need one or we're gonna lose for sure."

"Pick something special," Becca whispered.

I had an idea. "What about water?"

"What?" Tuyet said.

I jiggled my bottle. Becca glanced at me and frowned.

"Well, what about it?" Tuyet asked me.

One of Uncle Billy's Nieces shushed us.

I spoke softer. "We should do clean water, how much of a problem it is."

Tuyet thought on this a minute.

"That's dumb," Becca whispered. "Cook up something better."

"*You* cook up something better!" I said. "Why's it gotta be me?"

"Boy, I'm sure in the *wrong* group," she said. "Wendell made you out to be real smart. But you two are bad news, just like Pa says."

"Shush!" went somebody else in the dark.

Tuyet shook her head and whispered at Becca, "And you are one ornery yellow-haired scarecrow."

I laughed.

"*Hush up!*" someone else shouted.

Later that day, after Becca had got attacked and murdered, me and Tuyet couldn't stop screeching. The body just laid there in the dirt, gushing out blood everywhere.

The little scarecrow deserved that.

She'd got ambushed by another group's avatar, but instead of trying to fight, she turned and ran! They'd rushed after our guy and beat us to pieces.

After that, it didn't take long for Becca to find one of our resurrection stones in our game's survival kit and bring our avatar back to life. I hoped she'd learned a lesson.

When we found out how rare those stones were in the VR game, Becca getting our avatar killed was not as comical. We only got three lives. And after that, we'd be done.

Becca tugged off her headset and hand controls and shoved them at Tuyet, who tossed them at me.

"You go next," Tuyet told me.

"You sure like giving orders," I told her.

I didn't think she heard. I geared up and took over our avatar. Tuyet and Becca watched what I did on the small video monitor in our cubicle.

In the game, we had left the alien desert behind. Now I was climbing up a mountain range. I wondered if Wallace the Designer had named these mountains. They were a lot like the Blue Ridge. But he wasn't from around here, I knew.

Once I got to the top of one, I used my controls to spin our guy around. There was an entire alien universe here. As far as I could see.

Endless.

The valley below, or holler I guess, was made from dark red rock and speckled with boiling ponds that crackled like acid.

Every now and then, I could see the slippery flipper of some alien monster pop out of the acid pools. I decided to not walk too close to those ponds when I got down to them.

Any monster that bathed in acid must be hard-core.

The view was still kinda hazy. Some kinds of vapors blew in the wind back and forth in front of my eyes. This made it hard to see right.

I noticed another team's avatar rolling between the acid pools. This group's guy, gold and roundish like a basketball, had almost made it beyond the pools. They were way ahead.

None of us knew which avatar belonged to who. It was funny, with so many of the other groups' avatars in the game, we hardly saw anybody else.

This reality really was huge. I started down the other side of the mountain.

Suddenly everything in my VR goggles flashed red. And then I was falling down the hillside. I hit the bottom of the valley hard. My viewfinder in the game now looked like cracked glass.

I'd been pushed! Ambushed by another avatar.

"Oh my God!" I heard Becca yell. "You lost us *life* bars. We could die!"

"Javari, get up quick," I heard Tuyet say. "That kid that hit us is still around. They'll attack again."

"Who was it?" I asked Tuyet.

She was quiet for a minute, I guessed scanning around the room at the other campers. Five groups of Futureneers were logged in and playing right now.

"I don't know," Tuyet said. "Could be anybody."

Just then, my screen flashed red again.

This time, I used one of our life bars to get enough energy to leap high into the alien planet's sky. From up here, I was able to peek down at the valley and spot the avatar who ambushed me. It wore a red suit of armor and a triangular helmet with big beetle eyes.

I fell back toward the ground.

I aimed my body down toward our attacker, landing hard on top of it with a smash. They were hurt bad.

"Shoot!" somebody yelled from the other side of the room.

In the video, I stared down at my opponent, who started to quiver and then vanished. I wasn't sure, but it seemed like Beetle Face teleported before I could finish them.

"They're gone," Tuyet told me. "You mopped 'em!"

"Barely," I said.

I was about to remove my gear when Becca shouted out, "Wait! You need to pick up the prize!"

A virtual reality message flashed above me in the game's dark sky:

TO THE VICTOR GO THE SPOILS! PICK ONE OF YOUR FOE'S SURVIVAL KIT ITEMS TO TAKE AS TRIBUTE!

Next, a survival kit flashed above. There was an ELECTRO WHIP, a FLYING JET PACK and some POWER GRENADES.

Becca and Tuyet told me to pick the jet pack.

I shook my head. "But it says it's only good for one trip. I want the power grenades instead."

"Javari . . . ," I heard Becca start.

I reached up and grabbed at the grenades and they disappeared. A glowing note flashed:

ATOMIC POWER GRENADES ADDED TO YOUR
SURVIVAL KIT. CONGRATULATIONS! PRESS "E"
BUTTON TO CONTINUE.

Instead, I saved our game and snapped off my gear.

The girls gave me faces. "You better not ruin our chance," Tuyet said.

"You're dumb; I know what I'm doing," I said. She was about to say something, but I interrupted, "Who was that I battled? When I fought back, I heard somebody in here yell."

"I couldn't see," said Becca. "It sounded like a boy."

"Yeah." Tuyet nodded, scanning around. Her eyes finally landed back on mine. "Some dumb boy," she said, arms crossed.

21

"AUTOMATA."

Ethan waited for his word to echo in our classroom.

"Who knows what that means? Anybody?"

He sat an old wooden clock on his desk.

"Mechanisms," Ethan said. "Automatic machines that seem like real people, real things, but they're not. They're artificial. We fabricate them."

"Like the Terminator?" one boy yelled.

"Exactly!" said Ethan.

He wound the clock's arms a few times around its face. After he stopped, the clock chimed and clicked. A tiny wooden bird popped out of its doors.

Kookoo! Kookoo! the bird chirped.

"In 1515 AD, Leonardo da Vinci, the artist, constructed a life-sized mechanical lion that *walked*," Ethan continued. "Even farther back, in Baghdad in the Middle East, a *Persian* inventor built a water-powered mechanical clock! That was in 807 AD.

"Many other automata, or robots, were forged in Mesopotamia during this golden age of Islamic culture. Much of what we know today about engineering is actually based on work from back then."

I didn't know that robots were that old. Or that some Greek dude named Archytas invented a flying robot bird in 400 BC!

That was *thousands* of years ago!

"Today, drones are trendy," Ethan went on. "But modern drones are lazy. We won't build those this summer."

I felt our whole group sag, disappointed.

Ethan said, "Me? I prefer kinetic clockwork gears and cogs and pulleys. I prefer those to lazy battery-operated electronic motors. Skipping the electronics when you want to build forces you to absorb even more about how stuff really works!"

For the rest of our class, each one of us worked with mechanical parts to build our own little automata. It was hard at first, but after a while, it made sense.

Logical.

By the end of the activity, I'd made my own helicopter propeller.

I cranked it up, and it spun and spun and spun.

Unreal.

His old brown face flickered on the big video monitor. I smiled and leaned forward in the leather communications chair.

"Poppa George!" I yelled.

"Javari!" Poppa said, smiling. "I can figure the shape of your face. Yes. Well, look here. This thing sure does work."

"I told you, it's easy," I heard Shireen tell Poppa.

She was holding her phone for him, so I couldn't see her.

"Okay, okay, Shireen," he said to her. "Don't be boastful."

I knew Shireen probably frowned at him for telling her that. It was good seeing Poppa. I'd talked with my folks before now, but not him.

In the ARCC communications room, I settled back into my chair. I was the only one scheduled for this video call slot. I enjoyed the swishy room.

I felt like a don.

"Good to see you, Poppa George," I said. "What you doing?"

"Oh," he said. "You know me. Just stuck in this old apartment. You the one out there living his dreams."

"The STEM camp is okay."

"That's good."

"West Virginia is pretty!"

"Oh, is that so?" he said. "Never been. Now, I used to work the railroad through regular ol' Virginia. Yessir, along that Texas Eagle line. I met hateful rednecks back in them days."

"How's Bushwick?"

"Oh, you know, *fine*, I guess," he said. "These dizzy Negroes around here, up to no good as usual."

I heard Shireen tell him: "Poppa, my hand's tired. Hold my phone. Here."

"Okay, okay," Poppa told her.

His face on the monitor started to wobble. I knew it wouldn't be long before he'd drop the phone.

"I learn stuff, but it's hard to make friends," I said.

He kept trying to steady the camera phone.

I said, "There aren't many Black kids here, Poppa."

"Well," he said. "You there to make friends or are you there to learn? Don't worry about fitting in. Them little children down there probably ain't worth the effort, no ways."

He dropped the phone. The screen went black. But I still heard him call for Shireen.

It was great seeing Poppa, but the stuff he said scratched me like it hadn't before.

22

"ROTTEN-FRUIT GAS?"

"Produce pesticides?"

"Robot drones that shoot rubber bullets!"

"Nah."

"Or drones that blow bubbles?"

"Bubbles?"

"Your *idea* blows bubbles."

"Hey! At least it's better than your boring water plan, Javari."

"It's relevant," I said. "Do you know how many people in our country can't get clean water? I googled it. Millions drink polluted water: places in Nevada, Illinois, Cali . . . Remember Flint?"

"Texas too—" Tuyet said.

"*I know,*" Becca said, sounding annoyed.

We were in our group's cubicle in the Brain Cells under the auditorium. We had been here for forever, brainstorming about what our official STEM project could be, the one that might win us the treasure chest full of green.

Our idea meetings sucked.

Dr. Hunter had sent out descriptions of what our groups needed to do for our contest. We had to find a STEM topic, do research and come up with a final project supporting what we found.

"I heard mountaintop mining poisons their drinking water here," I said.

"Hmmm," Tuyet said. "So, if you dig up mountains, you contaminate the water?"

I said, "We can pick *that* for our final project. And find a solution. We'd blow 'em away!"

"Too much work," Becca said.

"Don't be lazy," Tuyet told Becca.

Becca's face looked irritated. "But it's bad pub."

"Huh?" I asked.

"Bad publicity," she said. "It just ain't popular round here, I mean."

"Science ain't about what's popular!" Tuyet added. "*Good* science is about understanding, explaining—"

"And *solving* problems," I added. "We'd really impress Hunter and the judges by trying to work out the local troubles. *Everybody* hates the water here."

Becca bit her lip and checked her watch for the time. It was a gold one with tiny gold mountains on its face. She looked even more bothered.

"Becca, don't you care?" I said. "You're *from* here—"

"God's sake, I'm from *Charlotte*!" she yelled. "My family left this dump *years* ago."

I didn't have nothing to add to *that*.

My eyes floated around the Brain Cells, at all the other groups of campers, bunched up in their own cubicles, either taking their turns on *Flexus* or working on their projects like we were trying to do.

One of the groups was crowded around a computer, taking turns at code. These other kids had filled a goldfish bowl with water and were now pouring in a bottle of Crisco oil.

No idea what was going on there.

And a third group had started to build something crazy out of ropes and pulleys, like some old motors Ethan had showed us. But that Church Dress girl and the other three girls in *her* group weren't snapping at each other at all. They got along good.

Another team of campers looked like they had almost finished the frame of a small volcano out of clay or mud.

What did they think this *was*?

Kindergarten?

I tried not to laugh too loud and shook my head. Then I looked back at these two girls in my crew and sighed. I wondered if it was too late to join up with the volcano crew.

Tuyet and me had volunteered most of our project ideas. Becca'd just sat there, reading a kids' science magazine and playing with her watch and saying no.

I yawned again.

That Cricket . . .

"*Dude,* why are you quiet-belching?" Tuyet asked.

"He's always bored," Becca said to Tuyet. "Or just plumb lazy."

I glared at her. "I been having trouble getting to sleep, *Becca*. I ain't the one just sitting on my butt, not contributing."

Becca kept on worrying with her watch.

"You should stay away from any *screens* before bedtime," Tuyet told me. "Screens before bed: your phone, tablet, TV, any of that spoils your sleep."

Becca nodded like she'd been about to tell me the same thing.

"*And,*" Tuyet added, whispering, "drinking and smoking ruin your rest too. . . ."

This got Becca's attention.

"*Do* you?" Tuyet asked me. She squinted at me like my mother when she's suspicious.

I rolled my eyes at the ceiling. "Veer snores."

Tuyet stared at Veer, who was across the room, meeting with his own group. They were all boys, the Virtual Gear Engineers. This also included Lester the Afro-Puff, Jerry in his wheelchair and Blue Braces. It sounded like the four were already working on their project.

I glanced back at Tuyet and Becca. Why'd I have to get stuck with them?

I guess they'd been thinking the same about me.

"Stuff a sock in it," Tuyet told me.

Smirking, Becca glanced up from her mag.

"If Veer tries that snoring crap tonight, I mean," Tuyet went on. "You being nappy-time all day is ruining us."

"We're gonna lose!" Becca said. "I'm just not any good. I told my parents I didn't wanna come to this stupid camp, but they forced me."

She really looked upset. I gave her a sympathetic look. "Becca, I don't even understand how ARCC let you in here," I said.

"You trying to make me feel better or worse?"

I went on, "You don't seem creative or even really talented, I mean. And *you're* the lazy one who whines all the time. . . ."

Tuyet snickered.

"But you're here and we're all on a team, so maybe you should try harder," I said to Becca. "Or maybe just *try?*"

Becca threw her magazine down on our table. She stood up, boiling, face deep red. "I don't have to sit here and be insulted. Especially not by you."

"Good!" I shouted. "Go outside and be insulted! We tired a' you."

Becca marched off.

Nephew Wendell, who had just entered, spun after her. "Miss Rebecca! Oh, Miss Rebecca!" he called out. "Everything okay?"

"Ask him!" she said, before stomping out the door.

The other groups in the room stopped working and stared. Veer whispered something to Jerry, and the rest of the Virtual Gear Engineers snickered.

"Don't take her personal," Tuyet told me. "That girl'd start an argument in an empty room."

I plopped my forehead down on our table and shut my eyes.

In my head, I pictured zooming down Foggy Gully Road on the back of Miss Daisy.

I missed hanging out with Cricket.

Horsewhip – Cricket = 0

23

OUT BEHIND BRISWOOD CHAPEL, kids were rolling down a grassy hill that ended onto a little field. Everybody rolling had started after this one girl did it, and we all followed her.

She looked like she was having *that* much fun.

I hadn't rolled down a hill like that since I was real little. I used to *love* doing that in Prospect Park during picnics.

I got down on my knees, tucked in my elbows and spun into it. My roll started off slow but sped up.

It was that crazy sense I remembered, tumbling.

By the time I hit the bottom of the hill, I felt *so* dizzy. And I'd wound up on the opposite side from everybody else.

"Your butt turned you the other way when you rolled!" some girl yelled at me. "I *saw* you!"

I think she meant my butt was too big.

"Okay, kiddos!" Ethan yelled. "Quit fooling around!" He'd set up a bunch of stuff on a table in the field. "Come here! I got something for ya!"

* * *

The talky blond kid named Scotty plopped down on the grass across from me and grinned. He had teeth that looked like pebbles. And I could, like, *see* his red blood just beneath his skin, he was that pale.

White people are weird like that.

He held the bottom of our crankshaft between the heels of his two sneakers. This shaft looked like a crooked rod that you could twist around with your hands or with something else, like a rubber band. When we released it, the crankshaft would be what spun our propeller inside the motors Ethan was teaching us to build.

Spin like a wheel!

Scotty's fists held the top of the crankshaft so tight, his knuckles drained off blood under his skin and turned white as chalk.

"Go 'head," he told me.

Just like Ethan had shown us, I started wrapping one of our big rubber bands around our crankshaft. It started off easy, but got harder, twisting that band.

"You got it?" Scotty asked. "You got it?"

I nodded. "Get ready to fix our propeller on the end. It's hard to—"

Schnaaap!

Our rubber band popped off and whacked me!

"Dang!" I shouted, holding my cheek. It stung.

Scotty cracked up. "Yeah," he said. "You got it, all right!"

I sat there, embarrassed. I could feel my blood burn under my skin where the band hit. I knew Scotty wouldn't be able to spot my red cells under my skin, though.

"We could build a *glider*," Tuyet said, behind her goggles. "I always wanted to fly."

"Hover board?"

"We should try gunpowder. Or fireworks!"

"Drones?"

"You said that already."

The Fractal Dactyls *still* hadn't decided on our final project.

Disgusting.

I kinda wanted to build something.

Lately, because of my coding and Automata sessions, I'd been wondering about creating things, inventing. I remembered Ethan telling us about that mechanical clock they made back in ancient Baghdad. He showed us pictures of it.

Well, not *real* pictures, but models of how it was built and what it looked like. It worked by a big tank of water dripping into a bowl and twelve metal balls dropping on a gong to let you know what time it was.

Nowadays, people didn't even need to invent things out of just metal and wood. We also learned about this super-smart software named Watson that was programmed by IBM, the big company.

Watson's so smart, it learns by itself.

And in Coding for Better Lives, our instructor, Mr. Wang, programmed his own app that we used. It was called Nightjar. Named after some magical Chinese bird, and it taught kids how to code.

Most of the kids in our class really needed it, since not all campers knew coding. We weren't on the same level.

I know some code, how to write simple strings, but Wang's Nightjar was mostly about choosing icons, or pictures, on our tablets and dragging each icon into a function box on the screen to create easy strings of code.

Like building blocks, or those hieroglyphics on Egyptian walls.

Nightjar was fun even if you already knew a lot of code. You could make your little Nightjar bird avatar do all kinds of things on your tablet—fly upside down, get messages from other kids, draw pictures, even sing like a *real* bird.

"Hey!" Becca shouted, throwing me back to the Brain Cells under the auditorium. "What about one a' those fun-size volcanoes for our final? You make 'em from baking soda?"

"*Volcano?*" I glared at her. I'd been dreaming about computers that learn, and *this* is what she came up with? "You mean, like those dudes over *there*? We'd get laughed off the stage, just like they will."

Becca's face flashed red.

On our *Flexus* screen, Tuyet steered our avatar through a few gullies until she reached the edge of a dark, alien forest.

It went on for miles and miles.

Becca and me stared down at the small video monitor, where we could see our avatar stand by the forest entrance. From what I could tell, there weren't any enemies near us. But we had to watch out, the other campers who also piloted their avatars through this game had been bloodthirsty!

"Should I step inside the woods?" Tuyet asked us. "Or slip around?"

"It's *big*," Becca said. "It would take too long to go around."

Tuyet said, "Too bad we don't have a jet pack so we could just fly over the forest."

In my head, I could see her cut her eyes at me.

Becca glared. "Yeah, Javari. Too bad."

"Shut up, Becca. That forest is too huge to fly over. Probably."

"Going in," Tuyet announced. She moved the hand controls. I watched our tiny pixelated avatar creep into the woods on the screen.

I got nervous.

Tuyet walked like that for a long time.

"What's it look like, Tuyet?" Becca asked.

"It's almost totally black, spooky," Tuyet said. "There are these huge dark trees everywhere. . . . And it sounds like somebody—or something—is crying, far off. You can hear it echo all around. Wait, what was that?"

"What?" said Becca.

"I thought I— You guys see anybody? Near me in the woods?"

I shook my head, squinting at our monitor. "It's hard to tell," I said.

"In this part of the game, the map's hard to see. It's confusing," said Becca.

"Oh, great!" said Tuyet. "Wait. Wait. There's— Crap! I'm hit!"

"We can't see!" Becca yelled. "The monitor's black!"

"Oh crap, oh crap!" Tuyet shouted. "Oh! I'm trucking. Straight ahead. He's chasing me. Wait. There's *two* avatars chasing me now!"

"Who?" I asked.

"I can't see," she answered. "I think the same from before! The gold one shaped like a big basketball and Beetle Face too!"

"What—?" I started.

Tuyet screamed. Then, she was quiet.

"*Tuyet?*" Becca said.

"We're *wounded*," Tuyet said. "Bad. But not dead. You guys want me to use another resurrection stone? Or stay at half power?"

"We gotta save 'em," I said.

"Can't we power up with a Dragmor pellet?" Becca asked.

Tuyet nodded. "I'll use one Dragmor and save our game." She removed her headset and controls and leaned back in the chair. From the look on her face, she'd wrestled in a real fight.

"Know which groups jumped us this time?"

"Naw, I don't, Becca," Tuyet said. "But it was the same

avatars from before. One all gold. And the other, flaunting that red suit of armor. With a helmet like a beetle's. They worked together."

We all glanced around the room at the other Futureneers who shared our game. Any of these groups could have just ganged up on us.

"Just before they jumped me," Tuyet said, "the red beetle shouted out 'oorah' over his mic." She shook her head and then left for the bathroom.

"*Oorah?*" Becca repeated. "That's a Marine yell."

"Well, you know Lester told me his daddy's a Marine," I whispered. "Over there with the green Afro puff?"

Across the room, Tuyet passed between the other groups. One group hid their monitor from her. Then, Veer, Jerry, Blue Braces and Afro-Puff busted out laughing at her all of a sudden.

She stopped and stared. They got quiet. After she left the room, Veer shouted, "Unbeatable!"

"Ugh!" Becca said. "I don't see how you room with that boy. I'd be scared he'd blow me up with a bomb. He's from *over there,* you know."

"He's from India," I said. "I mean, Naperville."

I was about to roast her for what she'd just said, but I left it alone.

I felt fake all of a sudden.

24

A DARK, FOGGY FOREST.

Creeping along at night, I followed Nature Boy Alcott Washington through this patch of woods he'd driven us to a couple of miles from campus. Way out in the middle of no-where. Before Cricket'd parked his bike beside a tree, he'd told me he had a friend out here who ran a cool nighttime spot where they played music and gambled.

Cricket called it rowdy.

I went along even though I maybe shouldn't have. I liked fun, but I couldn't decide if Cricket's kind of fun was too dangerous.

But when I heard that birdcall, I snuck out and followed. Something about hanging out with Cricket made me feel like I was really living, out in the world.

And something else . . .

Out of the dark up ahead I heard the music at first, then we saw the lights. It was a tiny old spot, wooden, like a cabin almost, out here on the far side of Mount Tackett.

Around us in the woods, I could almost feel the trees thump.

Wildment.

"I always go round back," Cricket said. He took me to the rear of the shack. After he tapped on the door in a code, it swung open.

Nobody there I could see. Like a ghost had answered.

We both stepped inside what looked like somebody's old kitchen. It was way hot and humid in here. Pots and kettles boiled on a stove.

This kitchen was stickier and mustier than the woods.

The door closed behind us. And the man that had closed it howled out so loud I jumped.

He was tall and bald with a brown goatee and a scar on his face. This man in the kitchen stood there beside the door, staring at me until his stares melted into an evil grin.

I musta gulped.

It was Dalton Spratt. Bald Dude from my bad bus ride.

The Beast.

Me, him and Cricket stood there alone.

Dalton said to me: "Crook Eye."

Cricket glanced at me. I lurched toward the door.

Dalton stepped in front. He laughed and leaned a hand on his hip. The big dude held a dirty rag, soaked black.

" 'Vengeance is mine. I will repay, saith the Lord,' " Dalton yelled. "I knew I'd find you, snitch. My little buddy done brung you right here."

I gawked at Cricket.

"Didn't even have to leave my kitchen," Dalton said.

Cricket tilted his head to one side. "You two knowed one another?" he asked me and Dalton. Then, to me, "How you know Big D?"

"The bus," I mumbled, eyeing the wooden floor. It was caked black with food and dirt. "He tried to steal my backpack—"

The Beast jumped at me, gripping me by my neck. I stumbled backward, his hairy fist the only thing keeping me from falling onto the floor.

"Quit lying!" Dalton yelled in my face. I could smell his cheesy breath. "The Devil talks *soft,* don't he, boy?" He pulled back his other fist, like he was about to pound me. "But God's hand is *hard.*"

I shut my eyes.

"Dalton!" I heard Cricket yell. "Quit!"

Eyes shut, I still hadn't felt punched.

"*Geez, Louise!*" Cricket went on. "He's my friend! I drug him out here to cut up, not to get whupped on."

I un-shut one of my eyelids. Dalton was still glaring at me.

Cricket was holding back his other fist. Well, not holding back as much as lying on top of. Cricket had slung his big body over the Beast's whole other arm, trying to block the blow.

I wished I hadn't come out.

More.

Wildment.

"Let go a' him!" I heard Cricket yell. His face was hid over the other side of Dalton's enormous arm.

"He's the one!" Dalton let him know. "I told you what happened. This little bastard lied on me!"

"Your *mama's* a bastard!" I yelled.

"What!"

"Leggo, Dalton!" Cricket grunted.

The old bum thought on this for a long time and he finally did let me go. But really, shoved me to the floor. I felt my butt stick to the greasy floorboards. I jumped up and stumbled back.

Cricket unwrapped from on top of Dalton's biceps. I nodded Cricket thanks. He looked serious for a minute, then busted out laughing. Cricket kept on laughing like that for, like, forever.

It got to the point when both me and Dalton were confused.

I cooled a bit. Just a bit.

"Holy spit!" Cricket wiped a tear from one of his eyes. "You two nitwits! Dalton, I thought you was gonna go ape on him."

Dalton squinted at me and wiped sweat off the top of his bald head. "I *owe* this inbred woodrat," he said.

"I ain't no rat, you crazy redneck!" I yelled.

He twitched. "Don't call me no redneck, boy. I'm *hill-billy* and proud of it."

I went on, "Well, like I told you, what happened on that bus wasn't my fault."

Dalton growled, "You lyin' sack of—"

"Hey, Mule Head!" another voice called out from the front room. Besides the sounds of R&B music, I heard more people talking from the other side of the wall.

"Yep?" Dalton called back.

Cricket turned to me and smiled. *"Girlfriend,"* he whispered.

Dalton growled at this.

"Well," said Cricket, "she's really more like his lady-boss!"

"Where are my dawgs and them beans, sweetie?" the woman's voice yelled. "And we short on corn mash! You back there taking a nap?"

"Hold up!" Dalton yelled back. "I got you!"

"Ain't she just lovely?" Cricket teased him.

Dalton rushed to the tiny, crowded stove to fix a plate of tired-looking hot dogs covered in some weird gray sauce and a bowl of what looked like beans and corn bread. He topped the dogs with cut-up vegetables.

In the trash bin, I noticed dozens of wrappers of Bushwick Starr Franks. While fixing plates, Dalton kept glancing at me and growled under his breath.

"It's okay, Bird!" Cricket said. "You with me." He whispered, "We really ain't supposed to be at Barrelhouse, on accounta we's too young. His lady don't like it when I sneak in the kitchen."

Giggling, Cricket sat on a rusty stool and spun around like a little kid.

Dalton grabbed the dishes he'd made and stopped to glare at me again before walking through the door to the front room. After he'd left, I could hear people on the other side hoot, like they'd been hungry and waiting.

"I'm gone," I told Cricket. I started for the back door, but he snagged me by the elbow.

"*Wait!*" Cricket said. "Come look!"

25

CRICKET DRAGGED ME toward a tiny window that was cut into the wall. Through it, you could see into the other side. A bunch of country Black folks sat around drinking and eating. There was R&B playing and they all seemed to be having fun.

Some musicians were setting up their instruments on a small stage. Getting ready for a concert, I guess. It sure was a grungy spot.

But also, there was something *alive* in there. Everybody was amped and chill at the same time.

Celebrating.

I almost wanted to join.

"That's the Pot-lickin' Brothers Band," Cricket told me, pointing toward the musicians. "Best chocolate hillbilly music you ever heard."

I'd never thought there'd be so many Black mountain people. I'd assumed hillbillies were all white. Here inside Barrelhouse, a whole lot of Black folks had turned out.

At least the old ones.

"Try this," Cricket said.

Before I could stop him, he poked some chunk of food in my mouth. I almost spat it out before I realized how good it tasted.

"*Huh?*" Cricket said, grinning. "What I tell you? Dalton made that. He is the best cook ever."

Just then, Dalton raced back into the kitchen. "Shut that casement!" he yelled, talking about the little window.

Cricket ignored him. "D, Bird was just telling me how good a cook you are," he said.

Dalton seemed to soften a little. "*Yeah?*" he said.

"Yep." Cricket elbowed my ribs and hopped down from his stool. "After Bird tasted your smoked pork meat, he told me he was sure glad he didn't get you arrested on that bus after all!"

"*Cricket . . . ,*" I started.

Nature Boy bent over roaring again. Dalton wanted to kill me, I knew.

"You really good at food, *uh,* Dalton," I muttered.

Dalton shook his fat head. "I boil hot dog meat mostly. They like 'em around here, though."

"Popular," Cricket agreed. "Bird, is there some matter you wanna tell to Big D?"

"Too bad your feelings got hurt," I told Dalton.

"You call that an apology?" Dalton asked.

"More of a *nonapology,* I reckon," said Cricket.

"I didn't do anything *to* him," I said to Cricket. "Some other dude claimed he was trying to rob me."

"I'm a righteous man," Dalton said to me. "You were mixed up with making me look like I done something I did not do."

"A man's reputation is important," added Cricket.

"Look—" I started.

Just then, somebody screamed from the other room. We heard noise, like people scrambling and tables turned up-side down.

Dalton snarled at us, "Stay here!" and rushed inside.

Me and Cricket peeked through the window into the other room. A bunch of people stood around one man who rolled around on the floor.

He didn't know where he was or even who he was. His bloodshot eyeballs took turns spinning back into his head. White foam slid out the sides of his mouth.

"Lord," Cricket said. "He's sure slunk down."

"What?" I asked Cricket.

"He's OD'ing. On them drugs," Cricket answered. "Opioids, probably. Bad round here."

Dalton stood over the sick man for a few seconds before shouting at us in the kitchen. "Crick!" he yelled. "Bring me that charcoal from under the window! Hurry!"

Cricket grabbed a white bag from a shelf and ran it out to him. Dalton's brown-skinned girlfriend frowned when she caught sight of me and Cricket.

Before long, her and Dalton had mixed some of that powdered charcoal from the bag into a glass of water and forced it all down the throat of the man overdosing on the floor.

Back home on the streets, I'd seen people messed up from drugs, but I never saw other people force charcoal water down their throats. After a few minutes, the man on the floor was more alert and able to sit up.

A dark-skinned dude in a wide white hat propped him against a window.

"Grady," Dalton said to some other man, "kin you run him down to Memorial Hospital in your pickup?"

Grady nodded.

"They're gonna need to pump his gut," Dalton said. "That charcoal we fed 'im is a short-term fix."

"Why charcoal?" I asked Cricket, who'd come back to the kitchen.

He nodded. "*Activated* charcoal."

"Why do they keep that in the kitchen?" I asked him.

Cricket seemed surprised. "You just seent why, Bird. To save these folks from OD'ing. Drinking the activated charcoal to keep from dying is cheaper than taking Naloxone."

I'd heard of Naloxone. In New York, it was a drug the cops carried to help people high on heroin and other drugs. It saved people's lives.

"Them sorta shenanigans happen all the time round here," Cricket said.

I was done.

I shot for the kitchen door we'd come in through. I was at least twenty yards away before Cricket caught up with me. He held my elbow to slow me down. I whirled on him and almost stole him in his jaw.

Cricket didn't flinch. He just stood there, laughing in the moonlight. I felt like slapping the taste out of his mouth.

"Yo," I said instead. "That was nuts. I gotta . . ."

I glanced around the woods where we stood and I felt suddenly scared of everything out there in the darkness that I couldn't see.

"Look, Bird," he said. "Settle down." He wiped my forehead. His hand was cool, chill. "Yer sweating like a snowman in heat, boy."

I felt stupid.

"Ain't you never seen nobody OD before?" he asked.

"Course I have," I said.

"Humph. Must happen every day in New York City." Cricket stared up at the night sky, then back down to me. "Tell me 'bout New York."

"Just take me back, man. Where's Miss Daisy?"

I was lost.

26

AFTER CRICKET DROPPED ME OFF, I got to the tree that sat beside my dorm room window and stared up at the branches. As I started the climb up, my reunion with Dalton the Beast was still hot.

Mule Head.

I really didn't understand how him and Cricket could be old friends. Dalton, to me, seemed like just any old hood from around the way. Even though he was country and lived in the woods, he reminded me of some of the street hoods back in Bushwick.

How he talked with a twang was the only difference. And that he was white.

Grabbing up to the next branch, I suddenly heard something.

"Pissshhh! Elrod, what's your twenty? Over!"

Other voices chattered too. Coming nearby.

I stared down from halfway up the tree and saw Rich the RA and Elrod strolling along the yard in the dark.

I froze.

Elrod's walkie talked again: *"Pissshhh!"*

They couldn't see me, I realized. Not yet at least, but they'd soon be staring straight up at me. And I still had another floor to climb on my tree before I reached my own window.

I could hear their footsteps come closer.

Without thinking, I yanked at the branch right above my head and my hand slipped. I almost fell out of the tree!

I cursed.

There was a window right across from me. One floor beneath mine. Holding my breath, I stuck close to the tree trunk and watched Rich and Elrod pass below.

". . . what's good for 'em," I heard Rich say. "Doc Hunter's on the warpath. She don't even want them warning the campers' parents."

"That's a crock a' crap," I heard Elrod say. "I told Wendell it's just some tater in a Halloween mask, is all. I seen that colored boy before. Just not up close. Running barefoot like some critter."

"An *ill*billy, huh?" Rich asked him.

"Yessir."

So, *that's* how they talked when I wasn't around?

Dang.

Rich said to him, "Well, I got faith in you, bud. We gonna . . ."

They drifted away. I could breathe again. I sucked my teeth, thinking about those two knobs. Then, behind me in the dark room, I heard a bed mattress go *sproing*.

"Hey!" somebody yelled.

I jerked around. Through the window, I could see Becca's pale face and gold hair reflected in the moonlight. She seemed to be looking at me, crouched outside her window.

"Tuyet!" Becca shouted.

I heard Tuyet call from the top bunk: *"Bec-ca?"* Tuyet sounded half asleep.

I shot up the tree.

Becca screamed as soon as I moved. Scrambling to the floor right above—*my* floor—I almost fell twice.

I tripped inside my own dorm window.

Veer was still asleep, of course.

I flew into bed. A few minutes later, Rich barged into our room to check on us. He asked me and a cranky Veer if we were okay.

"That damn creeper scared one of our girls downstairs," Rich told us. He was breathless.

"For real?" I said, pretending to be sleepy.

"Yeah!" Rich answered. "Same sucker's been sneaking around campus, I bet, snatching and wrecking everything."

I nodded.

I knew he meant Cricket. They didn't know it'd been me just now. Becca must not've got a good view at my face.

Rich's face was dark now, hid by the fluorescent hall lights behind him. He stood in our doorway, quiet for a minute, then suddenly shouted, "That *thug* tried to break in Ms. Becca's window!"

He was *way* perturbed. Like his own *daughter*'d just got scared. And Becca had *way* exaggerated. I'd been far outside her dumb window, nowhere *near* her!

Rich also told us the creeper screamed something un-Christian before jetting.

Fictitious drama.

Forget being a STEM scientist. Becca should be a *writer*.

Rich left. Veer started to snore again.

Sunk back into my bed, I chuckled at how *stupid* country white folks were. I wondered how Becca woulda reacted if she'd been in true danger. She wouldn't last a second on New York streets.

But I really worried how all this would hit Cricket. They'd already been on the lookout for him on campus because of his thieving and tricks.

Now, I realized, they'd really get after him. Believing him some kinda wild nut.

I'd just made him a bigger catch.

$a + b > a - b$

27

I WANDERED AROUND the main auditorium for what seemed like forever before I spotted them. Near the front doors of the huge room were Ma and Shireen.

Talking to Elrod.

What was *he* doing with *them*?

Shireen saw me first. "Jay!" she called out, and started to run toward me before she realized how goofy she looked and slowed down.

I smiled at her.

She smiled at me. "You got skinny!"

No, I hadn't. I'd only lost a couple pounds. I was still fat.

"Oh, Javari," Ma said.

She gathered me and Shireen together for a big family hug. I felt relief to see them, even though before, I couldn't wait to leave New York.

"My little king," Ma said, studying me. "Why haven't you been eating? You homesick?"

"Yo, Javari!" Elrod said. "We tried to find you, bro. I ran into your mother and sister out on the yard."

"Okay," I said.

"Yeah," Ma said. "We got lost. Thanks again, El. I didn't realize this campus was so big."

"Ma," I said. "Let's get some air."

I tugged her arm and led her and Shireen through the glass doors.

"Um, okay, baby," Ma said.

"Enjoy Family Day, ma'am!" Elrod shouted after Ma. "And don't you worry none, I'll handle our *problem*! I am on it!"

"Oh, thank you, El!" Ma called.

"Don't talk to him," I warned her after we were far away. "What problem was he talking about?"

"Oh. Your 'monster' on campus. I asked him. El said it's just some local punk pinching muffins."

She talked with him about Cricket? "Ma," I said. "Don't pay no attention to Elrod. He's one of them illogical human beings you hate."

"Oh, Lord," Ma said. "And he was so helpful . . ."

Outside on the campus grounds, all three of us strolled along. I was surprised Ma hadn't argued to go back inside. She usually didn't like outdoors.

But Shireen told me she wanted to see more of the campus before the Family Day lunch. So, I showed them.

On the way we walked past the big bush that hid the hole in the fence where Cricket and me crawled through. I suddenly grew nervous, worried that my moms and Shireen might be able to spot it.

I was a doofus, I realized. They would have to have X-ray vision. I guess there was something about that hole that made me feel guilty.

"Ma, I can't believe you came," I said. "Why didn't Daddy?"

She and Shireen looked anxious. Ma said, "*Uh*, your father had to work."

Sis said to her, "Ain't you gonna tell him about—"

"That's enough, girl," Ma snapped.

"*Okay*," I said. I knew enough about my mother's voices to know to change the subject. "I'm sure happy to see yow."

We sat down on Cricket's fountain in the middle of the yard. A few other families were nearby. Kids got hugs and kisses.

Ma squeezed my hand again. "Ain't these folks feed you?" She tugged a small bag of chips out of her purse and shoved it at me. Utz Salt'n Vinegar Potato Chips. "I know it's not healthy, these chips, but I want you to eat, baby."

Shireen snapped a picture of me with her phone. I had a potato chip in my mouth.

Ma said, "Jay, we *all* miss you—your father, George, even Shireen here."

My little sister rolled her eyes. Ma kissed my forehead.

"This sure is the boondocks," Shireen announced,

glaring around with a frown. "These white people ain't tried to lynch you?"

"Shireen!" Ma said.

"I'm sorry, Mommy," said Shireen. "I'm just saying . . . I heard that's what they be doing down here. Lynch Black folks?" My sister stared in the direction of the hole in the fence. She turned toward me. "You ain't scared?"

Ma squinted and brushed her braids out of her face. I knew she was paying close to what I'd say next.

"Well, actually," I started, "it's been okay. People been nice. *Mostly.*"

My moms tilted her head to one side. Shireen shrugged.

"They got Confederate flags here," Ma said. "In *this* town. We saw one on the ride up. Set up right on some fool's front porch."

"That redneck flag," Shireen said.

"*Shireen . . . ,*" Ma said, frowning. She glanced around.

"Well, that's how Poppa George called it," little sis said. She pulled up a pic on her phone. "See? I took this."

It was a picture of Fred and Dorothy's red, white and blue flag. The same one I'd seen when I first got here. The big X right in the middle.

"That's a racist flag," Ma told me. "Hate. It's the flag they used during the Civil War, the one the slave states chose to represent their ideals."

"I know, Ma. I seen it," I said.

"You *knew*?" Ma asked.

"Told ya!" Shireen said to Ma.

"*Shireen,*" Ma warned her again. Then, to me: "Boy, why didn't you tell me? If I knew, I woulda snatched you outta here so quick!"

And that's why I didn't tell her.

I just shrugged.

"Racist crackers," Ma whispered.

"Now, *that's* racist," Shireen told her. "What you said."

Ma whipped her neck. "I done told yow kids, Black people *can't* be racist. We can be prejudiced. There's a difference. To be racist, you need power, and we have *no* power in this country."

"What about Oprah?" Shireen asked. "And the Obamas? He was president."

Ma narrowed her eyes at her. "Next time, you stay in Brooklyn." My mother squeezed my hand. "Javari, I thought we can take you back with us, back home."

"What?" I said. "*Now?* Ma—"

"Don't you wanna?" she said. "You ain't scared, Javari?"

"I ain't scared," I said.

I wouldn't be able to say bye to Cricket!

"I *wanna* go home, only not now. I'm learning. It's fun. And I wanna finish this camp. There's a contest I gotta win. I don't wanna quit."

She nodded slow. "I don't like you down here, alone, around these Confederate-lovers. It ain't what I signed up for."

"There's Black people too," I said. "I met a whole mess

of 'em. They nice. And I can't go back now, Ma. I got a plan. To save us."

"Save us? From who?"

Across the yard, I watched this Asian boy stroll with his family. His mother, I guess, kept picking at his hair. They started to argue.

"You do seem different, more confident," Ma said. "I think gettin' you away from Poppa George's working some good."

She didn't know about our video calls.

"We gonna have to move?" I asked her.

Ma's mood instantly changed worse. I was sorry I'd asked her, but I wanted to know if we were still getting evicted. It had been on my mind so much.

"It looks like it, baby," Ma said to me. "We can't seem to pull the money together."

Shireen's eyes stared at the grass. I knew I had to win that cash prize now. It was the only way.

"I'm sorry, baby," Ma said. Her eyes got wet. "We already started making plans. We'll land somewhere."

She rubbed my head. I barely felt it.

28

MA AND SHIREEN STAYED the *whole* afternoon. They ate pork chop dinners with me in my dining hall and walked around some more. We skipped the official tour because that was corny, and Ma wanted to focus on me.

They liked Taylor Hall and even met Veer and his fam.

I had fun. I think the Harris women did too.

Uncle Billy's had sent travel vouchers to cover my bus fare, but Ma didn't get none of those. She got lucky and was able to score one of her coworkers' cars to drive down. A real long trip just to check up on me and see how I was doing.

But my ma was like that.

This afternoon, late, I'd hugged both of them goodbye. Held on extra long.

Tight.

"I could stay here all week," Ma said into my hair. She let go and shot me in the eyes. "But we gotta get back. I got work in the morning!"

Before her and Shireen hopped into the borrowed,

beat-up Toyota to ride straight back to Bushwick, I could tell Ma felt better about leaving me down south.

"Everybody seems so *nice*," she'd said. "At first, them being so nice made me suspicious, but I guess that's just how they are." Ma shrugged.

The next day in the Brain Cells, I thought about their visit and leaned back in my swivel chair. I wished they coulda stayed longer. That round trip they made just for me musta been brutal.

Ma really had been worried about me. And about something *else* too. As much as she had wanted to see me, she seemed just as worried to get back home.

Tuyet and Becca and me were back at it now, arguing over our final STEM project, trying to choose one that would win us the treasure. Our group was the *last* one who hadn't decided.

The other day at morning assembly, we watched this video on the jumbo screen called *Hi-Tech Christians*. It was about these developers using AI, or artificial intelligence, to solve moral problems in our world. I asked the girls if AI would make a good project.

They hated my idea.

Back in the Brain Cells, Becca was bored and ready for lunch. She sighed every few minutes and stared at her fancy gold wristwatch, like she did whenever she wanted to dodge a problem.

Across the room, Veer's group was already at work on their project. Something to do with hydrogen energy, from what I overheard.

One of them caught me staring. "Keep your eyes on your *own* project, Brooklyn!" Lester shouted at me.

Veer started to giggle.

"They don't *got* no project!" Jerry shouted.

The entire group laughed at us.

"*Oorah!*" Afro-Puff yelled.

Tuyet sighed. "These boys irk us in real life *and* in *Flexus.*"

That was correct.

Trying to escape, I went on our laptop and did a search. I found a fan-made site for Cricket's Barrelhouse group, the Pot-lickin' Brothers Band. I never did get to hear what they sounded like. I was curious.

I started to download some of their songs from the site.

Back across the room, the Virtual Gears steady continued to cut up. Lester, bobbing his green Afro puff up and down, hooted, "*Ooo-ooo-Oorah!*" over and over while the others clapped.

Becca whispered at us, "That kid with the green pompom acts like a big *monkey.*"

My eyes musta got *so* huge. I swung around. Tuyet had hid her head in her hand.

"I oughta shove that word back down your throat," I told Becca.

"*What?*" she said.

166

"Not cool, Becca," Tuyet said. "Why would you say that?"

"What you two *talkin'* about?" Becca asked. "Those boys are a real bunch of clowns."

"That's *not* the word you just said," I snapped.

"What is *wrong* with you?" Tuyet asked her.

"I don't get it," Becca said.

"You just called Lester a *monkey*!" I shouted.

Everybody heard.

We'd got the attention of the Virtual Gear Engineers now. They had been across the room. But after my holler, they *all* knew what had happened. The boys rushed over to our cubicle.

Lester was *really* upset. We both were.

"Is *that* what you call me?" he asked Becca.

"There's nothing wrong with that," she said.

Lester looked at her like she was crazy. The rest of his group had his back.

"You prejudiced or something?" Jerry asked Becca.

"Huh?" she said.

Lester flipped. "*This* chick called me a monkey!"

"That's why nobody wanted you in their group," Blue Braces told us.

"Who you callin' a *chick*?" Becca bit back at Lester.

"*Man . . . ,*" I said. I turned to Becca and Tuyet and stood. "I'm leaving the Fractal Dactyls. Becca, you got problems."

"She ain't the only one with problems, *Brooklyn*!" Lester shouted. "*You* called me the N-word!"

"You called Lester the *N-word*?"

"Shut up, Jerry," I answered. "That's different."

Jerry rolled toward me in his wheelchair. "But if *I* said that—" he started.

"Shut up!" Then, I spun back on Becca. "I can't be around you."

By then, Nephew Wendell had ran into the room from the hall. He scurried up, worried. "Boys, girls . . . We okay? What's all this caterwaulin'?"

"She just called Lester out his name," I said. "A slur."

"No, I did not!" Becca said.

"Didn't you?" Lester asked her. *"Didn't you!"*

"Now, everybody, let's all just settle it down," Wendell said. "Javari, Lester, are you sure you aren't being too *sensitive* with Miss Rebecca? What did she say?"

"She called Lester a big monkey," I said.

Wendell glanced at Becca and then at Lester and then back to me and then back to Becca. He said, "Becca, honey, is Javari right? Did you say that about poor Lester?"

"What's wrong with it?" Becca asked. "They're always *monkeying* around. He's the ringleader."

Wendell winced. "Honey, we don't . . . That's just not a word we use for—"

"What's wrong with it?" Becca snapped. "My *daddy* calls us that all the time. It's funny."

"Hmph!" said Lester. "Do I look amused?"

"But you cain't call other people that," Wendell told Becca. "Particularly not boys like Lester and Javari."

"Why not?" she asked.

Was she for real?

"Because there's a nasty history of folks like you com-paring folks like them to *animals*," Wendell explained. He almost whispered, "It's different when *your* daddy calls you and your sister that 'cause, well, y'all ain't Black. But calling some *African American* boy that name, well, is like calling them the N-word."

She sat there, her mouth a little loose.

"I'm *out*," I said again.

I left the whole thing.

29

MAYBE I SHOULDA GONE with Ma and Shireen. After lunch, I took my time wandering around the school grounds. *Anything* but going back to my evil Fractal group.

I really did want out.

Now.

Even if I had to be my own group, by myself.

I sat under a shade tree across from Cricket's fountain. They'd just turned it on. Fountain water misted my face.

Before long, that Elrod strolled by. He stopped to chat, though I really didn't feel like chatting with nobody. Especially not him.

"Yo, Jay!" he said. "Lil Hunk just dropped his new EP. You heard it, man?"

I shook my head.

Sucking on the end of a grass blade, I stared up at Elrod. He loomed over me. I was reminded of those tall trees in that fractal video.

Elrod said, "Okay, man. Let me know when you listen."

I nodded.

"I'm curious to hear what you think since you and Lil Hunk is both from New York. In fact, I kin stop by your room Sunday. So you can vibe to mine."

"I got plans Sunday."

He nodded all slow. "You going to Charlotte on that field trip?"

"I got plans" was all I said.

"Okay, Big Apple," he said. "I really liked meeting your mama and little sis from New York yesterday. Real cool *sistahs*."

I wanted to knock him in his big, dumb head. Were all these white people crazy?

Sticking the grass blade back in my mouth, I stared down at my phone. I still didn't have any bars no matter where I went here. I wanted to call Ke'Von. Talk with somebody who wouldn't instinctively drive me nuts.

Elrod finally said, "Cool," and left me alone beneath my tree. I laid on the grass and sighed.

$0 \times \infty =$ Elrod

Some folks were dumb times infinity.

The view from my back reminded me again of that *Is God in Fractals?* video. The sun shined down on my face through the branches of the tree above. Every limb, from the top to the trunk, was a copy of the others. These fractal shapes repeated down to the leaves. Even down to that leaf's little cells.

The universe was a huge fractal.

Endless.

Like the ∞ sign.

Though it seemed like infinity, I was actually alone beneath my tree for only a little while. Tuyet wandered over and sat down beside me.

She handed me a bluecherry muffin. "You like these, don't you?"

I nodded.

"Thought so," Tuyet said.

I sat up and took a bite even though I wasn't hungry.

"I'm sorry about Becca, Jay," she said. "After you left, she told me she was sorry. I don't think she really knew what she said was racist."

I laughed. "Do you know how you sound?"

"I think she's in trouble," Tuyet said. "Nephew Wendell took her to see Doc Hunter."

That made me feel better. "But if she's sorry, well, that's for Becca to say, not you."

"I know. But she's just . . . ignorant. I don't think she wants to be like that. But sometimes I just wanna introduce her to the back of my hand."

We watched three Futureneers roll sluggishly across the yard. Bits of fog started to drift across the mountains. Being up here in this cool, soggy weather slowed down everything.

"Plus," Tuyet said, "Becca's hiding something."

"Her KKK robe?"

Tuyet shook her head. "I don't know. But I can always tell. Just like you."

"Huh?"

"You're hiding something too, Javari."

I gave her a smirk and took another muffin bite.

Now Becca and Nephew Wendell walked down a footpath. They were coming from the main building. She made eye contact with us and floated a weak wave. For a minute, I was concerned they were gonna come over, but they kept walking.

She looked regretful. I didn't have time for that girl.

"What's wrong with her?" I asked Tuyet after they'd disappeared.

"I don't know," Tuyet said. "She's got these strange ways."

"Conceited too," I added.

"Yep," Tuyet admitted. "That girl's stuck-up higher than a streetlamp."

"You kill me, some of the stuff you say."

"So, will you come back to the Fractal Dactyls if she apologizes?" Tuyet asked. She planted her forehead on my shoulder. "Please, Javari! If you don't come back, I may have to strangle Becca and then I'll go to jail."

I grinned.

"Probably some ratchet Appalachian jail," she said.

"Okay," I said. "Only if Becca apologizes. And promises to be better."

"Oh, thank you!" She hugged me. "Thank you!"

"You're too bossy to go to jail," I said. "I just hope *I* don't strangle her and get caged up."

"I'd visit you."

Later, we had a special session in the Brain Cells with both Ms. Ferguson *and* Ethan. Though I usually liked their two separate classes, I was still sizzlin' from what went down.

I think Ms. Ferguson realized. She'd been extra smiley toward me.

I wondered if she'd heard.

Ethan went on, "But some computers, like the ones we have here, can do things in simulation that we can't do in real life. Or rather, do things that'd be harder in real life."

"Like our birdcalls we've been listening to?" Ms. Ferguson added. She smiled at me again. "Who remembers what the warblers sound like on God's Eye? Hmm?"

I kinda did . . .

"Logan!" Ferguson had whirled on him. His eyes bugged. Everybody laughed but me. "Don't panic, Logan. I want you to make our warbler call. You are very good."

He hesitated a minute, then pulled back his lips.

Shree-shree! Shurah-shurah!

"That was our Connecticut warbler," Ferguson said.

"Logan! Bud!" Ethan yelled. "This duck-hunting season, I'm taking you with me!"

"Ethan . . . ," said Ferguson.

"What!" Ethan answered her. "With him making duck calls, we'd catch all them great big, juicy mallards."

They all laughed again.

I still sat, heated and quiet.

Ferguson opened her birdcall program on her laptop. It ran on all the small screens we usually used for *Flexus*. I leaned in closer, curious.

Ethan strolled down my aisle. "Warblers, songbirds use their syrinxes—or their voice boxes—to regale! And ain't we lucky?"

This girl Kate nodded.

"The syrinx is a unique, two-sided organ at the top of their throats," said Ethan, cupping his neck. "It can vibrate and produce two different sounds from both of its sides at once."

"I wish I could do that!" Kate shouted.

"With this software, you can!" Ferguson said. "We want you all to create your own unique birdcalls! It's intuitive, the program. Use your arrow keys to control pitch and tone."

"And choose your notes with your number keys as a music scale," Ethan added.

"Keep adding up sound bites by toggling between Space and Shift," said Ferguson. "You can layer the bites on top of one another, just like real songbirds do."

"Once you all come up with your own birdcall, and name it," said Ethan, "we'll save 'em and we'll listen."

It didn't take long to pick up this program.

And after about ten minutes, our room was whistling with artificial bird songs. It was real loud. But also, real pretty.

Shreet-ta! Shreet-ta-heeee!

Churahhh-churah-toooo! Churahhh-churah-toooo!
Blooo-ahh-bluh-bluh-bluh!

Like sitting in a big cage full of singing birds.

It made me feel better, actually.

Like, lifted away.

"Miss Rebecca, what thing is most crucial?"

Becca sat speechless. She was so dumb.

"Eh?" Mr. Wang went on. "Besides your phone?"

We all laughed, except for Becca. Her phone had just chirped. She put it away.

"Um, what's crucial to *me?*" she asked him back. "Well, I guess my family."

"Good!" said Wang.

Becca continued, "My parents and my sisters. Our nonna."

"Yes! Very good!" said Wang. "Family . . ." He paused, slowly turning until he made eye contact with all of us. "What is bigger than family?"

"Nothing!" Lester shouted out. *"La familia* is *numero uno."*

Wang stuck his nose in the face of Afro-Puff, who leaned back. "Mr. Jones," Wang said to him, "are you and I family?"

Us sixteen Futureneers gathered on the grass laughed. Lester shook his head dramatically.

"No, sir. You're from China, right?" Lester asked. "My

ancestors come from *Africa*." He glared at Becca for a second. Then turned back to Mr. Wang. "By way of Atlanta. You and me are *way* apart." He spread out his long arms to show the difference.

Wang said, "This is true, Mr. Jones. But I propose to you all now that none of us is as far apart as we think. And the tools you forge, with your own tiny little hands, can help bring our world together. *Eh?* Bridge the gaps between the *human* family!"

He spun on me and Becca.

"*You* are no more different than *her*," Wang said.

I didn't laugh this time.

"Understand?" he asked. "I am not religious. You ask, 'Then why teach at this *Christian* college?' I teach because I believe the human race is crucial. Yes? Today's goal is to produce app ideas that we *all* care about. Everyone. Every human."

I snatched up my tablet from the grass. It was getting late.

"You mean using Nightjar?" one boy asked him.

"No! No coding!" Wang said. "Type only ideas."

"Thank the Lord," Becca mumbled.

"He wants you to use the other part of your brain," I said. "If you *got* a brain."

"Once you are done," Wang announced, "we will examine your ideas for their possible social impact. How they may help or hurt the *biggest* family. Yes? Okay, go!"

"Where's Tuyet?" Becca asked me.

"Robot Wars," I said.

"I thought that one was full!"

I shook my head. "That girl's clever." I began thinking about ways to bring folks closer together.

More car pools?

Free doughnuts?

Doughnuts were so good . . .

"Javari?"

"Yeah?"

"I'm sorry you took it wrong today. About what I said? I truly did not know that was bad. We say it all the time."

Becca frowned at her tablet. The sunlight made a glare.

"Did you even get in trouble for the name you called Afro— I mean, Lester?" I asked. "Did you sit with Dr. Hunter?"

"We spoke," she said. "They called my parents. I was told not to mention it."

"So, Becca, you're not really sorry for what you said, you didn't get in trouble, and you only feel bad that *we* got perturbed over it?"

She didn't say nothing.

"You right," I said. "I shouldn'ta responded that way. I got too upset. With an uninformed doofus like you, that was a waste of my energy."

I turned away from her on the grass and started typing ideas on how to make world peace.

30

"NAW, I AIN'T A BIT surprised that little white girl called him that!" said Poppa, rising up in his seat. "No, sir. But you can't let them folks run you down, grandson."

I nodded.

He glanced away from the camera phone. Shireen had left it in a holder on the dresser beside his chair. There was a stack of dirty plates behind him.

I thought back to lunch earlier.

Whenever I heard the noon bells ring at the top of Brigwood Chapel, my stomach started to growl. Because my belly knew it was time to eat. Even though I felt I'd been eating less and less.

I ate the most at lunchtime.

Today the dining hall served up pepperoni rolls, beans and corn bread. My favorite breakfast, I think, had been those buckwheat pancakes they made. Nothing like 'em.

"What have I been telling you all these years, huh?" Poppa asked me. "Didn't I tell you the truth?"

I nodded again.

He said, "White folks have been calling us *names* and *monkeys* and all kinds of *animals* since before they brought us over here from Africa! In the bottom of them ships!"

"I know, Poppa. . . ."

"That is how they got the power over us, making our own kind believe that we're *nothing*. That we're *less*, Javari. That's why I always tried to teach you and your sister and even that doofus father of yours that you're special, that you got special gifts!"

I frowned. "*You* used to tell *my* father that he's special?"

"*Uh-ruh*, a' course I did . . . What you mean? I was his biggest cheerleader, Javari! But *some* people, you can't do nothing with them." He shook his head and settled back down in his seat. "Some people ruin everything they touch."

I remembered how bad Poppa had talked to and treated Daddy over the years. Couldn't he see how that brought Daddy down?

It kinda reminded me of how Becca acted toward me. "Becca claims she didn't know any better," I told him.

His pale eyes grew wide. "Oh, she knew. She knew. That little girl sees you as competition. Let me tell you, if you want to keep somebody down, *anybody* down, then you call them out they name. Make them into an 'animal,' a *wild creature*. Something not human."

I wondered if Becca thought I was totally equal to her. She'd said my skin didn't look real, not *human*.

"If you can make somebody *think* they ain't a real

person," said Poppa George, "*and* make everybody else think they ain't, then you have won."

My head hurt.

He went on, "Even your doofus father can tell you that! Next time you see that, uh, *Miss Becca,* you put her in her place, ya hear? Put *her* down. Call her a low-down, lazy dog!"

"Take it easy, Poppa."

He squinted one of his clouded eyes at me.

The other day at the tater farm, they had horses. One of the older horses had cloudy eyes like Poppa's. The folks at those stables kept trying to get that old horse to listen to them and get led outside but it wouldn't budge at all.

Big, cloudy old horse eyes.

"Don't you let no girl treat you *any* ol' kinda way, Javari," Poppa said. "'Specially not no *whitey!*"

I got off the phone then.

I loved him, but Poppa George made me feel worse. Half of what he said made sense. The other half . . .

31

ANOTHER *HA-KAA!* through my open window had got me out.

At first, I'd been glad to hear that call to sneak off-campus again. Anything to get my mind off Becca and these other crazy folks around here.

But after we crawled through the hole in the fence, I'd remembered the last time I heard that birdcall. I didn't know why I was hanging out with him again.

Before we left ARCC, he'd said I'd meet the *real* Horsewhip Holler tonight. That got me curious. Plus, there was something about spending my afterhours with this kid.

Only . . . this time it sure was coming down *heavy.*

It was almost night and Cricket and me flew fast down a dark dirt road, heading somewhere else he'd said was special. I hoped wherever this was, it was at least clean and dry, because me sitting on the back of Miss Daisy in the pouring rain was not any good.

We were both soaked.

I'd gone to my room earlier than usual after telling Rich

I felt sick. Now I worried if all this rain might actually get me sick. It really seemed like it showered almost every day in the mountains.

I still couldn't believe what Becca'd said to me before. She'd really served me a plate of *nonapology* and tried to pretend like it was the real dish.

It all made me wonder about her family.

How was she even raised to act like that? Did she hand the same weak excuse to Afro-Puff?

Boooooooooooonkkk!

Just then, I almost puked.

A country pickup truck had just swung around the corner of the slick, wet road. It looked like it was driving straight at us. I never been so scared.

The pickup honked again.

Boooooooooooonkkk!

Cricket swerved our bike, and we ran off the road. I clutched on tighter around his waist. We skidded to a stop in the mud. Somehow, Cricket kept the bike upright in the rain.

I heard the drops hit the sticky mud around us. It was coming down even harder than before.

By the time I realized we weren't dead, that pickup had already stopped and backed around on the road. I looked up to see the driver, some white guy with a red beard and baseball cap, giggling at me and Cricket.

"Crick!" he shouted.

"Hey, Uncle Norm," Cricket answered.

Uncle Norm, he said?

I noticed this Uncle Norm was wearing that red, white and blue Confederate flag that Ma was scared of. A racist flag on his baseball cap! I knew if she was here, Ma'd be *hot*.

And probably curse him out for almost killing me.

"Boy, you are nuttier than a squirrel turd!" Uncle Norm said to Cricket. "I almost made me some roadkill outta you and your partner there!"

Uncle Norm laughed again. He didn't seem like he was really worried; this man seemed like he wanted to chat more than anything.

He went on, "What you doing out here on Miss Daisy? Ain't a fit night out to be on no bike."

"Got a meeting," Cricket said.

This got Uncle Norm's interest. "Uh-huh. This, uh, this one a' your *secret* powwows?"

Cricket kept his mouth shut.

"Up at Spoon and Shug's?" Uncle Norm asked.

What was Spoon and Shug's?

Uncle Norm giggled again. "It's okay, Crick! I am down with the cause!"

"Unc . . . ," Cricket started.

"All right, all right," Uncle Norm said. He pointed at Cricket. "Remember, you are my *Negro Numero Uno*! You fellers be careful." He grinned at me: "Pleased to meet ya." And Uncle Norm peeled off almost as fast as he'd torn around that corner before.

We rode Miss Daisy around the curve and higher around another corner up a hill. With the dirt bike climbing, I looked down and watched the gushes of water, like rivers, on opposite sides of the road.

I felt like I was underwater. Rain was everywhere.

Just when I was about to tell Cricket to take me back 'cause I couldn't stand no more, we turned another corner up another hill and rolled up a nice smooth driveway toward a big two-story white house.

In the front yard was a lamppost.

The house sat near the top, with a taller hill or cliff rising up behind it. The dirt cliff above the house looked like it'd been chipped away. Like somebody had scooped out half and left the rest bare.

Glancing around from up here, you could see that the tops of a few of the mountains were missing. Like they'd been stripped off too. I guessed it was because of that mountaintop removal mining, like I'd spotted my first day here.

Cricket pulled us into an open garage on the side of the house.

Ahhh . . .

Saved from the rain.

Cricket pointed out a chubby Black dude named Spoon and his pretty wife, Shug, who greeted me and him in their garage.

"Spoon's a smart doctor," Cricket told me before killing the engine.

"Howdy, stranger!" the man called out. The lady looked at me like she was curious.

"Hey, Spoon!" said Cricket.

The two of us yanked off our drowned sneakers. Then Cricket smiled and tossed Spoon his soppy wet duffel bag.

"For the kids," Cricket told him.

"Our man Alcott!" Spoon said to Cricket.

Shug shook her head. "*Uh-rum,* who is this?" she asked Cricket.

"Oh," Cricket mumbled, looking weird. "This here's my bud, Bird."

"Nice to meet you, Bird!" said Spoon.

Shug had the biggest grin on her face. "I don't think we ever met one a' Alcott's friends," she told me. "You must be special."

Cricket rolled his eyes. I felt embarrassed.

"I must got something dry you boys can put on," Shug told us. "Lemme go see."

32

THEIR HOUSE WAS BIG and decorated nice. But it felt cozy in here too, with lots of soft rugs everywhere. It was better than our place in Brooklyn.

Yeah . . . Brooklyn.

Who knew where my family'd end up after they threw us out?

It wouldn't be as cozy as this.

Anyway.

I understood why Cricket liked to visit here so much. The Johnsons were friendly too, Dr. Spoon and Shug. I liked them.

I followed Cricket up another set of stairs to a dark room. This space was in their attic, but they'd done something to it, fixed it up. There were two soft couches and wall-to-wall carpet.

Also, there were lots of things all around on shelves and special bookcases, like a museum. Dr. Spoon collected old typewriters, he'd told us downstairs.

But Cricket knew that already. That's why he asked Spoon if he could show me up here. By the way Cricket showed off the typewriter collection, you'da thought they were his personally, instead of Spoon's.

"Come here, Bird," Cricket told me.

I walked across the room to where he pointed. The dry socks Shug gave me felt good, sinking down into the deep carpet every step I took. It was dark and quiet upstairs. The steady thump of the rainstorm on the roof was the only noise.

"What?" I asked Cricket, who was pointing at this one dusty typewriter on a dark shelf in the corner.

Cricket said, "This is Spoon's best. You know, you put a piece of paper in there and type here to print the words."

I knew what a typewriter did.

Cricket added, "Bought it in Boston in Massachusetts."

I knew where Boston was.

"The redhead in the pickup was your uncle?" I asked.

"Yep. This typewriter belonged to Dorothy West," Cricket went on.

"Your *real* uncle?"

"Naw," he answered. "He ain't real, he's *plastic*. Dang right, he's real."

"I just wanted to ask."

"Well, now you asked. Satisfied?"

"I wanna know—"

"And people in hell want ice water," Cricket snapped. He pointed back at the typewriter. "Ms. West, who owned this, was an old African American writer who lived in the Harlem Renaissance. Wrote lots of good books."

How did *he* know about her?

I gave him a skeptical look.

"She wrote *The Wedding*," he said with a dopey look on his face.

Cricket probably had never even heard of Dorothy West until Dr. Spoon told him. He showed me something small that sat between two other typewriters. This was an old-fashioned pen that used to belong to some guy named James Baldwin.

"Heard of him?" Cricket asked.

I shook my head.

"James Baldwin is famous!" Cricket almost shouted.

The pen was thick and dark red with a fancy, flat gold tip. I didn't understand how you were supposed to write with it.

Cricket went on, "He was a writer too. Died years ago. He was also Black. And he was a gay. And he lived in New York too. Him and your poppa mighta knowed one another."

"I doubt it."

"Why not? Up in New York, I bet it ain't too hard to run into people you never met. Everybody lives there, it seems like."

Cricket didn't know what the hell he was talking about. New York was huge. But still, sometimes I was surprised by how many friends I bumped into in the streets there.

New York was big but could feel small.

I studied the pen some more before Cricket took it from me and put it back on the shelf. Our fingers touched when he took it. His were ice-cold. I wondered how mine felt.

I looked back at Dorothy West's typewriter more closely. I didn't think I'd ever seen a real typewriter in person. Only in movies and TV.

I reached out and touched it.

As I pressed down on one of the hard plastic keys, a metal arm raised up from the typewriter. It looked like it waved.

"Alcott, you should take Javari to Hawk's Nest!" Dr. Spoon shouted.

"Not tonight, Henry. It's raining like heck out there," Shug told Spoon.

"I *know* not today, Martha," Spoon told her. "That's not what I was getting at." He turned back to Cricket. "I mean when the weather's nice, you two boys should go." Spoon rolled his eyes at Shug. "This woman thinks I'm a spud."

"Don't be cutting your eyes at me, *spud*," Shug told him. "Now come over here and help with this pop."

Him and Cricket each yoinked a case of sodas and started stacking them on one of the tables next to all the food. The dishes, desserts and snacks that all their guests had brought took up two whole tables.

Just to look at that good food made me even more

hungry every minute. I heard my gut growl. This woman named Paula, sitting next to me, laughed at my stomach racket.

The downstairs living room at the Johnsons' had about a dozen people in it now. All of them Black mountain folks from around here. We had all gathered around two wooden chairs in front of the fireplace where I supposed Shug and Spoon would sit when they were done setting up the food.

The goodies were for after the meeting. They were all I could think about.

The hijacked snacks Cricket smuggled here in his duffel bag weren't for us. Shug told me she always donated whatever he brought to a local boys' and girls' club. For poor kids in Horsewhip Hollow.

I was stunned to find that's why Cricket took food from the college. Spoon didn't seem to mind it. Shug did seem to.

"Okay, y'all! E'rbody! Haul up a seat, please!" Shug shouted. "Take a seat, Shelton! We 'bout to begin." She plopped down in one of the fireplace chairs. "*Uh-rum,* Dr. Spoon and I welcome you into our home for another night of Affrilachian Book Society, where we read and discuss books that are important to *us.*"

I found out that both Dr. Spoon and Ms. Shug worked at ARCC. But they only worked there in the fall and spring when the college was really open.

They knew Dr. Hunter too. I could tell by how they acted when I mentioned her name that they didn't like her that much.

Dr. Spoon sat down next to his wife. "So! What y'all think of my book, *The Kingdom of the Happy Land*? Yessir."

I hadn't read this book he wrote.

I didn't even know we were coming here until we got here. But from listening to them all talk about *The Kingdom of the Happy Land*, it was a book about a real town of Black folks, former slaves, who really lived in the Appalachian Mountains after the Civil War. They planned their own Blacks-only town near Tuxedo, North Carolina.

"Writing this book, for me, was a long *haul*," Spoon told everybody. "The end result of a lot of research and work. Getting out in these hills and digging up history . . ."

The book club talked about the *Happy* folks for over an hour and a half. My eyes drooped. My stomach had got so hungry, it wasn't even hungry no more.

"These hills around here," Dr. Spoon continued, "the ones we all grew up in? Mountains. They kin sure hide an awful lot."

"Mmm-hmm!" some old lady agreed.

"Some folks like to hide our history from us," Shug added.

I watched Cricket's face. He was all into what they said.

"One of the biggest mountains, Black Boar Mountain, sits right above this here house," Spoon went on. "I wrote my book because most folks, when they think of Appalachia, they forget about *us*, the *Affrilachians*. It's like we ain't here, or never *was* here."

"We here all right!" that woman Paula shouted.

Everybody clapped. Spoon held up his book.

"These freed slaves founded their own Garden of Eden," Spoon said. "Right in these mountains, some of the most ancient peaks in this here Earth. We can't forget towns like the Kingdom of the Happy Land. Never forget who we are."

He had got emotional. His wife squeezed his knee. You could hear the wind whip outside the house and around the windows.

"Okay, y'all," Shug told us. "I think that's it! Another great book club."

"Yes, it was," Paula agreed.

"Thank you all for coming," Dr. Spoon said.

"Thank *you*, Spoon!" the man named Shelton yelled from the back.

"Let's dig in!" Spoon shouted.

The whole room dove at the food tables.

"Wait!" Shug shouted. "I forgot: next month, *uh-rum*, as you know, we will discuss *Buffalo Dance* by Frank X Walker. Get your books and get reading!"

"Did you enjoy the book talk, Bird?" Shug asked me.

"Yes, ma'am," I said. "It's cool that yow do this."

"It's crucial to come together, baby. Nowadays, we hardly ever touch one another in real life. Relationships with folks in the real world are the only ones that truly feed us."

"Yes, ma'am."

"Speaking of getting fed, don't let all this good food go to waste, hear? Healthy young man like you!" She left me to go chat with some young woman.

It was time for me to holla at these food tables. I saw somebody had brought some big chicken pot pies that looked just like the ones we had for dinner at ARCC.

I wondered if these tasted as good.

Just when I'd heaped all kinds of delicious food onto my plate, Shelton rushed back into the Johnsons' front door screaming.

He surprised me so much, I almost dropped my plate on the rug.

"Spoon!" Shelton yelled. "Spoon! Y'all come outside! You got trouble!"

Shug and Spoon and the rest of their crew froze in their tracks, staring at him. Shelton had only left the house a minute ago. He'd said he had to work a late shift wherever it was he worked.

The whole living room rushed outside after him, into the pouring rain. Except for me. For a minute, I stood right where I was between the food tables until Cricket glared at me from the front door.

I stuffed a spoonful of chopped pork and spicy pickles in my mouth and followed everybody else out into the rain. They all stood in the driveway in the dark.

I glanced down and noticed that the two "rivers" running on either side of the driveway had grown bigger and faster. I looked up to see what everybody else was staring at.

"See there!" Shelton yelled at Spoon. "I was 'bout to hop in my truck when I heard it groan and peeked up!"

I squinted into the dark, above the Johnsons' two-story white house.

At first, I didn't see nothing. It was so dark. But then I looked a little higher. There was just enough light from the lampposts in the front and back yards.

You could see the top of the mountain up there. The part that had been cut up from mining. The steady, hard rain had torn at what was left of the mountaintop.

We all heard another loud groan.

A huge chunk of the mountain, about the size of a delivery van, was breaking away from the rest. At first, I'd thought the cliff was standing still, but then I could see that it was moving.

Slow at first.

And then, fast!

The big brown piece broke away from the rest and slammed down onto the Johnsons' house. A river of water flowed off the mountain after it. Half of the enormous chunk of rocks and mud busted onto the attic and the other half fell into their backyard and garden.

The noise it made was like a howl.

As if their whole house cried out.

And died.

33

I LEANED FORWARD in the truck and squinted out the front windshield.

Through the glass, all striped with raindrops, I could finally see the sign at the entrance for Appalachian Ridge Christian College.

"Don't stop at the gate," I said. "You can drop us out here."

"Sure?" Shelton asked, peeking ahead.

I nodded and reached for the door handle. I didn't want the guard working the security gate to know I was out. I'd almost got caught once already.

"Come on, Cricket," I said.

We pulled his dirt bike from the back of Shelton's truck. It felt like the rain was letting up, I thought.

On the way over, Shelton called Cricket's moms from his truck. She was okay. No mudslides on their side of the mountain.

"Crick," Shelton said. "Boy, you sure you don't want

me to drop you at home? Or with one of your ding-a-ling uncles?"

Cricket shook his head. "Holler's too dangerous between here and our side of Black Boar. All these mud- and rockslides. I'll be okay till morning."

I hoped this weather'd let up by then. It was the worst. I tightened one of the blankets around my neck. The emergency workers that came to Spoon and Shug's had gave one to both me and Cricket.

We thanked Shelton and said goodbye. After stashing Miss Daisy in the bushes, we started to march up the hill in the woods toward the hidden hole in the fence.

I almost slipped a couple of times in the dark. Streams of water gushed down the muddy hill. It reminded me of how the inside of the Johnsons' house looked after the mountain fell.

Rivers flowed all over their nice rugs, everywhere in their house. The mountain chunk that had dropped on the roof was followed by a steady spill of water off the top of the cliff.

By the time the emergency workers arrived and me and Cricket left, that water was *still* rushing off Black Boar Mountain into their house. The rest of the people there blamed the local energy companies for mining in the mountains too much.

They said mountaintop mining killed hills and destroyed all the trees. The trees usually stopped rainwater like this from tearing stuff apart and making mudslides.

But if there were no trees to stop the runoff water . . .

I felt sorry for the Johnsons. I knew Cricket did. He'd been quiet since we left. He'd wanted to stay to help, but the Johnsons refused, saying it wasn't safe.

I was thankful I was almost back to my dry dorm room.

"Bird?" Cricket said. "Bird, I'll sneak into the fountain room tonight. I'll sleep there."

I thought about him lying in that wet, drippy room beneath the fountain. With all the smelly pipes and dirt.

It was probably flooded.

Now I felt sorry for Cricket.

"Okay, do not say a word," I ordered Cricket. "And keep your blanket drawn way up, cover everything." I paused in the dorm stairwell to yank up Cricket's emergency blanket over his head, like a hoodie.

It was too rainy and stormy to try and climb up the tree, I'd felt. And besides all that, Cricket hadn't done it before and the last thing I wanted was for him to fall from the tree, break his leg and wake up all of Taylor Hall.

I figured if we moved fast, we could make it to my dorm room another way. "And you know Elrod and security are searching for you more than ever," I warned Cricket. "Partly because they think you peeked in this girl's window."

"White girl?"

I nodded.

Cricket scrunched his face. "I ain't no perv," he said, angry.

I didn't want to tell him it was me they took for him.

At the top of the steps, I was glad to hear reggae coming from Rich the RA's room. I was ready to run straight past his room toward mine when Cricket, hidden under his blanket, tripped on the top step and crumpled to his knees.

Clumsy.

While I waited for him to get up, Rich's door swung open. Suddenly him and Elrod were standing there, eyeballing us.

34

I SULPED.

Elrod and Rich's eyeballs landed on me first, then went to Cricket. I helped him to his feet. He started to speak, but I interrupted.

"Elrod! Rich!" I called out. "What you dudes up to, man?"

They both seemed surprised to see me in the hallway. Rich yanked his door shut. The gust pushed a skunky smell into the hall. I inhaled and immediately recognized the odor.

They knew that I knew, then. They both looked nervous.

"Javari," Rich said. "I wasn't expecting . . . It's late, bro. You should be—"

"I am!" I said. "Went out for a stroll."

They frowned at Cricket, covered beneath his blanket like a ghost.

"Who's under there?" Elrod asked.

I froze.

Then, Rich to Cricket: "Veer, what you doing? Hiding or something?"

It took me a minute, then I added: "Veer and me just snuck out for a walk. But he got cold. It's very cold and wet out there. That's all. Come on, Veer."

I started to lead Cricket away.

"Wait!" Elrod said. "It's raining cats and dogs. What were you two doing?" He took a few steps after us.

I stopped. "We love these big, country storms," I told Elrod. "But, like I said, Veer got too cold. I need to get him back to our room."

"Hold it," Elrod said.

This time I turned and asked, "Elrod, what you doing in here? What *you* fellas up to, Rich?" I sucked in a loud inhale. "Smells like skunk."

Elrod choked.

Rich's face turned whiter. "Jay, get Veer back to your room. He needs to dry off."

I nodded.

"And next time, ask me before you go prancing around after curfew," Rich said. "Me and Leslie been lenient with you kids' hours till now. Don't take advantage a' me being a cool bro."

I waved my hand at him and kept walking with Cricket. Before I stuck my key in our door, I heard Rich tell Elrod: "They're cool, El. Just a tad dim."

*   *   *

"You Veer, ain't ya?" Cricket asked.

Veer nodded. He sat at his desk by the window, playing on his laptop.

After I shut our door, Cricket strutted into our room and shrugged off his blanket like it was a superhero's cape. It dropped to the floor with his old duffel bag. I snatched them up.

"I heard about you!" Cricket said, falling backward onto Veer's bunk bed.

Anxious, Veer stared at me. His mattress got soaked.

"Dude," I said to Cricket. "That one's Veer's."

Nature Boy jumped up and began snooping around our room, like it was one of the alien lands in the *Flexus* game. He stuck his nose into Veer's closet.

"That's mine too," Veer told him.

Cricket glared at him. Veer seemed worried.

"Uh-huh" was all Cricket said before glancing around the room some more. "Bathroom?" he asked me.

I shook my head. "It's down the hall."

He shook his head, all exaggerated. "*Gotta* be hard when you need to pee in the middle of the night."

"*Javari*," Veer said. "Does the RA know he's here?"

"Just met ol' Rich the RA in the hallway," Cricket told him. "Down there partying with that slimy rent-a-cop Elrod. Rich is a good ol' boy. Me and him go way back round here."

He busted out laughing and looped his beefy arm around Veer's neck like they were about to wrestle.

"My name's J. Wellington Barrelhouse," Cricket told him. "Of the Horsewhip Holler Barrelhouses."

Their noses almost touched.

"Pleased to meet you," Cricket said.

"You're local, aren't you?" Veer asked.

"Holy spit, Bird!" Cricket shouted. "Y'all got too many future geniuses round here!"

"Shh!" I hushed him.

Ba-knock, ba-knock!

The door! Somebody was there!

Ba-knock, ba-knock!

I shot Cricket a look. Without a word, he skidded under our bunk bed, out of sight. Before turning toward the door, I pointed at Veer and gave him my scariest glare. I think he got the idea.

Ba-knock, ba-knock!

"Who is it?" I called through the wooden door. "Rich?"

"Open up, meathead!" a voice whispered. "You trying to get us in trouble?"

I quickly opened the door and let them inside the room. Before I shut it, I glanced down the hall. No more music. I stepped back inside and locked the door behind me.

Tuyet and Becca stood here.

Veer still sat at his desk, with an anxious expression on his face. The two girls were giving him dirty looks. Veer palmed his laptop and rushed toward our door.

"I'll be in the lounge," Veer told me. Before he shut the door, he said, "You are very busy, Javari."

"What did that donkey mean?" Tuyet asked me.

"He is so gross," Becca said. "Ambushing us all the time."

"I don't see how you room with him, Jay," Tuyet said.

"Like I had a choice?" I said.

Tuyet was about to sit on Veer's bunk bed, but she paused, her butt hovered just above it. "Is this Veer's?" she asked.

"Yup."

"Eww! No, thanks!"

Instead, she sat cross-legged on the rug while Becca slid into a chair.

"Why are you guys even here?" I asked them. "It's after curfew. You aren't supposed to leave the girls' floor."

Becca said, "You think that dumb Leslie cares downstairs? She didn't even have a kind word after that creeper *attacked* me."

I rolled my eyes.

Hard.

"Dude," Tuyet said to me. She looked me up and down. "So, you shower with your clothes on now?" She leaned down onto the rug, propping her head up with one hand. If she just peeked under the bed right behind her, she'd be eye to eye with Cricket.

"You're all wet," Becca told me.

"No shiz."

"You been playing puddle jump in the rain," said Tuyet.

I sighed. "I wanna take off these clothes—"

"Eww!"

"Gross!"

Tuyet grinned. "I knew there was something sicko about you, Jay."

"They're *wet*," I said. "Why are you here?"

"Why do you think?" Becca asked. "The Fractal Dactyls need to pick our project."

"We refuse to lose to those *kidiots*," said Tuyet. "Why don't we pick wearables? Jay, you missed that morning assembly. It was this guy lecturing all about wearables—"

"It was *dumb*," Becca added.

I had missed morning assembly on Thursday. Too early to get up after hanging out all night with Cricket. I hoped he'd lay still under there now. Becca and Tuyet had big mouths.

"Wearables are cool!" Tuyet shouted. "They keep track of your health, and we could explore their privacy issues. What you think, Javari?"

"I ain't sure I'm back with the Fractals," I said. "Becca never gave me a good apology."

"*Lord*," Becca said. "I didn't even call *you* that name. I knew I shoulda picked another group."

"Nobody else wanted you, Becca," Tuyet said.

"Nobody wanted any of us," I said, remembering.

The girls got quiet.

In order to win the money, I *had* to be in a group; Wendell explained that to me after the monkey argument. And all the other groups were already full and planning their projects.

"What about my water idea?" I said. "If we pick water,

then I'd come back. Water's a smart idea. There's bad stuff happening in Horsewhip. You heard about them mudslides tonight? It's caused by runaway water and mining and cut-down trees—"

"I vote with Javari," Tuyet said. "We should pick water as our final. We'll get extra points for relevance."

We both waited for Becca to speak. "All right," she agreed. "It's dumb ol' water, I guess."

"Great! So, what's our focus, exactly?" Tuyet asked.

"Not tonight, man," I said.

"What?" Tuyet said.

"A lot turned up today, man," I said. "We will focus on our water focus tomorrow. Now focus on getting outta here. Both of you."

Tuyet stayed right on the floor and said, "See, Becca? The Fractal Dactyls are back! You need to be about less drama. Like Dr. Hunter says?"

Becca snapped, "No drama? That's all she is."

She sounded emotional now. Down and irritated.

"You guys don't know nothing about me," Becca said. She started playing with that gold wristwatch she wore. "This watch belonged to my granddaddy."

Becca was so spoiled.

I think this girl was used to people falling for whatever she said. She stomped over to the window. It had finally stopped raining outside.

"I shoulda told y'all before," Becca said. "My grand-father was William Whitt, the original Uncle Billy."

"Huh?" Tuyet said, sitting up.

I didn't say nothing. Gradually, more things made more sense.

"My family owns Uncle Billy's General Stores. And they expect me to 'shine like a diamond,'" Becca said. "In everything. *Always.*"

The room was quiet.

Uncle Billy's was worth millions. Billions, maybe?

Becca was a *banksta*.

"Uncle Billy?" a voice shouted from under the bed.

I thought for a minute, then slapped my hand against my forehead. Suddenly crazy tired, I skimmed down against the wall and crouched on the floor.

"Who was that?" Becca asked.

Tuyet now stared under the bed. She squinted and gasped and scrambled backward away from what she saw.

"There's a boy here!" Tuyet said. "Javari?"

I just squatted on the floor, shaking my head.

Cricket gently slid out. He stood and drilled his eyes at Becca. He looked like he wanted to crush her.

"You the one who's Uncle Billy's granddaughter?" Cricket asked.

"Who the heck are you?" Becca asked. "Javari?"

Cricket took a step toward her. "Are you *really* Uncle Billy's grandkin?" he asked again.

She nodded.

Cricket's chest started to heave. He got excited. His fists clenched.

"Becca," Tuyet said. "Let's go."

But Becca didn't move. She just stood there, red-faced, staring up into Cricket's hazel eyes. Like he had hypnotized her or scared her stiff.

Neither one of them could move.

"Your grandpa killed my grandpa," he said.

She flinched like a knife stuck her.

Silence.

Finally, Tuyet jerked Becca by her hand and steered her out the door. Even after they'd left, Cricket stood there quiet.

When I was about to ask him what he meant, he grabbed his duffel bag off the floor and rushed out of the room and down the steps.

I slid from a crouch to a slump on the rug.

What?

Uncle Billy murdered Cricket's grandpa?

C = True / False?

35

WAR!

That's how Ethan called it.

Over the past week in his Automata sessions, we'd constructed all kinds of motors from scratch. Today, our class had tromped across the wet grass to battle each other in the fountain on the yard. The lawn was full of huge puddles from last night's rainstorm.

I hadn't seen Becca at all today to ask her about the storm that went down between her and Cricket in my room. She wasn't even at breakfast. Probably for the best.

I needed a break.

Holding the boat I'd built, I hopped over a big puddle and splattered mud on my shoes. I groaned. I hated messing up my clothes. And I'd been messing them up all week, it seemed.

Ethan called it war.

But really—boat races.

We'd cut shapes out of foam core and glued them

together into bows, keels and rudders. We made crankshafts out of straws, pipe cleaners and rubber bands.

The propellers were little rectangles of metal we bent on opposite sides to give them an angle. The angled propeller blades would push the boats forward through the water.

Supposedly.

This was all really old-school, the way Ethan loved it.

Two at a time, we had to race and be the first boat to reach the opposite side of Cricket's fountain, our finish line. The distance across was about thirty feet at the diameter. This fountain was fuller than it had been before. I dipped my hand under the cool water.

All that rain.

Only problem was, my crankshaft kept coming loose from my propeller.

"Okay now!" Ethan called out. "Time for war!"

Nobody wanted to go, so he picked these two nervous boys, Duck and Manuel. Our instructor counted down from ten, everybody joined in, and the two boys released their boats into the fountain. This first race was close, but Manuel just beat Duck, who cursed.

A couple more races ended the same way. There was always one boat that cruised quicker than the other. They weren't really contests.

Ethan had taught us that the speed of a boat depended on how long it was and also how strong the force was that propelled it. That force could either be wind or a propeller or something else.

A ship's length was important because longer ones leave longer waves in the water they move through. And longer waves push boats faster than short waves do over the water, which makes boats skim, making them even speedier.

Next up in the races was me against Scotty with the funny teeth. He seemed more anxious than I was. Our boats were about the same length, but I had a bad propeller.

"Okay, boys!" Ethan shouted. "Scotto, Javari, I want you to sail straight across this fountain like Ferdinand Magellan crossed the ocean!"

"Ferdinand who?" I asked.

"Sixteenth-century Portuguese explorer," Ethan explained. "Headed the first European trip to circumnavigate the globe!"

"Oh."

He added, "Except Magellan died before his ship got back home."

"Bad example," Scotty said.

"Never mind," said Ethan. "You two ready? Crank your shafts. Let's go, kiddos!"

If my funky propeller broke free, my boat would lose speed and sink. But I didn't have no more time to worry about it. Ethan started to count down from ten.

Everybody joined in.

On the count of one, Scotty and me released our propellers. Our boats sped off across the fountain's pool.

Ripples.

Waves.

Skimming.

They both did good at first, cruising side by side. Then mine started to swerve a bit.

Soon my ship had swung so much it ran into Scotty's boat beside it. That spun his around and tipped it so his filled up with water.

My rival sunk to the bottom of the fountain. My ship had turned, but still wound up at the finish line on the other side.

Futureneers cheered.

"Javari," Ethan told me, "you scored an ugly win, but still a win. The crucial thing was, you stayed in the game."

Scotty tore off his socks and shoes to wade out into the fountain for his boat. He cut his eyes at me along the way.

On my tablet, I dragged the last two of the Nightjar icons into the function box at the bottom of my screen. I had added lines and lines of symbols there, each one standing in for a different string of code. I clicked Save on my tablet and waited for Mr. Wang to come over to my group on the grass.

Two other campers had finished theirs before me and we'd watched them. Their pieces were all about how to bring the world together. Becca was still working on her program.

"Another one?" Wang asked me. "You children are fast today! Okay, let's see what you have produced."

"Well, it's not really that fancy," I warned him. "But we were supposed to make something that everybody cared about, so I picked our environment. Everybody cares about that."

"Okay, okay," he said, sounding impatient. "Let's see. Everyone, everyone, gather around to watch Javari's piece of code. He worked very hard on it."

The whole group watched me and my tablet. I didn't really like the attention.

I pressed my function button, and my little Nightjar program began. It started with some hip-hop music I found on the internet. An animated version of Earth spun into view in outer space.

My Earth had a smiley face.

And then, my Nightjar avatar, a bird, flew over the planet and dropped a chunk of coal into Earth's mouth. The planet swallowed the coal.

Another bird flew over and fed another chunk of coal.

And another bird.

Another.

And even more birds, until my Earth got sick and breathed fire.

Flames.

My birds circled around it and that was it.

The end.

I looked at Mr. Wang, who grinned at me, clapping.

"Very good!" he told me. "*Eh?* Children, Javari's

message of caring is what? Too much coal makes the earth sick?" He laughed.

I felt relieved.

"Don't shout your message too loudly around *here*!" he told me, still laughing. "Very good!"

36

THE GOLDEN BASKETBALL AVATAR went crashing down over and over again until it cracked like a big egg.

"Ah!" I heard some Group Six kid cry.

"I bet that's the last time you ambush *us*," Becca yelled at them.

A *Flexus* virtual reality message flashed above us in the sky:

TO THE VICTOR GO THE SPOILS! PICK ONE OF YOUR FOE'S SURVIVAL KIT ITEMS TO TAKE AS TRIBUTE!

Next, Group Six's survival kit's contents flashed above. They owned a WATER BOTTLE, MULTITOOL and AZOX SPRAY.

"Ah. Nothing good," I told Becca and Tuyet.

"Move on," I heard Becca say.

We left Group Six's survival kit alone and I walked down the mountain I'd just thrown them from. The old, abandoned city at the bottom looked like it'd been bombed out.

As soon as I got near the town, I noticed a warning flash up in the night sky above my head. So far, it had always been night here.

The sky warning read:

CAUTION! HIGH RADIATION LEVELS DETECTED.
LINGER HERE AT YOUR OWN HAZARD.

Our avatar's energy was low after fighting Gold Basketball. Almost no life bars. We needed to discover more Dragmors, or energy pills, or we'd lose another life. We had two lives left.

Maestro Island was still far off. I think most of the other teams were way ahead of us. Earlier I saw a big silver lady avatar jog past, but they hadn't bothered us. I kept on into the city, not wanting to be bothered by any other attackers.

"Be careful, Javari," I heard Tuyet say.

Becca had been mostly toned down this afternoon. I think she was afraid I'd jump down her throat. Neither me or Tuyet had asked Becca about what Cricket said about her granddaddy. But Tuyet had asked me who the crazy boy in my room was.

I told her: "J. Wellington Barrelhouse."

I kept wondering if Cricket was serious. He sure seemed serious.

What Cricket told Becca was a surprise, obviously. But since Becca was one of the Whitt family, I wouldn't be surprised about anything one of her family mighta done in the past.

Just then, a security guard peeked into our room, glanced around. Some new guy they hired. Before leaving, it looked like to me his eyeballs stayed stuck on me longer than anybody else.

That made me feel guilty for no good reason.

This morning at breakfast Rich had told us that last night Elrod got shot in the face with a white paint pellet while he was on patrol.

Tagged by Cricket.

Nuts.

Rich said ARCC had hired more security to deal with this "secret threat." I knew it was Cricket he meant. I hoped dumb Becca wouldn't tell anybody what she saw in my room.

"See that?" Tuyet said. "Something's alive in the center of town, Javari."

Becca said, "It might be a bug, more energy pills."

"It's very small. Keep on straight," said Tuyet.

I kept walking through the empty town. It was falling down, dusty. I felt like I might see a zombie pop out around any corner.

Sure was a creepy game.

"I feel like we're about to get ambushed again," Becca said.

"Yeah, Becca, maybe by one of your family!" I said.

"Your friend is psycho," I heard her say. "And he's scary. You shouldn't let him in the dorms."

"He's scary 'cause he's Black?"

"See, Javari, I was born and raised in Charlotte. I'm not used to certain *characters*."

"They don't got Black folks in Charlotte?"

"Lots."

"Then why you act so weird about us?"

"I don't!" she said. "I feel weird about *everybody*. Especially when some goober jumps out of nowhere, screaming jabber about my family."

"Your feelings are convenient," Tuyet said.

"Uh-huh," I agreed.

Tuyet: "Javari, right at this next corner."

I saw something, like, glowing up ahead. There was a pile of shiny gold nuggets in the middle of the street. I settled down and focused. One foot ahead of the other one. Soon I stood directly over the rocks. I recognized them.

"Dragmor pellets!" Becca shouted.

"Bag 'em, Javari!" said Tuyet. "Those are just what we need."

Dragmors, we'd learned, gave your avatar more energy, or life bars. I reached down to scoop up the gold pellets, but the image began to shake.

The energy pills altered shape into a bomb. There was even a countdown timer on the explosive. My screen flashed red.

"Get outta there!" Tuyet yelled.

I could hear Veer's group on the other side of the room roar.

I made our avatar run as fast as it could out of that town. But we ran slow because of our low power bars. A glowing sky message suggested that I teleport or use a jet pack to escape the bomb.

We didn't have neither. Thanks to me. By the time I reached the end of the block, the bomb exploded.

We died.

I snatched off my headset. The Virtual Gear Engineers crew fell over, laughing.

"Where was your jet pack?" Jerry hollered at us.

"Oorah!" Lester yelled.

I hated those dudes. Tuyet and Becca were steamed.

"I told you to pick that jet pack the other day, meat-head!" Tuyet yelled at me.

Dang . . .

I walked down the long brown hallway toward one of the communications rooms. I reached the door and put my hand on it. They were almost the same color, my hand and the door.

When I'd first arrived at camp, I'd thought all these tan and brown colors as decoration was soothing. I'd changed how I felt about it. All these tones had begun to bother me.

I felt smothered.

I rubbed my bad eye and stepped inside the room.

Pretty soon I was talking to Daddy back in BK. I had him on the speaker phone in the communications room. He was still at work at the hardware store. Sounded like he was moving boxes, he was so out of breath.

As much as he complained about his job, I also knew that my father liked it and appreciated it. He enjoyed his coworkers there and he sometimes told me when he came home from work, he was tired, but he felt like he was needed.

It must be nice to feel that way.

I told him about my failure in our VR game.

Me getting our avatar murdered meant that my group, the Fractal Dactyls, only had one life left. I didn't know exactly why this *Flexus* thing had got so important. It wasn't like you won any money for reaching Maestro Island.

Daddy and me didn't talk about the eviction. I did tell him I'd got used to living without my phone.

"Good!" he said. "You stay on it too much anyhow. Burn holes in my wallet, you and your sister."

I said, "Not having a usable phone here only makes me more hungry for a new one when I get back."

We laughed.

"I'm glad you called, son. I been feeling a little down."

"Yeah? I'm sorry, Daddy."

I heard him drop a box onto something. "Tell me something good!" he said. "I need it."

"Well, we got an excellent final project picked. It was my idea."

"That's good."

"And you know Uncle Billy? The dude that created the stores?"

"Yeah."

"Well, his granddaughter is part of my group."

"You kidding? For real?"

"Yup! And you know what that means."

"What?"

"We gotta win, Daddy," I said. "With Uncle Billy's granddaughter on our side, the judges got to pick us."

He laughed. "Son, sounds like you having that summer!"

But I was serious. "What you mean?"

"Well, you know . . . ," Daddy said. "One of those summers to end all summers."

"Oh. Maybe."

"And I see you developed an analytical mind like your mother's," Daddy said. "Her and Shireen are fine, by the way. They say you look good."

"How's Poppa?"

My daddy got quiet, then. "Poppa George and me really had it out. Big, big argument. When it was over, he wasn't feeling good. I almost called his doctor."

"He okay now?" I asked.

"Seems so," he said. "We don't talk at all now. Your mother has been the go-between. I been feeling bad for getting him so upset. He's real worried about . . . things."

"Poppa's so old, I'd spend all the time I could with him,

221

just listening. But . . . but I'm beginning to think he don't always give the best advice."

Daddy laughed. "You finding that out, huh?"

"He can slip bad ideas in your head too," I said. "I like to visit his room and listen to his music with him. Sometimes we don't talk. Just listen to his music."

"That don't work for me and him, son."

We chatted for a little bit more. Then, Daddy had to go. His boss, Rudy, wanted him.

"Be good, baby boy," he told me. "Hey, I love you, man. Proud of you."

"Thanks, Daddy. Love you too! And no matter what Poppa George say, I think you always improve yourself. And you never give up on me—you a black diamond!"

37

THiS SUNDAY WAS THE BEST day since I'd come to
Horsewhip Hollow. It was warm but not too hot. For once,
the weather wasn't misty. There was even a nice little breeze
that ran through the trees around the main yard.

I walked down the steps of my dorm to go meet Cricket.

Dr. Hunter'd told us that we'd have this Sunday off to do
whatever kinda junk we wanted to get into. Most Futureneers were headed to Charlotte again to sightsee and shop.

But yesterday, Cricket had tossed a rock into my window
with a paper note wrapped around it. Veer actually found it
and gave it to me.

I *really* wanted to ask Cricket about what he'd claimed
about Becca's family.

Uncle Billy murdered his grandpa?

I reached the bottom of the dormitory steps and heard
voices. Yeah, it was Rich and Elrod again, in one of their
debates. I felt like I couldn't go anywhere without running
into Rich, Elrod or both.

I waited just around the corner, eavesdropping.

"You are *not* serious," Rich said. "El, Ban-she is *way* hotter on the mic than Big @ss."

"You're jackrabbit crazy," Elrod replied.

"It's freestyle!" Rich said. "You never freestyled? You *flow!*"

"That's the *problem,* I'm telling you," said Elrod. "They don't *think* nowadays. Everybody reacts. No creativity, man."

I decided to walk right past these two. I didn't feel like waiting around for them to end their stupid convo.

Neither knew what they were talking about. They acted like they'd grown up on the streets of New York and not the hollers of West Virginia.

"There he is!" Elrod said, grinning when he saw me.

"Yo, Jay," Rich said to me. "Who do you think is the best on the mic: Ban-she or Big @ss?"

Elrod added, "This dude thinks it's Ban-she—"

I said, "I ain't into battle rap like that."

They both just stared. I kept walking.

"Have fun in Charlotte!" Rich yelled.

I wasn't going to Charlotte.

Cricket broke around another curve. We both leaned into it. Instead of slowing down, he sped up.

Dirt bikes were cool.

We zoomed!

On the left-hand side of Meadow Bridge Road, long white houses. They were flat and in rows maybe ten deep and made out of metal.

Cricket slowed down. "Trailer park!" he yelled.

I heard of these, but never seen one.

The long trailer homes had porches and barbeque grills out front. Screaming kids ran through water hoses. Two men stood under a tree swigging bottles.

These were regular folks, but some of the profiles I saw whizzing by belonged to poor faces. By poor faces, I meant you could tell they were used to worry.

Worry burnt into them.

I recognized those faces from back home. In my hood. In our three-story walk-up.

But not this one old woman!

She was not bothered.

With a grin like the Joker, this old lady in a yellow dress was out by the road, walking her dog, with a can of beer. When we blew past, she waved in the sunshine and gave us the greatest smile.

Her skin was like red leather.

"Howdy!" Cricket yelled.

"Hey, sugar!" she yelled back.

At first, I thought he knew her, but soon I realized they were just being friendly. I heard him gun the accelerator.

Our little Honda flew even faster.

Along the road, old barns popped up with pretty horses, big, ugly cows and some real sick'nin pigs. A few of the farms, you could smell before you even saw them.

Stunk.

I liked them, though. I wondered what it was like to live on a farm.

In front of a wash plant, I got a chance to grab a piece of coal. Wash plants were factories that rinsed and crushed huge lumps of coal into smaller ones, Cricket said. This one was owned by the Ball Creek Energy company. We found my piece of coal on the roadside, along with other bits.

I never held coal.

My black chunk, about the size of a quarter, shined after I rubbed my thumb over it. Like black glass.

"Anthracite," Cricket analyzed. "Hard coal."

It left a smudge.

It was smooth, but rocky at the same time. I knew that coal was made of carbon: plants and animals that'd been dead a long time.

Old dinosaurs and ferns.

Same as diamonds.

This teeny piece of coal coulda been dug out of that same mountaintop above Spoon and Shug's house. That would be something.

"They call 'em black diamonds," Cricket said.

"Black diamonds?" I asked.

"A nickname."

"This ain't no black diamond," I told him. "*Real* black diamonds are from Africa. They're rare and powerful."

Cricket laughed. "Not *these*. That's just the nickname around here. They ain't real diamonds."

I tucked it in my back pocket.

We stopped at a dusty convenience store in Landisburg. Cricket wanted soda, or pop, like he called it. But I got him to buy water instead.

The munchies in the store reminded me of the junk food you found in bodegas in Brooklyn. Same salt and sugar snacks, just different brands.

Moon Pies, Mister Bee's chips, Mountaineer Popcorn.

Cricket picked a TrixieLand pound cake.

Behind the cash register, the store also sold bumper stickers with that Confederate flag on them. The stickers said: HERITAGE, NOT HATE.

I asked the young white dude behind the register what that meant.

"Folks get the wrong idea about our flag," he said. "Need a straw? Yeh, well, there ain't nothing vulgar about the Southern Cross. She's a symbol of the *true* South, our pride in Dixie."

"But the slave states flew it during the Civil War," I said.

"I don't know nothing 'bout no dang slaves," he told

me. "Matter of fact, the only slave round here is the one you looking at now, working behind this here counter."

"It's *hate*," Cricket said to him.

"This ol' flag means more than that," the dude said.

"So you agree there's hatred in it?" Cricket asked him.

"Well now . . ."

"We heard you the *first* time," Cricket snapped, and snatched up his water. After we left the store, I asked Cricket if he was okay.

"That dang flag is around so much, I hardly even see it no more." Cricket shrugged. "Just some hateful hog slop for white trash to be proud of 'cause they ain't got nothing else."

I didn't like that flag.

It seemed to me like it actually meant both heritage *and* hate, depending on who you were. I guess you could own a heritage of hate. I didn't see why it had to be either one or the other.

We hopped back on Miss Daisy.

Gliding along, I sniffed something bad again. This time it was another skunky smell. Somebody had hit one on the road. I glanced around but couldn't spot any skunk before we left its odor behind.

A bit farther, we sped past a road sign on the right. It said: GAULEY BRIDGE 5 MILES.

And pretty soon we rode over a river gushing with water.

There was construction going on there, but they musta been gone for the day. I was quick enough to read a sign near the site that read: HYDROELECTRIC POWER BROUGHT TO YOU BY BALL CREEK ENERGY!

Later, Cricket stopped again to let us stretch our legs on the softest field of grass. Two black dogs zipped in the distance, wrestling with each other. It looked like part of an old farm.

The whole meadow was coated in yellow flowers.

We laid in this big field and stretched out in the sun awhile. Ate these purplish-red berries that Cricket had plucked off some bushes at the side of the road.

"*Sour,*" Cricket said, spitting one out. "You gotta know which ones to pick, Bird. You pick the wrong kinds of berries and they're poison. They'll make buzzard bait out of you."

"Unless maybe you sip some activated charcoal."

"I don't even think that'd help."

I inspected the berry I was about to stick down my throat. Just then, Cricket started heaving like he was about to throw up!

"Ah no!" he hollered. "Bad berry!"

Choking, Cricket rolled over still on the grass. I knelt over him and his eyes popped open. He grinned up at me.

Our faces were close.

"Skeered?" he asked.

I shook my head.

"Oh, why you all up in my eyeballs?" he shouted, laughing.

I jerked backward. "I knew you were playing, dude. You ain't fool nobody."

He sat up and ate another berry. "I fooled *you*, son," he said, laughing some more.

I noticed the sun shined off his skin, making him look like a light brown nut. This Cricket *was* nutty.

I musta been nutty for hanging so much with him.

38

WE FINALLY ARRIVED.

It was right on the bank of a river called the Kanawha. Which sounded Native American to me. Where we'd arrived was some local memorial that Cricket was interested in.

It was a nice place.

There was a dam and waterfalls on the water. We yanked off our shoes and socks and rested on the edge of the river, dipping in our toes. After a minute, I flew up out of the stream.

Something in there had nibbled my legs!

It didn't hurt. It just felt funny, ticklish.

Cricket didn't seem bothered by it. I knelt down in the grass and peeked into the water surrounding his bare feet.

There were maybe a dozen little green fish there, swimming around his toes underwater. They took turns pecking with their little fat lips. Every now and then, Cricket would jerk and sploosh them away.

They always came back.

He sat there on the river, sulky.

"What's this about?" I asked. "This place, why'd you wanna come here today? I mean, it's cool. . . ."

"Hawk's Nest Tunnel," he said. "Spoon suggested I bring you. Him and Shug say hi. They sucked all the water out."

He splashed.

"Can they fix their house?" I asked.

Cricket shrugged. "Dorothy West's typewriter got smashed," he said, sad. "Busted to pieces by that rock."

I'd meant to ask him why the Johnsons called him by his real name, Alcott, and not Cricket. They were the only ones I'd met who did that.

"Across those waterfalls is a tunnel?" I asked.

Cricket nodded.

"With real hawks in it?" I asked.

He shook his head. "Folks round here slap labels on things that ain't even factual. Hawk's Nest Tunnel is just a name. It's how I come to West Virginia."

"You walked through a tunnel?"

"Naw! Man, a long time ago—decades—my grandpa Al come here from Georgia to help dig that there tunnel. A lot of the diggers they hired were Black. And a lot of them Blacks died from breathing in the dust from tunneling out all that sand and rock."

"What?"

He sat up out of the water.

We walked over to the memorial plaque and read it.

232

Cricket plopped down on a bench. He closed his eyes like he was looking deep into his head.

The plaque said that this spot honored 109 dead people who perished here drilling and digging the Hawk's Nest Tunnel.

"That's a lie," Cricket pointed out. "Over a *thousand* died actually, Spoon told me."

A *thousand* dead?

I couldn't understand how so many could die like that.

"Yup. Over one thousand deceased. Probably more," Cricket said. "Most of them was Black migrants, including my grandpa, Alcott Washington the First. Back then, Uncle Billy came here too—your friend's grandpa."

"Becca ain't my friend."

"See, Uncle Billy got his start making money off those miners, selling them supplies. But he refused to sell the Black folks masks to protect them from breathing in that dust from their dig: *silica*.

"So, they died. Because Uncle Billy felt the white miners needed masks more."

I said, "That's why you said Uncle Billy killed your grandpa."

"All them Black miners died from silica, sand, in their lungs, Bird," Cricket explained. "And because of their color, the white folks didn't want them in the local cemetery, so they buried the bodies at that farm nearby. In that same field where we ate berries today. My father was a little boy when *his* pa died from dusty lungs, digging that tunnel."

"Yo . . . ," I said. It took a few minutes to take all that in. "My poppa George is alive, but he has bad lungs too. Sick from cigarettes." Cricket didn't seem to care. "Where's your father now?"

"Dead too."

"Cricket," I said. "I'm sorry."

He grinned. "What you sorry for? That was a *long* time ago. It don't make me heartsick. Just makes me think, is all. About life. And how life treats you . . . your own blood and kin."

He tossed a rock at the memorial.

"My mama's people, though, they go back in these hills even longer," he said. "Just like the Kingdom of the Happy Land that Spoon wrote about?"

I nodded.

"Locals say Uncle Billy's a hero," he said. "Bird, why do you think people's so mean? Why they gotta *hate* all the time? Huh?"

"I don't know," I said.

I thought about what was happening in our VR game. How Lester and Jerry and them ambushed us for fun. And how we ambushed them right back.

Lately, I'd begun to realize how full of hate my own grandfather was. How he'd let the way whites treated him influence how he feels. Even how he feels toward other Black people.

Finally, I spoke up, "I think folks hate—*attack*—when

they're afraid of getting attacked: 'I better kill *him* before he can kill *me.*'"

"That don't make no sense when you ain't never attacked nobody."

I shook my head. "It don't matter. Everybody's scared. If there ain't nothing real to be afraid of, we make something up."

Monsters.

Monkeys.

Thugs.

Beasts?

"You know, you *are* a future genius," said Cricket.

"I'm actually starting to realize how clueless I am. I don't know nothing."

Cricket picked up another rock, a bigger one, and hurled it at the plaque. It just landed to the left. He hopped up.

"Let's go," he said.

"*Cool,*" I said.

39

THE NEXT DAY AT LUNCH, I'd been waiting for forever for dumb Jerry to end his video chat. I didn't know who he was talking to in the communications room, but it musta been like his whole entire family and friends list.

I sighed and sat on the hall floor outside the room.

I thought back to this morning out on the yard during coding with Mr. Wang. He was cool.

But I hadn't been ready for the nasty news he laid down. It shook me.

This morning, like I'd been doing for the past couple of days, I'd helped Becca with her strings of code. She just needed stuff explained to her a few times. Wang was teaching us to translate his Nightjar bird symbols into their real lines of code.

More than once, I wanted to ask Becca about her granddaddy but held off. I was curious to know what her family'd told her about how Uncle Billy got his start.

With Wang's app running on our tablets, we sat on the grass.

"You repeated this Nightjar symbol again down here," I told her. "But you *already* translated it into code."

"I see. It's redundant," she agreed, deleting it. "Unnecessary."

"And . . . ," I said, squinting, "your variable here is bad because you translated the wrong bird symbols."

"Oh, okay."

"It's too common." I didn't know why I was helping her. Maybe these mountains had made me nicer.

Becca said, "Coding ain't as hard as I thought! His app sure helps."

Mr. Wang peeked over our shoulders and made a funny sound with his mouth. He read Becca's translated file, nodding.

"Miss Rebecca, your code is *very* strong," Mr. Wang told her. "The nightjar has worked its magic!"

Becca grinned.

"A good tutor you have, I think."

I grinned too.

"You would make a good professor, Mr. Harris," Wang told me after Becca'd left with the others. I'd stayed behind to help him carry the tablets.

"I thought about it, teaching engineering when I'm old. But your app makes learning easy. You like teaching at ARCC?" I asked him.

"I like my students," he said. "The *school* . . ."

"I think Uncle Billy's built a real nice school," I said.

"Only, the Uncle Billy's company did not build ARCC."

"Nephew Wendell told me they *owned* ARCC."

"This is true," Wang said. "But the Ball Creek Energy company founded ARCC many years before. And then, Uncle Billy's *bought* Ball Creek."

"Ball Creek Energy?"

"Yes," Wang said. "The coal company. Ball Creek Energy mines coal from the mountains here and ships it all over the world. Very rich business for Uncle Billy's. Over five million tons of coal sold every year."

We continued toward the computer building. What he'd said was news to me. But did he *really* just say what I *thought* he'd said?

"Uh, Mr. Wang . . . Uncle Billy's actually *owns* the company that's been decapitating all the mountains and making mudslides around here?"

My code instructor didn't answer at first. Then, "I am afraid so, Javari. Ball Creek Energy, or Uncle Billy's, mining for coal, killing trees, destroys the local environment. Cutting down trees causes runoff water to rush across the ground, unchecked. That runoff and mining helps *pollute* Horsewhip's drinking water."

I musta looked at him like he was crazy.

He sighed. "It is all very, very sad, I am afraid." Wang dunked his head with one big nod, grabbed the rest of the tablets from me and carried them into the building.

I stayed out on the yard.

So, it was *Uncle Billy's* mining, ruining the local water? *Polluting?*

Disgusting.

I told Tuyet and Becca about it right away. Becca said she'd known all along. That was the reason she was so sluggish about picking water pollution as our project.

Embarrassed, I guess.

Ever since then, we'd been pretty busy in the Brain Cells, researching about bad water and the environment and looking up more facts. Tuyet found a bunch of news articles online about how mining spoils water and how other places dealt with it.

It *was* a lot of work.

And we'd waited way too long to start our project.

Back in the hall outside the communications room, I was still waiting on Jerry to get out of there. I was just about to bang on the door when it flung open. Jerry rolled out all slow. I think he took his time only because he could tell I wanted in.

He even got one of his wheels stuck on the door there. I helped him unstick it. Jerry started to roll off toward the camp cubicles without even saying thank you.

He was an irritating kid.

And then, just before he wheeled around the corner to leave, he looked back and said something about "bars."

"Huh?" I said.

"You Fractal Dorks," Jerry said. "You been screwing up so much, you must got only one life bar left on your avatar. If you lose that life, game over!"

I waved him off.

"Right?" he asked. "One last life, right? The Silver Lady and the Witch avatars are way ahead of you too."

Irritating.

He rolled away.

I daydreamed about pushing him and his chair down those stairs that led beneath the auditorium. I musta still felt cheerful about that thought when I spoke to Poppa George a few minutes later.

But his voice was bad.

"Your daddy's right," Poppa told me. He almost whispered. "You do seem in better spirits. I like this new attitude."

He wasn't whispering as much as he sounded weak, tired.

"Since when you and Daddy been talking?" I asked him.

"Oh, you know," Poppa said. "With you gone, ain't nobody here to talk to but your doofus daddy."

"What about Shireen? Or Ma?"

His old brown face wrinkled up even more. "What they know?"

Poppa George.

Folks around here would call him ornery.

"How you been feeling?" I asked.

His face drooped. He waited a while before answering, "We got a mess on our mind around here, Javari. Your daddy . . . I'm just worried is all. I'm old! I am tired of the worry."

He closed his eyes like he went to sleep.

"Poppa?"

He opened them. "Yes, grandson?"

I stared at the video screen. Half of his face you could not see because he was holding the phone wrong. The parts that you could were a frown.

I frowned back at him. I knew he couldn't see me clear. I also knew there was a lot he wasn't telling.

40

THAT AFTERNOON, our two buses sped over Fox River Bridge, toward this nearby town called Ballton. It was still in West Virginia, in the next county, twenty miles from ARCC.

We parked in a slanted lot on the side of a hill.

Above, I could see what looked like a small, old-fashioned town on the mountainside. There were homes, a small church and a bigger building.

We all followed Wendell off our bus, on another field trip. But this field trip I was *really* interested in seeing. Thanks to recent discoveries.

Ms. Ferguson led me, Tuyet, Becca and our entire Futureneers STEM camp up the hill, toward the main building of the Ballton Coal Camp. Just in front of the entrance up top was this tall metal statue of some man, dressed in overalls, and raising what looked like a tool over his head.

"He's swinging a pickaxe," Wendell said, smiling at the statue. "My granddaddy owned one *just* like that. When he was a miner."

Inside the main building, which they called the company store, there was a little museum that had all kinds of objects and information about the history of coal mining in West Virginia. This was interesting, but I didn't see nothing about what I really wanted to know.

This one girl got yelled at for picking up a lantern. It was like the ones the miners used to use when this coal camp was still open. A sign said the mine here shut down back in 1916 when it ran dry.

I wasn't even sure if Poppa had been alive back then.

"Okay, everybody!" Ms. Ferguson yelled. "Queue up! We're about to go down!"

We lined up single file and climbed into some seats in this funky old train. It looked like a chain of shaky wooden roller-coaster carts, linked together and pulled by a head cart.

All of a sudden, our train jerked ahead, loud and scary.

Wendell grinned at me, saying, "Y'all gonna *love* this! A real live mine!"

I wasn't sure.

Our carts slowly wobbled on train tracks into a dark tunnel connected to the camp store. It got all black with only one or two dim lights every now and then. I could feel the ceiling of the mine lowering closer to our heads. Until there almost wasn't no room left above us.

It got cold.

"I don't like this," I heard some kid say in the dark.

"Woo-hoo!" another kid shouted.

And the mine's ceiling was wet and dripping, just like in

the room beneath Cricket's fountain. Drops ran down my forearms.

"Gross," I heard Tuyet say in the dark. Her and Becca sat in the cart behind me and Wendell's.

I tightened the hard hat they gave us after we got inside.

The old man driving the head cart told us he'd worked in a mine like this one for over fifty years! He said for all that time, there was never more than enough space for him to crouch above four feet.

Fifty years he spent digging in a mine, bent over.

I was sitting there in the dark, creeping along down those train tracks, trying to imagine being bent over that long, when suddenly the whole cramped tunnel began to shake.

Stuff fell off the walls and our carts swung from side to side!

"Ihh!" Wendell squeaked.

"Cave-in!" somebody yelled. *"This here mine's collapsin'!"*

Everybody started to scream. The narrow tunnel kept shaking! Scared to death, I crouched against Wendell and shut my eyes.

Then, it all stopped, and our train started creeping along again.

"False alarm!" the old miner up front yelled back to us. He was cackling.

After a minute, kids started to laugh. It was all some joke. It wasn't funny. I'd almost peed my pants in this cave.

* * *

We all shined flashlights.

Pete Kressner, the old miner who drove us, now bent over in the dark tunnel to show us how miners used hand drills and dynamite to break out the coal buried in the cave walls.

"Now, once a miner tucked his sticks a' dy-no-mite in the holes he drilled and was ready to light the explosive, who knows what he yelled?" Pete asked us. We all stood around a big, dark crack deep in the mine.

"Ooo!" Wendell shouted. "I know! They'd shout out, 'Fire in the hole!' before lighting the boom sticks! To warn everybody else!"

Pete smiled. "That is correct, young man! You must come from mining folk!"

"*Yessir!*" Wendell answered, proud.

Another drop of water splashed my shoulder.

Becca whispered, "I'm ready to go."

"It's too cold," Tuyet agreed.

"Well, coming from miners," Pete went on to Wendell, "you must know then that coal turns out forty percent of our world's energy and West Virginia is the *second*-largest coal-producing state! Now, if you young'uns will step right over here, I'll show you all how to know if your air is safe for breathing."

The others started to follow Pete the Miner toward another corner. A few kids kept teasing Blue Braces for almost jumping out of his cart during that fake quake.

I dropped back with Ms. Ferguson. "How do they poison the water?" I asked her. "Coal mines, I mean."

245

"Several ways," Ms. Ferguson said, talking low. "The smoke from coal-powered energy plants gets into the environment, poisoning groundwater. And when they dig out all this rock and toxins to get down here, they scatter it all outside, which seeps into the local water table. There's also the wash plants that create sewage and pollution. Wash plants are—"

"I seen one," I said.

She seemed impressed.

"Coal use kills environments," Ferguson said.

But before I could ask her my next question, Pete the Miner rolled up on us and held out a tiny metal cage. I didn't know why.

"Peek inside," he told us.

I looked. In there was a small yellow bird. About the size of somebody's big toe. It was laying on its side, dead.

I leaned back.

"Ms. Ferguson?"

"That bird was *fake*," she answered. "Don't worry."

"Oh," I said. I was happy to be back outside, inhaling fresh air.

"Like ol' Pete said," Ms. Ferguson went on, "*birds* were how miners knew if there was enough oxygen to breathe. Or if there was any deadly methane gas. If the bird in the cage died, those miners knew to get out quick before *they* died."

"Okay," I said.

"Canary in the coal mine, they used to call it."

"But that wasn't what I was gonna ask."

"Oh?"

Our group strolled back down the coal-camp hill, toward our buses. Even downhill, it was hard keeping up with Ferguson, she always walked so fast.

I asked her, "Do you know Uncle Billy's owns Ball Creek Energy—the one that's been digging all those *new* mines and spoiling the water?"

"So, you found *that* one out?" she asked. "Bright young man!" Her slap on my back stung. "And, yes, Javari, I know all that. I do."

"Well, I don't understand something," I said. "If you're so into sharing nature and teaching us to appreciate it, listen to birds, how come you work for a school that *destroys* all that?"

I marched beside her there, waiting.

She smiled at the ground. "I'll answer that with *another* question," she said. "Why are *you* here?"

"*Me?*"

"Yes. Why'd *you* come to this STEM camp, all the way in the heart of *Appalachia*? From New York? You must have a reason."

I thought about what she'd asked.

Last year, when I applied, it seemed like a good opportunity. To get out of New York and see something new. And once I got here, I realized that winning that Lost ARCC of STEM treasure chest full of cash and prizes could save my family from the streets.

I had *lots* of reasons to be here.

"I came because I like science. I came to learn," I said.

She nodded her head and slipped on a pebble. "We all get some reward out of this place, Javari. All of us have different reasons, different needs. Understand?"

I nodded my head but didn't really get it.

What she'd said, I concentrated on the whole trip back to ARCC.

41

HA-КAA! HA-КAA!

Laying in my top bunk late at night, I laughed out loud when I heard that fake birdcall.

I jumped out of bed, already dressed, and ran toward my window.

Wind in my face, I flew along a dirt road on the back of Cricket's bike. He parked Miss Daisy at the base of a hill with a house at the top. In the dark, I couldn't tell the size of the house but could see one square of light coming from a window.

He left the bike, and we climbed a steep path made out of flat rocks that led up to the front door. Now I could see more. It was a larger house than I thought.

There was no lock on the front door.

Two huge dogs came running out from behind back. They were about to jump up until Cricket shouted, *"Down!"* at them. They both stopped and bowed their heads.

I think they were shepherds. Black and white mixed. I knelt down to pet and baby-talk them. Man, did those dogs stink. They were definitely pets you keep outside.

"Mama's still up," Cricket told me before we stepped through his front door.

Inside sat a big room. There was an old brick fireplace in the wall farthest away. A round green-and-red rug sat underneath a dark wood table in the center of the area.

There wasn't a lot of lights.

Up above, the wooden ceiling was made out of beams. Long, thick beams that made me feel like I'd suddenly stepped into a cabin. There were four doors in the main room leading to other rooms. An old-fashioned stove sat against the wall of a large kitchen.

Maybe I had been thinking prejudiced because I'd expected Cricket's crib on Black Boar Mountain to look like a barn, a total mess. Except for a few country things—and no door lock—it was pretty regular.

I felt let down.

A skinny white woman leaned back in a blue velvet chair in the corner of the main room, listening to the radio and sipping from a bottle of soda. She was younger than my moms but with dark red hair.

Though it was dim in here, I could see she was freckled in the face like Cricket. When she caught me staring at her, she smiled. Missing two of her front teeth. And there was something about her grin that seemed childish, like she was even younger than she looked.

It smelled funny in here too. Like something I'd never smelled before. Kinda like the wet woods.

"Alcott Washington!" she yelled. "Home early? Wasn't 'spectin' to see you till Monday, a week." She turned down the radio volume and tilted her head toward mine. "Who's your handsome friend?"

"This is Bird," Cricket mumbled.

"Well, pleased to meet you, Mr. Bird," she said. "Don't get to meet many of my boy's running buddies."

I stepped toward her. "Nice to meet you too, Mrs. . . . ?"

"Likewise. And it's just Miss," she said, smiling with that gap in her front grill. "Call me Miss Maddie, baby."

I nodded and grinned. "Nice to meet you, Miss Maddie."

She stood. "You that boy from New York City this one's been rattlin' on about."

Cricket was embarrassed.

I told her, "I'm in the STEM camp at ARCC."

"Uncle Billy's," she said.

I nodded.

"Well," Miss Maddie started, "I'll try not to hold that agin you." She laughed loud.

"I need cash for gas," Cricket blurted.

She frowned at him. Then, at me. "Gas and food! Food and gas! If it weren't for them two, I'd never see this one."

Cricket crossed his hands behind his back and stared at

the floor. I grinned. He was usually so loud and grown. I'd never seen him this tame. Like his dogs outside.

His mother walked up on him. "You ask ol' Luke for credit?"

Nature Boy shook his head. "I already owe him for gas."

His mother sighed. "How much you want?"

"Twenty bucks'll do," he said.

"Twenty!" she shouted. Miss Maddie seemed to be *acting* more than really meaning it. She glanced at me. "Mr. Bird, do I look like *Aunt* Billy to you?"

My mouth hung open.

"Close your mouth, honey," Miss Maddie told me. "You'll catch flies."

I shut my mouth. She cackled again. Cricket rolled his eyes.

"My little angel thinks I'm made a' moolah," Miss Maddie told me.

"You *look* like new money, Mother," Cricket said, kissing her hand. He was performing right back with her.

"Nice try," she said, swaying away.

"*Mama . . . ,*" Cricket whined like a little kid. I felt sorry for him. But they were both funny. I was starting to like his moms too.

"Oh!" she yelled, and leaned in her cheek toward his. "Show your mama some love! Come on!"

Frowning, he pecked her cheek. That seemed to make her feel better. She reached into her bra for two five-dollar bills and held them up in the dim light.

"This is all I got, Crick," she said.

"You got tons more mashed down there," he said.

"Is that sass I hear?" Miss Maddie started to tuck the money back in her bra.

Cricket shut up.

She waved the bills. "Same sass as your daddy."

Cricket smirked.

"I know as soon as I give this to you, you'll cut straight outta here like a cat on a quilt," she said, handing him the money.

"Wait here," Cricket told me, and rushed toward another room.

" 'Thanks, Mama!' " his mother yelled after him.

"Oh," he said. "Yeah. Thanks, Mama. 'Preciate ya."

He ducked behind a curtain and fought with pushing a door open. If that was his bedroom, then there musta been enough crap on the floor in there to make it impossible to walk. From inside the room, I heard the sound of junk tumblin' around.

Miss Maddie stared at me like: See what I gotta put up with?

"Set a spell, Bird," she said. "My boy's run back there to plunder his stash." We sat down on two soft chairs. "He thinks I don't realize he got his own bank vault a' funds back in his room." She laughed again. "Want some cookies, sweetheart?"

She handed me a red tin of sugar cookies. I picked one. "Thanks," I said.

"Grab a bunch."

I took some more. Miss Maddie asked how I liked ARCC. I said it was okay, but I wished I could meet more Appalachians. She frowned.

"You say it wrong," she told me.

"Huh?" I asked, inhaling another sugar cookie.

"It's Apple-*atcha*," she told me, pronouncing the name different than I had. "You need to say the second part like you was saying 'at ya.' Like 'coming at ya'?"

I understood.

She went on, "You say it like I tell you and the hill people round here'll think you grew up in Horsewhip."

We both laughed.

"I don't think so," I said. "Does everybody in the mountains hate Uncle Billy's?"

"I cain't speak for everybody around here, but if I coulda got my hands on ol' William Whitt—the one what started this mess—I'da snatched him bald-headed."

I almost coughed up my cookie.

"You like that one, huh?" she asked.

I nodded. But I couldn't stop hacking. Miss Maddie brought me a glass of water that she poured from an old pitcher.

I took one sip of water and wished I hadn't. I swallowed a bit, but it tasted like rusty pee.

"I kin tell by your face, you ain't used to water round here," she said. "*That's* Ball Creek's water. Courtesy a' them same folks at Uncle Billy's paying for your fancy camp."

I'd stopped coughing but was still frowning. I couldn't get that bad water taste out of my mouth.

"Yessir. Our dear ol' Uncle Billy," Miss Maddie said. "All the coal ain't enough! They gotta support drilling for natural gas in our mountains. Killed our lovely trees. *Rurnt* our water. When I was Crick's age, you used to could drink it."

"It's *terrible*."

"I apologize," she said. "Forgot you weren't used to things around here. I bet at that school they give you water in bottles."

I felt like Miss Maddie was pretending with *me* now. She tossed me a bottle of springwater from her kitchen.

Why didn't she give this to me in the first place?

I chugged down that small bottle in one gulp. When I was done, Cricket's mother looked at me funny. The same way my mother looked at me when she wanted me to remember something she'd just said.

"Miss Maddie, how would *you* solve your water problem?"

"Well, I ain't no scientist," she said. "Who am I, *really*? But after all the dirt Uncle Billy's done on us, I'd just be happy if they'd fix our water."

"*Fix* it?"

"*Clean* it. Set it back to how it *was*, Bird. Before Ball Creek's mining, ours was some of the best-tasting water in the world."

Miss Maddie leaned forward. In the dim light, her freckles looked like they glowed.

"Nobody in Charlotte hears us," she said, shrugging. "They all think we're poor, dimwitted hill folk."

"Uncle Billy's says you love 'em," I said. "Like they're the best thing ever."

"All that glitters ain't gold." Miss Maddie let out another laugh. "Welcome to our world."

42

WE RODE DOWN Black Boar Mountain and along a little river to stop at a gas station. It was the same spot where that bus had dropped me off. But tonight, the gas station was wide open.

Cricket said the old man that ran the station only kept it open when he felt like it. That man turned out to be the same old Fred who sat on the porch next to Uncle Billy's original store in Old Town.

Since Fred didn't act like Cricket owed him nothing, I'd assumed this wasn't the gas station Cricket said he owed money to. I also realized Cricket mighta been lying to his moms about owing anything. Just to get some more paper out of her.

Cricket was slick.

After gassing up, we rode across the parking lot and over those train tracks, headed toward some more mountains on the other side of the holler. Looking up at the silver peaks from the back of Cricket's dirt bike, I understood how you could fall in love with living here.

The blue mountains were "everything," like my uncle Melvin would say.

Over the holler tonight, a mist settled down from above. It was summery and humid outside. I could feel the warm wind gust over my face.

It was cool that people around here mostly let you did what you wanted without bothering you. If I'd been back in Bushwick, riding a little motorcycle everywhere, the cops woulda stopped and arrested my butt by now.

Before we could make it up the other mountain, Cricket slowed down, staring at the train tracks far away. I could see a little light flicker there. Cricket turned us around. Before I knew it, we were at that light—a campfire—and talking with two old men who were friends of his.

They were dressed shabby and about the same age as Daddy. These two looked like they hadn't seen a bath. But seemed cool. Their names were Sloan and Chauncey. They said they were out there waiting on a train.

I didn't understand it.

The train station was way back near the gas station and bus stop.

Sloan crouched over their fire, adding some dry sticks to it. He seemed to be really enjoying that fire. Chauncey did too. I could tell by his smile when he stared into it. He had a face that reminded me of a cat's.

Smart and silent.

They were both homeless. Sloan and Chauncey used to have residences and real jobs before, though, according to

Cricket. Even though they had nothing now, you couldn't tell by how glad their faces looked.

"Yeah, boy," Sloan said. "I was an assistant manager at the dollar store in Fayette. Before that, I worked security at ARCC."

I wondered if that was how Cricket got those keys.

"I was a teacher," said Chauncey.

"What happened?" I asked.

Chauncey inhaled deep.

Sloan spoke up: "What had happened to us both was substance abuse."

"We're addicts," said Chauncey. "The recovering kind."

I glanced at Cricket, who stared into their fire.

"I got addicted to prescriptions, Vicodin, Percocet, all a' them," said Sloan. "*Meth*. Couldn't handle that one. Messed me up *real* bad. Got me fired from my job. Lost my place. Almost kilt me."

"But for the grace of God," said Cricket, sounding religious. I didn't think he was.

"Mine was OxyContin," said Chauncey. He glanced at Sloan. "We met, us two, in a program for drug addicts." Sloan smiled back at him.

"How'd *you* two meet?" Sloan asked me and Cricket.

"That STEM camp?" Chauncey asked.

"Yup!" Cricket answered.

"So, you know about the secret gap in the fence?" Chauncey asked me. I didn't say nothing. "Sloan here is the one who showed Crick that."

Sloan grinned. "I used to sneak food off that campus." He jerked toward Cricket. "You still do that? Best be careful, them rent-a-cops they got now—some carry heat."

He meant, *guns*.

"I kin *truck*," Cricket bragged about sprinting. "I run barefoot at night. Like a cheetah."

We all laughed.

"Whatever you do," Sloan said, "stay away from them drugs. Both a' you. At first, you think you kin handle 'em 'cause they're just prescription, but it's too tenacious."

"Buddy, they'll take you down *every* time!" Chauncey added.

"Ain't that the truth!" said Sloan.

Cricket nodded.

I was ready to go!

"Where you fellers headed?" Cricket asked.

"We fixin' to ride the rails," Sloan said.

"Down Florida way," Chauncey added.

Sloan nodded toward Chauncey. "He's got a little sister down there we kin stay with till we're both back on our feet."

"My sister runs a motel in—" Suddenly Chauncey looked all serious. He'd spotted something in the distance. "Sloaney-boy! Over yonder!"

I looked over my shoulder. A train was far off, headed down the tracks toward us. The two old dudes hopped up and kicked dirt over their fire. They scooped up their backpacks from the ground.

"Safe travels to your Florida kin," Cricket said. He stood and stretched.

"Good Lord willing and the creek don't rise," Chauncey said to Cricket.

Then Sloan said to us, "And you two young men, God bless you."

"Keep one 'nother safe," Sloan added.

Chauncey and Sloan exchanged goofy grins. I didn't understand why. I really was ready to leave them behind.

Cricket knew some strange folks.

Soon after, I learned what they'd meant by "ride the rails."

While Cricket and me hid in the trees by the train tracks, Sloan and Chauncey ran beside that train. I wouldn't have believed those two could run that fast if I hadn't seen it that night.

They musta been forty years old!

Right when the train slowed down at an intersection before the next bend, the two old dudes leapt onto it and hauled themselves up on top. They were safe on board the train, waving back at us, when it let out a whistle, chugged around the bend and picked up steam.

"Next stop, Flo-ri-da!" Cricket yelled after their train.

We hopped back on Miss Daisy. Sitting behind Cricket, I held around his waist and leaned into his back. We kept up the mountain.

43

"OH!" I YELLED. "What the—?"

Whatever it was had scared the mess out of me. Something small, furry with claws and yellow eyes had just ran through the bushes near my sneakers.

I sprinted ahead on the path in the woods, zooming past Cricket. He didn't seem bothered at all by the animal in the dark. I could barely see my hands in front of my face.

I heard him giggle in the night.

"Keep cool, man," Cricket said. "Probably just a possum or a coon!"

I'd seen opossums and raccoons. We had them back in Brooklyn. If it *was* one, it was a crazy big one.

"How much farther?" I asked.

We'd left the bike against a tree. My legs were logs. I hadn't been getting good rest the past week, staying up late, running all around Horsewhip with Cricket.

"Just over the top of this hill," he said, passing me. "If we lucky . . . I'm hoping it ain't too late."

Cricket still hadn't told me what this was all about. Whenever I'd asked him why we'd rode across the holler to hunt around this particular mountain, he'd only answered with a grin and the words "It's magic."

We kept on walking up the hill, through the trees. The crickets really thundered tonight. More than usual. It was hotter on this side of the ridge. The mountains weren't as high.

"So . . . ," I started. I was way out of breath and sweating. "How do you know them?"

"Who?"

"You know, those two," I said.

"Oh, Sloan and Chaunce? Well, Chauncey used to be my teacher. Back in fourth grade. Before he got hooked on drugs."

"That man was *your* teacher?"

"*Used* to."

I couldn't believe it. "Wow," I said. "And you call him Chauncey?"

"Sure," Cricket said. "After he got fired, Mama took pity on him and used to give him food, try to help him out and stuff. About then, he went from being Mr. Bartleby to just ol' Chauncey. Maybe he'll be a Mr. Bartleby agin someday."

"That's sad."

"Yeah, it *was*, but he's better now. They both are. I hope they bounce back in Florida. I wouldn't mind traveling someplace else. Something different."

We walked for a while, listening to the cricket songs around us.

"Your crickets are crazy loud down here!" I said. I was starting to get used to them. "Ms. Ferguson told us crickets don't have lungs. They breathe through tiny holes in their bodies. And in Thailand folks eat fried crickets with beer."

I could tell he didn't believe that last part. She said it was true, even if it was nasty.

"My granny nicknamed me Cricket 'cause when I was born, I came out *dark*. Like a black cricket? And I reckon that was a surprise to everybody. Particularly for my mama's boyfriend back then, who was a white man."

"You let them call you Cricket? That's messed up."

"Ever since *before* I kin remember, that's been my nickname." Cricket had reached the top of the hill before I did. "Here we go, baby! Down yonder! See? Hold on to yer butt!"

He disappeared quick down the other side of the hill. I was feeling ready for my bed, I was so tired.

I reached the top.

Nothing.

Nothing but trees and more trees and rocks and leaves and probably even more little beady-eyed monsters, waiting to chew my ankles in the dark.

"Bird!" Cricket shouted from the black ink down the hill. "Hurry up! They still here! It's about to start agin!"

"What?" I yelled.

I followed him. I didn't really have no choice. Just when

I'd decided to start making better choices in my life, I suddenly saw.

I'd thought it was an illusion, like some VR images had flashed inside my eyes. Then, it exploded all around me. I lurched to a stop, settled on the side of that hill.

A hundred, no *thousands,* of tiny yellow and orange lights were winking on and off, straight down into this little secret valley, as far into the trees as I could see.

It was like being planted in the middle of a silent fireworks show. Then, just as soon as the lights had started, all the twinkles stopped.

I ran down the hill until I bumped into Cricket at the bottom. We both laughed. There was a creek here. I could smell the water before I saw the moonlight bounce off its top.

"Dude," I told him. "That was amazing!"

"Told ya to hold on to yer butt!"

"Yeah," I said. "All those fireflies lighting up . . . but they stopped?"

Just when I said that, they started up again. All around us, tiny little lights spun around. These were no ordinary lightning bugs.

Nah.

Some summers back home we get them too: One light flicker here. One tiny bug spark there.

But right now, in this gully, what looked like thousands of fireflies were having a block party, blinking on and off their little beams like concert strobes. And then, all at once, they stopped. . . .

Waited a couple of minutes in pitch-black.

Then, they'd all light up again.

Winking.

Together.

I'd never seen nothing like it. Almost like somebody was controlling the whole thing, timed with a gazillion light switches.

Mouth open, I sat down on the grass.

"How do they do it?" I asked.

"Flying beetles," Cricket said. "Synchronous fireflies. Only a few like 'em in the whole world. Right here in Appalachia!"

"Lucky," I said.

All around us, clouds of bug lights were popping on and off.

"Chauncey took my class here on a field trip when I was little. Us and our parents, late at night. He said these fireflies are special, rare. They're only here and some spot in the Smokies."

After a minute or two of darkness, the bugs burst into twinkling again.

I said, "It's like they talk back and forth. With light."

"Yep! Chauncey said they're all sweet-talking one another. It's the men fireflies flashing to the lady fireflies."

"Oh . . . right. I get it."

"But there could be some male bugs out there trying to

get with other males," he added. "I read there's a lot of gay animals: penguins, ducks, cheetahs, chimps, tigers, lions (lions—*that's* something) and, heck, even *worms*!"

I laughed at this. "Gay worms? How do they tell?"

"Don't ask me," he said.

"Well, they're not *all* that way," I said. "A few in each species, I think."

"*Anyways,*" Cricket said, "our bugs here use these lights to show off." Yawning, he plopped down next to me. "Basically, they're trying to get some bug booty."

He elbowed me. I heard him giggle.

"Bird?" he said.

"Yeah?" I said.

"When you gonna tell me 'bout where *you* from?"

I didn't wanna think about that right now.

This here was beautiful.

This *was* magic.

44

NEXT DAY, WE HAD a Futureneers field trip. Exploring even more nature in a whole different part of Horsewhip Hollow.

We rode buses down into Foggy Gully, where we hiked and river-rafted and collected insects and rocks and stuff. Ms. Ferguson ran some lessons with our class where we collected samples of different types of plants and then arthropods.

Arthropods were small, spineless animals. I was surprised by how many different varieties we found.

There was all kinds of stuff hiding out here in these woods. I didn't mention Cricket's firefly gully to Ms. Ferguson. I kept that private.

My favorite bug today was the cottonwood borer. It ran big and had this black-and-white design on its beetle back. Like a tie-dye. We also uncovered a colony of cow killers in a field. These little ants were covered in dark orange fuzz, like little fur coats.

Ms. Ferguson told me those ants had a powerful sting. I showed her a ladybug I found crawling up a flower stem.

"Ah! Ladybug!" she said. "My favorite. Nice, Mr. Harris."

"Pretty bug," I said. In my hand, I turned the flower upside down. The ladybug U-turned and started climbing back up again.

"Oh, that's not a bug. She's a beetle," Ferguson said.

"What's the difference?"

"Bugs eat liquid. Beetles don't; they have little jaws to chew."

A girl tried to snatch my ladybug flower.

"Do you know how Miss Ladybug got her name?" Ferguson asked us. "No? Well, many, many years ago, farmers in Europe prayed to the Virgin Mary to save their crops from aphids, crop destroyers, and then, ladybugs appeared and ate up all the aphids! Isn't that something? So they named them after Our *Lady* Mary."

It was a nice story, but I wasn't sure if I believed it. I mean, why did they name them lady*bugs*, when she just told me they were actually *beetles*?

Later, we hiked around the hills beside another creek and looked for old birds' nests. When one of us found one, Ms. Ferguson would analyze it for us, telling what type of birds used to live there. We were careful not to touch the nests or break them. She said that even a nest that looked deserted could be recycled next year by a new bird family.

I wished human families could do that just as easy.

Then we learned how to build our own birds' nests. Long reeds and blades of grass and ribbons all wove together like baskets. Weak stuff built into something strong.

After a picnic lunch, we had time to swim.

That was interesting.

Where I'm from, when we wanna swim we go to a swimming pool. There's lots of pools open in New York in the summertime. Sometimes, we even go to the beach, Coney Island, Rockaway Beach, the Atlantic Ocean.

I never swam in a creek or stream in the country.

It's a different thing, I discovered.

For one, instead of all sand, the "beach" was mostly hard pebbles and mud. And the creek water you were supposed to swim in was muddy too. Especially when a lot of kids jumped in.

Tuyet, Becca and me laid our beach towels out on all these rocks and waded into the creek with the other kids. The girls wore one-piece bathing suits. I wore swimming trunks with one of my undershirts, the one with the hole in the back. Niece Nickie and Niece Verity were the lifeguards.

Ethan Cunningham waded out into the creek and powered up a two-foot-long motorized submarine he'd constructed. Him showing off his muscles got more attention than his ship.

Scotty challenged Ethan to some body-builder poses, which made everybody laugh. Scotty was so pale and skinny.

Becca was the first one of us to jet. Said she was gonna practice some more with Wang's Nightjar app. One of the

Nephews had brought the tablets for an outdoor session here, and Scarecrow had got pretty good at programming them bird avatars.

But Becca got back to where we left our stuff on the rocks and started wagging her hand toward me and Tuyet in the water.

"Who's she waving at?" Tuyet asked.

"You," I said. "Her roomie."

Tuyet waded out of the creek and stood there talking to Becca for a minute. Pretty soon Nieces Verity and Nickie were hovering around Becca, who was starting to cry. The two Nieces ran off, it looked like to get help.

I didn't know what was going on and I didn't care. I was tired of Becca.

No drama! Like Dr. Hunter said.

Tuyet waved at me to come out. When I got to the place on the rocks where we'd left our towels, I could see that Becca's face was a mess. She couldn't stop bawling.

"What happened?" I asked Tuyet.

"Javari," Becca started, "you saw me leave my grand-daddy's watch here, didn't you? I hid it under here, under my hat."

"No, I didn't see," I said. "What happened? Somebody stole it?"

"Looks like it," Tuyet said.

Becca nodded. "Why would somebody do that? My granddaddy's watch! Pa's gonna kill me. I mean, *literally* kill me!"

"Honey, calm down," Tuyet said. "Nickie and Verity went to find Wendell and Tom. They'll find out what happened. You check all around here?"

They both knelt down, searching.

I wasn't about to hunt for nothing. "If it fell in these rocks . . . ," I said. I looked away and spotted a familiar face peek out from behind some trees.

Crick!

I chuckled out loud.

"Why are you laughing?" Becca asked. Her voice sounded like a moan. Both her and Tuyet saw where I stared and musta seen Cricket's grinning face too.

When Cricket saw them, he disappeared. Becca jumped up and rushed after him, down a dirt path. Me and Tuyet followed.

"That boy!" Becca shouted. "He took it!"

"Becca!" Tuyet called. "Wait!"

But Becca kept running.

45

WHEN ME, TUYET AND BECCA reached the end of the path, we saw a pond that'd been mostly hidden by the trees.

It was a very small pond with a tiny island at its middle. On the sandy island sat a concrete building with no windows and one door. The gray building couldn't have been more than ten feet around.

Somebody had spray-painted onto it: RIP HH.

This was Cricket's work, I could tell. "Rest in Peace, Horsewhip Hollow?" I said, translating the grafs.

And Nature Boy himself was sitting a few feet from us, at the edge of the pond, looking like he was on vacation in Hawaii. Spread out, coolin' it, grinning. Waiting for us with his duffel bag beside him.

Cricket looked wet.

"Howdy!" he said.

"Where is it?" Becca demanded, rushing up to him. "Where's my granddaddy's watch?"

Without saying a word, Cricket waved a hand toward the small gray building on the little island. Becca squinted out at it.

She spotted something over there. I saw it too, small, glistening in the sunlight.

Becca gave Cricket a disgusted stare. "You must not think I can swim," she told him. As she waded into the water, she said, "Watch this!"

She dove into the water and swam like a dolphin straight to the other side. From the doorknob on the little building, she plucked her granddaddy's gold watch and strapped it around her wrist like a conqueror.

Becca grinned, shouting back at Cricket, "I finished *second* in the hundred-yard breaststroke!" She stepped toward the island's edge.

Cricket hollered, his hands to his mouth. "That's fantastic, Miss Whitt!" he shouted. "I reckon that means you good at swimming through raw sewage water too! 'Cause that's what you just did!"

On the little island, Becca froze. She had been about to wade back into the pond for the short swim back. On our side, Cricket stood up with a wide smile.

He yelled across to her, "That little building there is the Horsewhip Holler sewage facility! All the wastewater from our toilets empties into this here pond you just swam through!"

Me and Tuyet exchanged looks. I thought of those acid pools in *Flexus*.

Becca freaked out. She glared at her skin, and started to rub, like she was trying to wipe off all of the sewage water.

"Oh my God! You!" she yelled. "Why'd you do this?" She left the water's edge. Her back pushed against the graffiti on the building.

"Miss Whitt!" said Cricket. "Your grandpa killed my grandpa!"

"I asked my father!" she shouted back. "He said it's lies! My granddaddy was good!"

"Not likely!" Cricket said. "Men like Uncle Billy don't get gold from being good!"

"What do you want!" Becca shouted, frantic.

Cricket smiled. "I don't know. Maybe I just got what I wanted."

"You expect me to apologize for something that *might* have happened before either of us was even *born*? What did *I* do!"

Cricket: "Miss Whitt, you wouldn't be as rich as you are today if it wasn't for the grief and death of folks like my grandpa. You only here 'cause of dirty work your kin laid out."

"What do you want!"

"You broke us," Cricket said. "The way I see it: you break it, you fix it."

"What does that even mean!"

"I just told you!" he cried. "Fix it. And fix yourself."

After that, Cricket snatched his duffel and strolled off into the gully.

Becca collapsed on the sand over there. "What am *I* supposed to do?" I heard her sob. "I'm a kid."

About a minute later, Wendell and Nickie ran up beside us. They asked why Becca was crying on that island in the middle of the pond. When we told them it was because of the sewage water, they both laughed hard.

"Well, butter my butt and call me a biscuit!" Wendell yelped. "Wait till I tell Larry!"

"Who told you kids that nonsense?" Nickie asked.

Wendell cupped his hands to his mouth. "Miss Whitt! Ooo-whooo!" He told me and Tuyet: "That ain't no sewage processor. That's the boathouse. Only thing in there is kayaks."

Tuyet and me let out the biggest howl.

Becca still looked panicked until Wendell and Nickie waded out into the water to get her.

46

"NOT TOO SHABBY, JERRY!" Tuyet called out.

She reached over him to pick a small box of Honey Nut Cheerios.

"Huh?" Jerry said. He spun his wheelchair around in a perfect wheelie in the dining hall.

"You know," Tuyet said. "Your little shape-changing bomb trick you flipped on us the other day?"

Jerry grinned like a villain.

"Oh, yeah," he said. "That was hilarious. Veer won us a shape-changing gem and we really wanted to use it." Jerry glanced up at me. "Sorry to blow you up, but . . . you know."

He wasn't sorry. None of the Virtual Gear Engineers were. I shoulda known Veer was behind using that shape-changing gem. Keep your eyes on the quiet ones, Poppa says.

Jerry wheeled himself toward his group's dining table.

Tuyet grabbed a box of cranberry juice. *"Dân quê,"* she muttered, glaring at them.

"What's that?" I asked.

"Hicks," she answered, frowning. "That's what they are."

"Oh."

We headed back toward Becca, who was sitting alone at our table, picking at her turkey sausage. She'd been almost silent since her island adventure yesterday. I bet she'd never remove that watch again. Even in the shower.

"Here," Tuyet said, handing her the juice.

All of the Virtual Gear Engineers brushed past our table. "Well, look what's happening at the KKK rally!" Lester roared.

"Don't be late for your cross burnin'!" Jerry added.

Becca's eyes teared up. I rolled my eyes at her. As he left, I heard Lester call me a Black Klansman.

"We gotta beat those meatheads," Tuyet said.

"It's *on*," I agreed. "*Black Klansman?* Black folks can't be racist! They gettin' *five across the eyes*."

Tuyet whispered in my ear, "We think Jerry's down in the meadows. Looks like he just killed off the Silver Lady and the Witch avatars."

I lifted the headset off my eyes. Tuyet and Becca sat beside me at our VR cubicle. Tuyet wore a sneaky look.

"On my way to the bathroom, I overheard the Virtual Gears say they were somewhere called Redrix Meadows," Becca whispered.

"Our map says that's just ahead of our guy," said Tuyet.

"Let's *get* Jerry and them," I said.

They nodded.

I went back into the game. We had full energy but only one life left, so I had to be careful.

"Use the power grenades," I heard Becca say. "Blow him up like they did us."

After searching around Redrix Meadows for what seemed like forever, we found the Gold Basketball avatar there and defeated them again. What a dumb choice for an avatar!

That VR message flashed:

TO THE VICTOR GO THE SPOILS! BUT YOUR FOE OWNS NO PRIZE. GO FORWARD IN TRIUMPH!

I told Becca Jerry'd probably meant for her to overhear them. To throw us off. Those guys were sneaky. Their avatar wasn't here nowhere.

But there was something else.

I saw something huge shining up ahead in the tall orange grass. There was a big silver spider crouching. It throbbed like it was breathing in and out, staring at me.

"Holy spit!" I shouted.

The spider musta been six feet tall.

"Silverback sac spider!" Becca shouted.

"That's what the monitor says, Jay," Tuyet added.

"Another trap!" Becca yelled.

"Scoot!" Tuyet shouted.

I almost turned and ran, but then I remembered what

that Wallace had told me about his game's bugs. He'd said most insects were misunderstood.

Folks feared centipedes, worms and cottonwood borers because they were ugly. Folks loved butterflies and lady-bugs and lightning bugs because they were beautiful.

I knew what it felt like to be judged based only on how you looked.

Facing this silverback sac spider, I settled down and focused. One virtual foot ahead of the other one, I walked toward it.

"Javari, you'll get us killed and out of the game for good," Tuyet warned. "This is our last life."

"I *know*," I told her.

Soon I was standing directly in front of the silverback sac spider. I held out my hand. The spider looked like it recognized me.

Then it rose up on its legs and dropped something out of its thorax, its underside. After that, it leapt away. High over a clump of weeds.

What it left for us in the grass was one silver pellet.

Above, the game's floating note read:

PRIZE! SILVERBACK SAC SPIDER PELLET! WOULD
YOU LIKE TO ADD THIS TO YOUR SURVIVAL KIT?

I snatched up the pellet for our group. We had no idea what it did.

After I logged out, Tuyet asked me: "Holy spit?"

Later, we worked on our final project.

Water.

Pollution.

Horsewhip.

In our cubicle, Becca used Nightjar to work on a presentation, using pictures we found online and some other graphics and music. I was surprised by how hard she was working.

What Cricket did at Foggy Gully seemed to affect her.

Me and Tuyet were the ones writing the speech we had to give. It was hard. And it was only a speech. We really needed something to *show.*

Something more than a presentation on a screen.

We needed to make something real.

Becca told me, "I'm using this Pot-lickin' Brothers Band music in our presentation. I like them!"

"Yeah," I said. "They ain't bad."

"Where'd you find 'em?" she asked.

I remembered that night I saw the Pot-lickin' Brothers set up their instruments at Barrelhouse. And remembered almost getting beat down by Dalton. Plus, that man OD'ing and them saving him by pouring charcoal down his throat.

I suddenly sat up. I had the start of an idea.

"You know what'd be good?" I said.

"What?" Tuyet asked.

"*Charcoal,*" I said. "Like Ethan's water clock . . ."

"Huh?" Becca said.

"You wanna build a *clock*?" Tuyet asked me.

"No!" I said. "But what if Uncle Billy's *fixed* Horse-whip's water—made it right?"

"*Hmmph,*" Becca grunted, over her shoulder.

Tuyet tilted her head to one side. "Or *maybe,*" she started, "if Uncle Billy's made a way for *Horsewhip* to fix it."

Becca suddenly stopped typing. Spun away from her laptop to face us. She covered her eyes, groaning.

It was dusk.

My Automata class with Ethan had climbed the steps of the tower above Whitt Hall. It was named after Becca's granddaddy, I'd found out. A lot of buildings around were.

Looking out over the mountains with the bright orange sunset behind them was something else. We musta been a hundred feet up in the air inside this tower.

I peeked down below and saw most of the other campers standing across the yard, looking up. They were down there waiting on us to do our thing.

That day, we'd formed lanterns out of wire frames covered with different sorts of bright-colored papers. Ethan told us these paper lanterns'd been invented by the Chinese back in third century BC.

Nowadays, the lanterns were legal here in West Virginia,

Ethan told us. Other places, people were afraid of their flames.

These lanterns looked like small hot-air balloons, but a tiny candle was where the basket would be. When the candles were lit, the balloon filled with hot air, and because hot air's lighter than the cool air on the outside of the balloon, the lanterns rise!

But they'd only burn for minutes before they come down.

One by one, Ethan lit the candles and we released them. Scotty's lantern got caught by some wind and rustled up into the air. I held my lantern out over the rail. I felt the wind tug on it, so I let go.

My sky lantern drifted out. Glowing in the warm sky. Pretty soon you couldn't see any of the balloons no more. Just their lights.

I'd named mine Firefly.

We watched them all float off into infinity.

Ethan spoke out to nobody in particular: " 'The balloon stands still in the air, while the earth flies past underneath.' Or something like that."

I didn't know what that was, but I liked it. I wondered what it would feel like to really fly.

Endless.

But everything had to end.

47

ANOTHER OL' LATE NIGHT, hanging with Cricket.

I asked him and he grinned at me and we rode back to see the synchronous fireflies again. He wasn't sure if they'd still be out, flashing. They only come out like that for a couple weeks each year, I guessed.

Then, no more fireworks until next summer.

Cricket told me that these fireflies live for years under the dirt, until they mature into adult bugs. When that happens, they fly out of the ground and put on a show for just them two short weeks.

They flash lights at each other and mate.

And then die off, leaving their babies, growing underground, to continue the same way. The same thing over and over and over . . .

Tonight, we'd made it back.

Our fireflies were still out, but not as bright. You could tell they were about to die. I wondered if these lightning bugs knew their death was around the corner.

Could they feel everything was almost over?

Did it make them mad?

I had named this little gully the Holler of the Fireflies.

It already had another name, but I forgot what Cricket'd called it. And also, I liked my name for it better.

After watching the lightning bugs, we decided to swim in the creek at the bottom of the holler. The weather was still hot. I was happy to roll off my Mets T-shirt and jeans and slip into the water.

Cricket did too.

I was surprised he had a keloid on his shoulder. He said it was a scar from when he fell off his bike.

I usually didn't like keloids, but his looked neat.

The creek was not as cold as I'd wanted it to be, but it was cold enough. Cricket called it a swimming hole. We splashed around a bit in the hole until I remembered that my STEM camp time was next to done. Soon I'd have to head back home and deal with who knows.

"Jerry, that kid in the wheelchair," I told Cricket, "he could win the whole thing tomorrow. His group's almost at this alien city on the map called Harmonee. Maestro Island sits right across the bay from there."

"And if you get to Maestro Island, you beat out every-body else, right?"

"Right," I said. I slapped the water.

"That's where you win the treasure chest?" he asked.

"No, no," I said. "That's totally different. Whatever group

produces the best final project wins all the money. Winning *Flexus* by beating everybody else to Maestro Island . . . that's only bragging rights."

"Okay. I'd be more worried about the one that wins you the cash."

"Beating the other groups to Maestro Island means you the best. I hate Jerry. He's like a woodrat."

Cricket laughed. "You even know what that is?" He kicked closer. "*You're* a woodrat," he said.

I laughed in his face.

"Just like Dalton called you," Cricket told me. "Come here, rat!"

He trapped me in a choke hold. Giggling, I yelled and tried to break free. I couldn't dunk him under the water, he was too strong.

We laughed and tangled until I felt something on the back of my neck. It tickled. It felt like Cricket had just kissed me there.

I froze.

My face got hot.

"Cricket?" I asked him.

"Yeah?"

"Uh . . . leggo," I said. "For real."

He let go. I swam to the edge of the stream and spun around. I could just make out his pale freckled face in the moonlight.

I could tell he was embarrassed.

"I . . . um . . . ," I started.

Cricket waded toward the grass. He reached up to rub his upper lip in the dark.

"You made me knock my lip on the back of your neck," he said without looking at me. "It hurts." He waited there, rubbing his lip.

"Okay, well . . . I wanna go back to my dorm. Like, *now*."

"Okay, Bird," he said. "Hey! You feel them fish in this hole? I felt one suck their slimy lips on me." He scanned around for his clothes on the grass. "You feel them fish?"

I squinted at him in the dark.

We slid out of the stream at opposite ends and gathered up our stuff.

48

I STAYED IN BED the next morning.

Veer went down to breakfast without me. I avoided all of my STEM activities, not leaving my room.

I just laid there. I didn't feel like it.

Poppa woulda called me idle.

I didn't care until Rich the RA came to check on me and I had to get up.

49

I STILL FELT WEIRD.

I thought about video-calling Ke'Von, but that was a bad idea. When we were kids, Ke'Von used to call me Sweet Jay because he thought I used to sound like a girl.

I tried video-calling Daddy, but I couldn't reach him.

I hadn't really wanted to video-call Poppa George for advice this afternoon, but I did.

Would Poppa understand what happened with Cricket?

Sitting in the ARCC communications room, I waited for Shireen to answer her phone. When my little sister finally picked up, she looked real nervous.

"Hey, Jay," Shireen said.

"What took you so long?" I said. "I need to speak to Poppa. Alone."

"Okay. He's here. Mother, it's Jay."

"Jay?" I heard Poppa say. He still sounded weak.

"He wants to speak to Poppa," Shireen said. She passed her phone, and I could tell that she wasn't at home. *Wherever* it was, was a bright white space, white walls. A few

289

electronic monitors flashed by as the phone's camera relayed.

Instead of Poppa George's face, I saw my moms's.

"Hey, sweetie," she said.

"Ma," I said. "What's going on? Where's Poppa?"

"He's here."

"Where are you?"

"We at the hospital," she said. "Your granddad wasn't feeling well the other day, so we brought him to the ER."

I stared at her.

"Charles?" she said, off-camera. "Charles, it's your son." Her face popped back on-screen. "Is everything all right?" she asked me.

"What's wrong with Poppa?" I asked. "Where is he?"

"Hold on," Ma said.

The phone bounced again and soon Poppa's face came on the screen. He looked tired.

"There he is," Poppa said to me. He smiled a bit. "My smart son . . . I mean grandson . . ."

"Poppa," I said. "What's wrong? You all right?"

"Me? I'm fine as frog's hair!" he said, and chuckled. "How's, uh, camp?"

I asked him, "Why'd they take you to the ER?"

"Well, I wasn't feeling my best the past week," Poppa said. "Ever since . . . I think I worried too much and got myself in a bad way. You know. Things had got kinda stressful with our, you know, rent situation."

"I know."

"I've lived there so long, Javari," he said, sounding like he was about to cry. "That's me and your grandmama's place. It's all I got of her."

"I know, Poppa. You really loved her."

"Yes. So, your mother brought me down here to the hospital. Thought maybe they could give me something to calm me down is all. It worked. I'm calm now." He grinned, almost falling asleep on me again. *"I'm . . . calm . . ."*

Ma took the phone from him.

"Why didn't you tell me?" I asked her.

"You couldn't do nothing, Jay," she said. "He's been worrying too much lately. Worrying himself sick. He feels better now."

"Where's Daddy?"

"Yeah, your father's here, baby," Ma said. "Hold on. I'm walking into the hall now. Hold on. Hello?"

"Yeah."

In the hall, her voice changed a little. "Your daddy can't talk right now, baby. He's kinda broke up over everything. Taking it bad. We all are."

I froze.

Ma's eyes got wet. She said, "Baby, while George was in here, they did some tests and . . . they found cancer. Cancer in his lungs."

What?

$$2x + 5x + 4x + 20 = 2x + 9x + 20 = 5 \times 15$$

50

THE DOCTORS FOUND a *nodule,* or small lump, in one of my poppa's lungs.

They said it was basically stage one cancer. Though stage one wasn't the worst kind, for somebody as old and weak as my poppa, it was serious.

The hospital would release him tomorrow. Over the next two weeks, they'd decide on a way to try to heal him.

I'd be back way before then.

He was okay for now. . . .

"Are you okay?" Tuyet asked.

She and me had been walking for over half an hour along this mountain road. I'd been guiding our way from memory, since the last time I'd been over here was at night.

"I'm okay," I told Tuyet. I was lying. "Actually, I'm not."

It didn't make any sense, not telling her the truth. Lying now felt like it would eat at me just like that cancer inside of my poppa.

I decided to stop standing off so much from people.

I told Tuyet everything about Poppa. I did right away feel a whole lot better.

I still felt guilty that Poppa had got so worried sick about our future eviction that they took him to the hospital. But if they hadn't done that, the doctors might not've found his cancer.

I *had* been lazy, like Becca'd said. Was having too much fun.

I knew I needed to win that money for my family, but I hadn't been trying hard enough on this final project. I'd argued with the girls too much.

I had also let that Cricket distract me, hanging out with him.

When all the time, he was . . .

All that had changed now.

I was determined to win more than ever.

Before we'd left ARCC's campus this afternoon, we'd all decided Becca was too busy making our Nightjar presentation to come.

"Stage one is the least-worse kind," Tuyet said. "My aunt survived stage *two* breast cancer. I think your poppa'll be okay."

"You think?"

"Sounds like they caught it early, Jay."

A motorcycle's engine buzzed closer. I thought it was *him*.

But we watched two white teens race by us on the road. The boy in front shouted, "Niggers, go home!" and the girl riding on back yelled, "Nigger!" before their bike dove around the corner.

They were gone.

Tuyet stopped walking. I kept on but glanced back at her. She was shook.

"What just happened?" she asked.

"That's *nothing*," I said.

"I been called chink before," Tuyet said, shaking her head, "but never *that*. I mean, what did they even *mean*?"

"It don't have to make sense. It's just stupid," I told her.

" 'Go home'? Where? There's always been Black people in this country."

"So, do you think *they're* racist on that bike?" I asked.

"Are you crazy? Of course."

"Okay. I wasn't sure if that was plain enough for you. When Becca said what she said, you doubted whether she knew it was wrong."

Tuyet thought on this a minute, then, "*White people*" was what she said. "Sometimes I don't get them."

"Yeah. Let's sneak through here," I said.

We cut into the woods.

More green bushes and wild birds' whistles.

Trees hiding red squirrels.

Rocks, mushrooms.

And dirt.

Through some thick forest, we walked farther along the

side of Mount Tackett. The closer we got to where we were headed, the more nervous I was getting. I stepped over an old log.

"Wait," Tuyet said. She stooped down to analyze a green plant growing out of the branch. Bright red berries speckled the shrub.

"Don't touch it," I said. "Could be poison."

"It's not poison, silly. It's ginseng."

"You sure?"

"Positive," Tuyet said. "This is very healthy for you. My grandma grows it. Wild ginseng."

There was a whole bush there.

We crept more up the mountain. It got steep. Tuyet was on the higher side of the hill, so I had to stare up at her as we went.

"Have you ever had somebody with a crush on you?" I asked Tuyet.

She sighed. "I knew this would happen," she said. "Okay, Jay, I think you're very charismatic, but I'm trying to stay focused on school and getting into a good college."

"Huh? College? You're in middle school."

"Plus, I live in Houston and you're in Brooklyn. Even though I have cousins in New York, the long-distance romance situation never works—"

"Not *me*, dummy," I said. "I don't like you."

She sighed again and threw me a pitiful look. "I know it's hard."

I glanced from side to side, then, "Another dude kissed me."

Tuyet hopped into the air and gasped. She landed funny and almost tumbled down the hill.

"No. Way," she squealed, staring around the woods.

It was like she was suddenly back in our lab, scrolling through faces of other boys in her mind. Everyone else, besides us, was back there, working on their final projects. Well, we were out here working on our final project too. Just in a sneaky, shady way.

Tuyet whispered, "Is it Veer? Did he make his move?"

I shook my head. "This boy's not in our program."

"Oh!" she yelled. "Freckles! You're in love with that freckled kid!"

"Shh!" I said, even though there was no one else around.

"The Rebecca-hater!" she said. "I approve."

"I'm not . . . I'm not gay. Okay?"

Tuyet looked confused. "Are you sure? Becca thought you were."

"Never mind, girl!" I said. "I hope she's almost done with our presentation."

I stopped.

"Look at this house."

We'd crossed over a dirt road that led up to a little wooden house hidden amongst a set of trees. The house was made of planks and gray rocks. It had a porch and looked really old. The roofing was coming off in pieces.

"I know," Tuyet said. "Held together with Gorilla Glue."

I tilted my head to one side. "Is the top slanted?"

"Oh!" Tuyet shouted.

This toddler leaned on the screen door from the inside. She wore a long pink T-shirt like a dress and watched us. The girl wanted out.

"Look!" Tuyet said. "Hi! Hi!"

That was all it took. The grubby little white kid ran over and tackled Tuyet around the knees. The girl would not let go.

"*Aww.*" Tuyet sighed. "She's so cute! Look, Jay!"

I noticed the girl held in her fingers a *bluecherry* muffin. It was one they baked in ARCC's dining halls. I wondered if she got it from that boys' and girls' club where all of Cricket's stolen snacks went.

Nuts.

"Jodie!"

Shouting, this crazy big lady had stumbled out the front door. She was a giant version of the toddler but scowled at us.

"Howdy," Tuyet said with a grin.

"Howdy," the woman said. She suddenly relaxed. "I see my little jellyfish stung you. Jo-girl, let the young lady go, now. It's almost time for supper."

"I'm sorry," Tuyet said. "We were passing by and your daughter is so cute!"

"*Grandkin,*" the woman explained. "And you'uns is all right. I just didn't know what was *what* at first."

"We gotta go," I told Tuyet.

"Bye! Bye!" Tuyet told little Jo. "Bye!"

"Say bye-bye to the purdy girl," the woman told her granddaughter. The toddler waved.

We moved on.

After walking farther up the hill, Tuyet tripped up beside me.

"She didn't look *old* enough to be a grandma . . . ," my Fractal partner said. "Javari, I don't really care if you *are* or aren't gay. Becca said she didn't care either—though I ain't sure I believe her—but you say that freckled kid wanted to lock lips?"

I nodded.

"How did *you* feel?"

"What you mean, how'd I feel? I feel guilty now. I ain't sure why. I didn't do nothing."

"Was it— Did he *attack* you, that kid?"

I shook my head. "We were goofing around, and it felt like he, you know, like he tried to kiss me on my neck. It felt weird."

"How old is he anyhow?"

"A year older . . ."

"*Hmm* . . . ," she said.

"What does that mean?" I asked.

"Well, you have to be careful," she said. "You haven't experienced this like I have, 'cause I'm a girl, but boys can be the worst. My father always tells me to be on the lookout for boys and old men touching me wrong, trying something gross—even *saying* gross stuff is not cool."

"I know that," I said.

My own daddy had a long talk with me last year, about how to be a "man of honor" when it came to girls. He'd said to never make them feel scared or uncomfortable.

"I mean, Cricket was my friend," I told Tuyet. "He showed me all around."

"He probably still *is* your friend, Javari," she said.

"I thought he was cool."

"We gotta watch out for predators. But Freckles sounds different," Tuyet said. "He's probably scared."

"*Him* scared?" I said. "Why? I know gay people, my uncle Melvin is way gay, but having one try to suck on my neck is different."

"You should go by your gut. That's what Ba tells me."

"*Ba?*"

"Daddy," she explained. "You feel like Cricket meant to hurt you or make you feel bad?"

I shook my head.

"Jay, if you see him again, you can just say you aren't into that and see how he acts. Then . . . then, if he *still* tries to grab some, kick him in the *cojones* and dash."

This girl actually made me grin despite how rotten I felt. "*Ba* taught you that too?" I asked.

She nodded.

"Are all the daughters from Houston like you?"

Tuyet shook her head. "I'm special. Me and Beyoncé."

I stopped walking again and stared dead ahead.

Dalton Spratt's Barrelhouse sat in front of us, up the hill.

I couldn't see any lights on, though. Maybe because it was daytime now and the last time I was here, it was at night.

"Is that it?" Tuyet asked.

"That's it," I said.

Tuyet studied the wooden shack for a minute before sighing. "God, all this STEM camp drama makes me miss H-town more and more," she said.

51

"KNOCK AGAIN," TUYET ORDERED.

"I don't think anybody's home," I said.

"It looks deserted," she said.

"I think it always looks deserted. Except at night when it's crowded."

"You came here at night? *Hombre valiente.* I can't believe the same bald dude from your bus ride was in here waiting for you. You sure him and Freckles aren't working against you?"

I shook my head. "Cricket wouldn't do that." I started to walk around toward the front of the shack when Tuyet pushed on the back door and it swung open.

"People around here don't lock their doors," she said.

We stepped inside.

"Here it is."

I showed Tuyet the white bag filled with dark powder. It was the same one Cricket had grabbed from beneath the window that night.

"'Activated charcoal,'" Tuyet read. "This is the stuff."

I looked around the empty Barrelhouse kitchen. It looked even worse during the day. The dark shadows at night hid exactly how worn down and dirty it really was. I gagged remembering I'd ate something cooked in here.

"How does this stuff work?" Tuyet turned the bag over to read the back.

"If you put it in water and drink some after swallowing poison or drugs, the charcoal sticks to the poison in your intestines. Prevents your body from absorbing the bad stuff."

"Cool. Let's pull some and go."

A bird chirped.

Above my head, there was a small hole in the kitchen ceiling where you could see the trees and sky. The chirps reminded me of that stupid birdcall Cricket made.

"Javari?" Tuyet said.

She'd got the plastic bag out of her sack and was holding it for me to pour. I emptied about two cups into her bag. She zipped it up and smiled.

"Easy-peasy!" Tuyet said. "Let's go before somebody comes!"

"Wait," I said. "Where's the money?"

"I'm poor," she said. "I thought you brought money."

I frowned and tried to unzip my fanny pack with my money stashed inside, but the zipper was broke. I tugged some more. It wouldn't give.

"What are you doing?" Tuyet said.

"It's caught."

"Let me."

"It's too stuck."

Tuyet yanked an old butcher knife from a counter and moved toward me. I stepped back.

"Take off your fanny pack," she said. "I'll cut it open."

"I can't take it off so easy. My stupid moms . . ."

I stood there in the middle of that greasy kitchen, trying to force my fanny pack down my waist and thighs. The buckle was taped shut. I was happy I'd lost weight since Ma taped it together. It was easier now slipping it on and taking it off.

"Hurry up, Javari. What if somebody finds us?" Her eyes were huge.

"Shut up!"

Finally, I'd managed to work the pack down around my ankles. When I lifted my leg to get to the pack, I accidentally fell over sideways. I landed on that nasty black and greasy floor.

Tuyet laughed.

I sat up from the floor and my T-shirt had a hard time pulling away from the gook there. The palms of my hands were sticky from landing on the floorboards.

"So gross," Tuyet said, giggling.

"Help me!" I said. "Quit and help me up!"

Of course, now that I'd removed my fanny pack, all of a sudden, the zipper worked fine again. I rolled my eyes. Tuyet thought this was even more funny.

I left five dollars on the kitchen counter to pay for the

charcoal. We stepped out of the rear kitchen door as quiet as we'd come, feeling like we had really accomplished something.

I gotta say I was proud of myself for having this idea that could save our final project, win us that cash and rescue my family.

We shoulda brought Becca, I thought. She needed to get out here in these woods and see how these people really lived. That girl was way too ignorant about things.

Standing outside the shack, Tuyet shoved our little bag of activated charcoal into her sack.

We stepped around the building's corner.

We came face to face with Dalton Spratt.

52

THE BEAST WAS AS SHOCKED as us. He carried two dead animals in one hand. I think they were rabbits.

"Crook Eye," Dalton said.

My words got caught in my throat for a second. "D-Dalton."

Tuyet froze when she saw the long rifle he held. For a minute, I thought she was about to run.

"What you doing here?" Dalton asked. "Who's this?" He glared at Tuyet and hiked his rifle up onto his shoulder.

"Dalton, this is my friend. From camp?"

He blinked at her.

"Nice to meet you, sir. Javari's said a lot of really nice things about you," Tuyet said.

He just stared.

"Well," I said. "I just ran through to . . ." I didn't know what to say.

"Apologize!" Tuyet finished. She glanced at me. "Right?"

I stared at his gun. "Yeah. Yes, Tuyet. I came to apologize

for, you know, what happened on the bus, Dalton. You getting blamed and everything."

His eyes narrowed.

"I really am sorry, D," I said.

Dalton lifted an eyebrow. "You came all the way up here to tell me that?"

Tuyet added, "When Javari told me what happened, I told him that his apology actually sounded like a *nonapology*!"

"Exactly!" Dalton agreed.

"Causing all that trouble for a really nice man like you," said Tuyet.

"Yeah, so that's that," I said. "Bye, Dalton!"

Me and her hurried off, but he shouted after us, "Hold it!"

We stopped.

Our backs to his, I braced myself for bullets. I began thinking that this would be how I ended up. Shot down on the side of a hill in Appalachia. Right in front of Barrelhouse.

He'd probably cook us up in one of those tasty stews he made. With those rabbits. Well, at least I wouldn't die alone.

"Turn around," Dalton told us.

We did. He got up in our faces. I could see his scar good now. Too good. Dalton nodded his bald head.

"Yeah?" I said.

"You almost had me fooled," Dalton told us. He stood on his long rifle now, like a cane. "All this time, I thought you was a bad dude, son. One a' them troublemakers. But you all right. I see why that little woodpecker likes you so."

He raised his fat knuckles in the air. We fist-bumped. I'd never been that relieved. I grinned ear to ear.

"Thanks, man," I said. "You're different than I actually thought you were too."

"I'm sorry for my part," he said.

"We better go," I said, turning to leave, but I did still have one thing that was bugging me. "Dalton, back on the bus, were you *really* just picking up my backpack after it fell?"

Tuyet looked at me like I was nuts.

"What?" Dalton asked.

Tuyet gripped my arm and led me away, telling him, "I'm not surprised he blamed you, Mr. Dalton. Javari is a congenital liar."

"He is?" Dalton said.

I am?

Tuyet nodded. "He makes stuff up all the time. He can't help it!"

"No kidding . . . ," Dalton said.

"Bye!" Tuyet yelled.

"Look after him, sweetheart!" Dalton called back, waving one of his dead rabbits at us.

After we were crazy far away, Tuyet grew more calm.

"Okay, Javari, that was like a really, *really* bad idea!" she said, squishing my arm.

"Yeah," I said. "You're right. But after a while, I didn't think he was gonna kill us."

"He could've done anything. We were stupid. And lucky."

"Maybe. But he kinda reminds me of some of the dudes around my way in the Shwick."

Tuyet had finally started to slow down her pace, the farther we got away from Barrelhouse.

I went on, "Dalton looks a certain way and acts a certain way, so people treat him a certain way. I don't really know if he tried to steal from me or not. But I do know that I *believed* he tried to boost my bag—'cause of how he looks, mostly."

"You're dense if you think that man didn't try to steal from you," she said.

"Tuyet, if I hadn't brought my cash belt with me, were you about to take from him? To get our charcoal?"

"What? That's different. You know it is."

"If you say so, girl."

53

WE GOT BACK IN TIME for our field trip, though for this one we didn't even leave campus. They gave us campers a tour of ARCC's new engineering center—the one the Nieces had pointed out way back on my first morning here.

The center wasn't all done yet, but Dr. Hunter said it would be by fall. Besides having some of the latest hardware in the area, the engineering school was supposed to teach something called spiritual and emotional mindfulness in technology.

I asked Dr. Hunter what she meant.

"*Well* . . ." She paused and went on. "We often create new technologies without asking first whether or not we *should*. Whether it is *right* or *wrong* to do so." Hunter looked me dead in my eyes. "We must do *right*, baby."

Later that same day in the Brain Cells, me and the other Fractal Dactyls used the laptop to finish up our final presentation. After a while, I snagged Nephew Wendell and asked if he could help.

"We just want you to sit here and listen to our presentation and let us know if it's okay," I told him.

"Oh, Javari," he said. "It will be my privilege to hear what y'all cooked up." Wendell plopped down in our lab cubicle and crossed his legs.

Becca pressed Return on the laptop. The presentation started in big letters: DON'T DRINK THE WATER. The Pot-lickin' Brothers Band played.

Wendell frowned. *"Okay,"* he said, hesitating.

Tuyet said, "Uncle Billy's is one of the companies that, by proxy—"

"Proxy!" Wendell shouted. "Big words!"

"Uh, yes, by proxy Uncle Billy's spoils local drinking water," Tuyet said.

Wendell's eyes narrowed.

"We know the company would never do such a thing without offering a solution," I said. "So we invented one: a portable water filter to help fix the damage."

Wendell swallowed and then looked sick. "But I told you we couldn't find no charcoal," he said. "How'd you—?"

"We found some ourselves," Tuyet said.

"We almost caught bullets," I said.

"Bullets?" Wendell asked.

"He's playing," Tuyet said, glaring at me, cold.

Wendell's face suddenly squashed. Like the blood had been sucked out of it. Probably what he ate for lunch, I figured. Those pepperoni rolls . . .

His head swung toward Becca. "Uh, Miss Whitt, what do you think? About all this . . ."

"Well," Becca said. "We all decided on it and it's a good idea."

"Uh-huh," Wendell said. "Well, well, well. Bless your hearts. *All* of 'em." He stood up like he was about to leave.

"Wait. You said you'd listen," I said.

"For feedback," Tuyet added.

"Yes, about that . . . ," he started. "I forgot I got a meeting with Larry right now. . . . Actually, it's a meeting for all the Nieces and Nephews. Sorry, kids!"

Wendell flew out the door.

I didn't get it. None of the other Nieces and Nephews left for any meeting.

But I felt good about our project. And the best thing was, I knew that with Becca Whitt in our group—the original Uncle Billy's real-life granddaughter—there was no way we couldn't win.

I thought about the money waiting for me inside that treasure chest. And how much it could save my family. I didn't want nobody worrying themselves sick no more. At least Poppa wouldn't panic about getting kicked out.

He only needed to worry about getting better.

I couldn't *wait* for our presentation tomorrow.

"Seventy-one percent of our planet Earth is covered in water," I announced from the stage. "But less than one percent of that water is drinkable."

I could see the bright lights from our presentation reflected on the auditorium's floor in front of me. Based on the Pot-lickin' Brothers music playing in our presentation, I knew the picture we found of the ocean would be showing behind us on the jumbo screen.

"Today," Tuyet continued, "about two million Americans don't have clean drinking water or even running water."

This was where a child's sad face appeared on the screen.

"Around the world," Tuyet said, "there are *many* causes for this: pollution, waste dumped in our waters, man-made global warming . . ."

Next, Becca was supposed to speak her part, but I didn't hear nothing. Tuyet and I were standing right beside her on the stage in the auditorium. When Becca didn't speak, we both leaned over to stare.

She was so nervous, she shook.

I looked out at the adults in the audience and the rest of the Futureneers. Some of the kids started to snicker and whisper. Even our presentation judges were saying stuff between themselves.

Their faces looked confused.

Mr. Ethan leaned over to whisper to Ms. Ferguson. Mr. Wang was the only judge that sat there quiet, but his forehead was all wrinkled.

The judges hadn't acted like that when the other groups presented.

I'd watched their faces carefully for signs.

When Group Eleven projected their interactive dance video on the jumbo screen, the judges hadn't blinked. When Church Dress's group showed off their crazy Everywhere Elevator, no whispers. Even when the Flyin' Achievers' Garbage Drone couldn't lift off the stage, no wrinkles in the judges' area.

But now . . .

The Pot-lickin' Brothers kept on.

I swallowed hard and glanced at Becca, still standing there quiet. Finally, she cleared her throat and read from her phone what we'd written for today's competition.

"Indeed, our environment suffers *all* over the world." Becca's voice quivered. "In fact, e-e-even right here in Horsewhip Holler, there's a severe shortage of clean water, created by *dangerous* mining from companies like Ball Creek Energy. *And* Uncle Billy's—"

"*Oh snap!*" some kid shouted.

Becca continued, "We *hope* that Uncle Billy's, who owns Ball Creek, wouldn't create a problem and *not* try to fix it." She glanced up from her phone at the audience. "Uncle Billy's digging mines *contaminates* the groundwater by pouring toxins into this here environment. It's *wrong.*"

She tried to keep on.

"S-s-so . . . so . . . Uncle Billy's . . . *uh.*" Becca's face was red as an apple. She was about to cry.

I took over: "And *that's* why, for our Futureneers final project, we designed a portable water filter."

"Our filter," Tuyet continued, "could be distributed at Uncle Billy's General Stores and aid those *without* clean drinking water. . . ."

"Our filter could help them clean the water that comes out of their own faucets," I said.

I glanced up at the jumbo screen behind us. Our presentation was way off. The video of grains of charcoal was already playing up there. We hadn't even *got* to that part yet!

I turned away as our photo of brown, rusty water appeared.

"*Uh, yes!*" Becca spoke up, her voice sounding stronger. "*Yes.* We know this filter doesn't fix what caused the dirty water. Only our governments, businesses and us can solve that problem."

Out in the audience, I heard somebody sniff.

"And now . . ." Tuyet waved at our portable water filter set up on the table.

The filter was made of two pitchers (one sat inside the other) with three separate layers of mesh and charcoal sandwiched in between. The bottom pitcher you could remove to empty out the strained water.

We built it using junk we found in that cupboard in Ethan's Automata class. The big cabinet had been packed with rods, wires, springs, tubes, containers . . .

Once we got the charcoal, it wasn't that hard to slap up the rest.

Tuyet announced, "Using genuine *activated* charcoal filtration, we'll show you how we make good drinkable water from a glass of Horsewhip's ol' tap water that we've all been warned *not* to drink."

Like we rehearsed, Becca scooped out a glass of pale-yellow water from a bucket we had onstage. One of the kids in the audience shouted, "Nasty, man!" A few others laughed. Tuyet held our tube-shaped filter as Becca poured in the dirty water.

Right as our presentation's music stopped before *we* had, I announced, "The charcoal filters out the contaminated particles in the H_2O."

It took a minute, but the water gurgled through clean. It *looked* more drinkable. Smiling, Becca held up the glass of water to the audience. Then, all three of us grinned.

Mr. Wang started to clap. Most of the audience started to clap. I elbowed Becca and whispered, "You're supposed to drink it!"

She frowned. "I'm not drinking it. *You* drink it."

I wasn't drinking Horsewhip water *again*.

But I think, out of all the final presentations we'd heard all morning, ours got the loudest applause. At least it felt that way to me! And we also got some hoots and whistles.

I was relieved.

I could tell by their expressions, Tuyet and Becca felt good too. Especially Becca. She looked like a different girl standing there on that stage after we finished.

Down front in the audience, Dr. Hunter spoke into her

microphone. "Thank you, Fractal Dactyls!" she said. "You obviously put so much *thought* into your final project. . . . *Er,* yes, next group, please! We've got *five* more groups before our judges make their decision."

I *knew* we nailed it.

The Fractal Dactyls!

54

"THE WINNER OF THE third annual Uncle Billy's Futureneers Finals is Group Two, the Virtual Gear Engineers!"

Huh?

"For their *hydro-fan*," Dr. Hunter went on, "based on principles of clean hydrogen energy!" Lester, Jerry, Veer and Blue Braces hollered.

What was Hunter talkin' about?

"Come up and get your prizes, boys!" she called. Screaming, they ran and wheeled onto the stage.

I think Hunter made a mistake, announced the wrong winners.

The boys broke open the Lost ARCC of STEM treasure chest and dove their hands inside, snatching. They whipped around the game consoles, gift cards and tech equipment.

In the audience, my mouth hung open, catching flies.

I glanced at either side of me. Tuyet shrugged. Becca inhaled deep.

"Clean water's not popular," Becca said. "Not round here."

I spun, trying to get somebody else's attention, but they were all too busy clapping and yelling for the Virtual Gear Engineers.

Nephew Wendell seemed to be the noisiest. He stuck his fingers in his mouth and whistled. He would not check my way for nothing.

After a minute, I understood Wendell was actually avoiding me.

On the stage, the Virtual Gear Engineers hugged around Dr. Hunter, who grinned wide. They all posed for pictures.

I could not believe what I was seeing.

The rent money.

My family.

Poppa.

"I told you," Becca said. "Hunter doesn't like drama."

The spongy cushions of my auditorium chair seemed to reach around me, swallowing me up.

"Unbeatable!" Veer called out from the stage.

"Oorah!" Lester and Jerry yelled together.

55

MAN, WAS I A BiG DOOFUS!

Numb, I wobbled out of the auditorium, surrounded by the rest of the kids. They were all electric, gossiping about the Virtual Gears' hydro-win. Plus, everybody had already been extra excited to leave camp tomorrow.

I'd let Poppa down just when he needed me the most.

I wondered how much longer we'd stay in our home. I sure would miss my room across the hall. I hadn't realized how much I would until all of this happened.

It really seemed real now.

Me and Tuyet stood in the lobby as the others flowed around us. Becca kept on walking, straight out the swinging glass doors to the yard. I knew she felt bad.

She cared so much about impressing her family.

I just wanted to save mine.

"We got screwed," Tuyet said.

"Yeah, we did. We shoulda won," I said.

"We had a proven need," Tuyet said. "We'd done our background research. Tracked down our own elements—

319

almost got shot! Even used extra-large pix in our Night-jar presentation so their decrepit old eyes wouldn't have to squint!"

Dr. Hunter brushed past. Tuyet straight-up scowled at her.

Mr. Wang paused in front of us. "I enjoyed your presentation!" he said.

"Nightjar," I mumbled. "We used Nightjar."

"I *saw*," Wang answered. "Very nice! You are a very good teacher, Mr. Javari Harris. You taught all of us something today." He glanced at Tuyet. "And you young ladies too!" Mr. Wang grinned and leaned into us. "I voted for you. But *Chairman Mao* disagreed." He glanced at Dr. Hunter and left with a frown.

"*Evil*," Tuyet said, glaring again at Hunter. "I'll get even. My family carries an exceptionally long *grudge* gene."

"Wasted energy, plotting to get even with *her*," I told Tuyet.

"Spoken like a dumb boy," she said.

Ethan Cunningham didn't say a word but handed me something and left. It was a slip of paper that read: *THE BOOK OF INGENIOUS DEVICES* BY BANŪ MŪSĀ IBN SHĀKIR.

Some dude.

"Jay?" Tuyet asked.

"Yeah?"

"The other day at Barrelhouse? I *did* bring money to pay for our charcoal," she said.

"Well, why didn't you say?" I asked.

She shrugged. "My daddy says, never use your own cash when you can use somebody else's."

I shook my head.

"It's an investor's secret. Ba is a dope businessman." Tuyet got serious. "Actually, it was great being your partner, really. I'd do it all again. We were *right*."

I pushed her. Giggling, Tuyet hugged me, then went to look for Becca.

Ahead of me in the lobby, Dr. Hunter stood there like she was posing, chatting with the other judges. Wendell and a few of the other Nephews and Nieces hung around.

I stepped up. "Um, Dr. Hunter?" I said.

She turned to me and grinned. "Yes? Oh, our young New York City man! *Jayden!*"

"Javari," Wendell corrected her. "Javari Harris."

"*Javari* Harris!" Hunter said to me. "I enjoyed your presentation, Javari. That took a *mess* of . . . resolve."

I nodded. "*Messy*, all right."

Dr. Hunter stared at me a minute, like she was waiting on me to say something. Finally, she said, "We hope you learned something *valuable* this summer at Futureneers, baby."

"I did."

"*Good*," Hunter said. "Did we blast those brain cells?"

"Yup."

"I'm sure." She placed her hand on my shoulder. "And, baby, some lessons we learn in books. But most of life we learn through *living*. If we're lucky, God willing, we learn and we *grow*."

I stared at her.

"No drama," Hunter said. "Understand?"

I nodded. "Some folks got more growing to do than others."

For a minute, Hunter looked like she'd been stung by a cottonwood borer. Then, "Safe travels, dear." She swung away. "Wendell?"

The two strolled off together, not saying nothing else.

56

CAMP WAS ENDING TOMORROW.

I'd be heading back home to my city.

But this evening, the last of our *Flexus* game, the entrance to the alien city of Harmonee was just ahead. And we all knew Maestro Island sat just beyond Harmonee.

To meet the Maestro was our final target.

For the last time, I walked our avatar along the top of a mountain ridge. Way in the distance, I could see the Black Lizard avatar. They were far in the lead.

I sighed.

The 3-D view from up here was spectacular. It also made me think.

"He's down in Casselac Gully," I heard Tuyet say. I knew she was talking about Jerry. "Use our power grenades to take them out, I think?"

"Sure," Becca agreed.

I nodded and slid down the side of the mountain, kicking up dirt as I went. It was a smooth ride. Over the past couple weeks, we'd all learned to control our avatars way better.

If I found Jerry, this would be a real battle.

I checked our avatar's life bars. They were low. I hoped we would have enough energy left. Our guy reached the bottom of the mountain and I scanned around Casselac Gully.

Nobody.

At least that's how it looked. I started marching, all aware of everything around me. I'd already lost the prize money and probably got my whole family evicted onto the streets.

I couldn't lose again.

I thought, there was a lot I had to learn about things.

Back home in BK, I hadn't really considered too much about how all those new people with money moving in would affect me. The fact that they had more money to spend meant the landlords could charge us all more for rent.

And if you couldn't afford to pay more, you were out.

Right now, life seemed to be about paying for things. If me and my group had picked a different final project, we might have won. But instead, we made Hunter mad—or embarrassed—by picking on Uncle Billy's.

I'd pay the same price again. I just hoped Poppa wouldn't have to pay.

Thoom!

All of a sudden, everything in the game flashed red. I hadn't been paying attention. Now, somebody was beating up our avatar, punching our guy around and around so fast I couldn't get my footing in the game.

I knew who it was.

"Virtual Gears!" Becca yelled.

"Get him, Jay!" Tuyet yelled.

I tried to fight back, but Group Two's Beetle Face was knocking me all over the place. Finally, I held down button B. That released our last power grenade. He fell backward, shook it off and raced back at me.

I leapt high up into the air, avoiding him. I landed yards away. Jerry shot a lightning bolt at me. I just dodged it. I knew that if that lightning had tagged me, our game woulda wrapped permanently.

"Careful, Jay!" Becca said.

"He knows what he's doing," I think Tuyet said about me. Did I?

Before I knew it, the Virtual Gears' red beetle was on me again, this time grabbing me from the back. We wrestled for a minute before my avatar's whole body shook. Jerry had shocked me with a stunner stick.

My game's viewfinder suddenly looked cracked.

I fell to the ground.

He stood over me, staring down, with the alien mountains behind him. My life power was down to our last bar.

This was it.

Across the room on the other side of the lab, I heard the Virtual Gears shouting: "End him! End him, Jer!"

The room was all excited.

Back in Casselac Gully, my avatar still knelt on the

ground. I motioned for him to stand, but he couldn't. Like he was still recuperating from that last shock.

My opponent whipped out a splitter gun.

"Jay . . . ," Tuyet warned.

I went into our survival kit. All I saw there were: SNOW BOOTS, WATER BOTTLE, MULTITOOL, SNAKE-BITE KIT, MAP and SILVERBACK SAC SPIDER PELLET.

As Jerry charged his splitter gun, I picked one of the items from our kit. It opened in my hand. I slung it at him as fast as my finger could press F on my game pad.

Just as Jerry was about to fire, the silverback sac spider pellet that I'd shot sprung out and folded around him like a spiderweb bubble! His gun went off inside the bubble and knocked his avatar off its feet.

The folks in our lab grew quiet.

Recovered, our avatar stood up. I could see Group Two's avatar lying knocked out in the dirt, still trapped in our web-bubble.

OPPONENT DEFEATED!

flashed in the sky. Kids in the room cheered. I felt Becca and Tuyet hug me.

The Virtual Gear Engineers were done.

I walked over to where their avatar laid, trapped inside our web.

Another VR message flashed above:

TO THE VICTOR GO THE SPOILS! PICK ONE OF YOUR FOE'S SURVIVAL KIT ITEMS TO TAKE AS TRIBUTE!

Next, the Virtual Gears' survival kit contents flashed above their guy for me to choose.

"Ladies?" I said. "Only one choice, right?" I floated the pointer over their survival kit and clicked.

"The jet pack!" Tuyet screamed. "Yes! We got a jet pack!"

Across the lab from where I sat, I heard a boy groan.

"You had to go after them!" Veer yelled.

"Now they got our jet!" Afro-Puff yelled.

And just then, everything started to rock. At least the landscape inside the *Flexus* game went all shaky. A loud boom in the alien world, like a bomb, went off.

It was an earthquake, I realized. A *huge* one.

"What's going on?" Tuyet asked.

"It's the mountain!" Becca shouted.

Inside the game, I glanced up at the mountain I'd slid down. The top peak was all red and glowing and spurting out hot pieces of rock. Before long, there was another boom and the whole mountaintop blew.

A wave of hot lava rushed down into the valley where we stood.

I gulped.

By this time, the silverback web-bubble had disappeared from around Jerry's guy. He now stood staring up at the lava rushing at us. His life power sat at one bar.

I popped open our survival kit and clicked on the jet pack I'd just snagged from him. The jets engaged. I watched the other avatar's body grow smaller and smaller as I whooshed up into the air above the gully.

Their tiny avatar below turned to race away from the hot lava flow, but it was way late. Jerry and them's guy was too slow.

Roasted.

I felt sorry for them.

But there was also something pretty about it all.

Now high in the sky above everything, I turned toward the city of Harmonee in the distance and shot across the clouds. Down below, I could spot the Black Lizard and Purple Tiger avatars fighting it out in a field.

We jetted over, leaving them behind.

Based on the fuel level in the jet pack, I figured it might get us past the woods below and all the way to the city's gates. Our stop after that would be Maestro Island.

The last stop.

"Tuyet!" I called out as I flew over the forest. "You were right. This is the best view."

Passing the VR headset between them, the girls took turns taking in the sights as our guy flew on.

We flew right over Harmonee and landed at the edge of a big ocean. Not far away was a small island. Floating above were the words:

WELCOME TO MAESTRO ISLAND

57

IT TOOK US A WHILE to figure how to cross the ocean.

Turned out, you just needed to climb into a little boat hidden on the beach. Tuyet found it. Becca moved our avatar into the boat, and it glided right across to Maestro Island.

Since our group was the only one to make it this far, the other Futureneers in the lab room had gathered around our cubicle. Even the Virtual Gears dudes had wandered over, straining to see.

I could tell they were still salty for being burned alive in lava and didn't really want to be here, but I guessed their curiosity about the Maestro was too much. If they hadn't waited around just to attack us, they coulda made it here already.

Once on the island, it wasn't too hard to find him—the Maestro—either.

Becca marched our avatar along the beach until we came to the mouth of a big cave that faced away from Harmonee.

She told us the cave's entrance was shaped like the jaws of a large dinosaur. Through the jaws: a tall cavern with a sandy floor and stalactites hanging from the ceiling. At the far end was a stage made from stone with a throne carved into it.

"It's the Maestro," Becca said. "He's sitting on the throne."

"Ooo!" some kid yelled.

"You made it!" somebody else said.

The whole room's attention was on Becca, sitting at our station, wearing the headset. The Group Two boys were quiet. Jerry had rolled up his wheelchair to Becca's elbow. Twitchy, he peeked up at me, then at our *Flexus* monitor.

Lester gazed in a trance, stroking a few hairs on his chin. "I wish I was still in the game, Brooklyn," Lester said to me. "Seeing."

I knew what he meant.

"Seeing what she sees," Lester repeated.

The game was amazing. But it wasn't real.

The real part, I realized, was what we were all going through now. That feeling we got from being real people experiencing something special.

"We all feel the same, Afro-Puff," I told Lester.

Lester jerked his neck. "Afro-Puff? *Hmph* . . ." He laughed. "Afro-Puff. . . ." He seemed to like it.

I had hated the Virtual Gears' guts.

They really tormented us. And they constantly fought us in and outside the game, like Tuyet said. It was an intense experience. But I guess I learned from it. And, I guessed, after I left camp tomorrow, I'd even miss it.

"What's going on in there?" Tuyet, restless, asked Becca. "The Maestro?"

"Yeah," I added. "What's he look like? Becca?"

"Shh!" Becca shushed. "He's still talking."

"What's he say?" Tuyet asked.

"Shh!"

Becca sat for a minute, listening to whatever it was dude told her. I leaned in closer toward the headset, trying to overhear.

She spoke up: "So, everybody, the Maestro announced he will ask one question. One question only. But it's the oldest question, the very first question anybody ever asked. And the *last* question we'll ever ask ourselves. The most crucial question in the world you can ask yourself."

I wondered what could be the most crucial question in the world.

I stared at Tuyet, who stared back at me. Both our eyes wide.

"And," Becca went on, "if we answer truthfully, we'll become our own maestro or *maestra* or master."

The whole room went still, listening. Becca concentrated on the Maestro's next words.

"'Answer me this question,'" she repeated after him. "'Answer it true. . . .'"

You coulda heard a mouse wheeze, it got so quiet.

This summer was *that* summer, like Daddy said.

58

I LAID WIDE-AWAKE IN BED.

I'd been trying to fall asleep for like an hour but couldn't make it.

Everything was so quiet.

Even Veer had turned over on his stomach, no snoring. I worried that I'd got used to hearing his snores and wouldn't be able to sleep when I got back to Bushwick. I glanced down at his treasure chest prizes stacked on the floor in the dark.

I sighed.

I sat up.

"No 'cricket'?" a sleepy voice asked.

"Veer?" I said. "You awake?"

"No, I am sleeptalking," he answered. "Of course I'm awake."

"Why aren't you 'sleep?"

"I been having trouble getting to bed ever since you stopped going out on your late-night excursions."

He knew?

333

I heard him say, "You thought you were keeping this secret from me?" He giggled. It sounded weird. I heard him turn over in his bunk. "For the past couple of nights, you talked about 'crickets' in your sleep. Mumble over and over and over."

I had?

"Drives me totally insane, man," he said.

"I'm sorry."

"Is that what you're afraid of?"

"What?"

"Crickets."

I grinned. "I don't think so. Who's afraid of crickets? They're just bugs."

"*Nice* bugs," Veer added. "I like their sound."

We didn't say anything for a while.

"Go on one of your outings," I heard him say. "I won't tell. It's the last night. It will help both of us sleep better."

"Thanks," I said. I hopped down from my bunk. "I might."

"I can't stand roommates," he said. "That's all."

Before I had jumped down to the second tree branch outside, I could hear Veer's loud snores booming from our window.

Late at night, the main yard hummed with crickets but oozed calm. I walked around the campus, thinking and stopping and thinking some more. What we'd all learned from the Maestro game was still fresh in my dome.

It really affected Becca.

Her and her family confused me. That girl says she's a good Christian, but how can you be that *and* a racist too?

She only started to treat me better after getting to know me.

I remembered back to all the times that Becca had hinted that Uncle Billy's might not like our water purifier idea. Bad publicity, she'd said.

She knew it'd make waves. She knew her people. Knew they wouldn't want to reward us for pointing out a problem to Uncle Billy's that Uncle Billy's had helped create.

I shoulda guessed.

Now, after everything, it seemed easy to see. In the future, I wouldn't get fooled like that again. In the future, I'd know.

This made me wish for the younger me, from fourteen days ago, that one who hadn't known as much. Being ignorant is bad, but at least you don't know any better.

I'd actually thought because Becca was on our team, we'd be sure to win. Like they'd have to give her group the award because her family owned the company. I did have a lot to learn about how things work in life.

Questions, I had. Lots of questions.

But what about that most important one? The Maestro's most crucial question in the world? How could there be only one?

Confusing.

That was why I preferred mathematics and science.

In algebra, I knew some equations could have infinite solutions. With these equations there ain't one answer.

$2x = x + x$

If you graphed both of these numbers on paper, with a good solid pencil, they'd both look the same.

Everything not on that piece of paper was too messy.

Ha-kaa!

I spun around.

This dude.

There Cricket was, lurking in the tree shadows, dressed up in his rubber Beast mask, the one he had the first time I met him. I felt a giant lump in my stomach.

Part of me felt mixed up, messy. Another part of me felt magic.

That all seemed like Crick, I realized.

Everything at once.

59

I WAITED FOR HIM to plop down on the edge of his fountain before I did. The painted yellow eyeballs of the crazy Beast mask stared at me, then he pulled it back and let it sit on his head like a durag. Instead of looking at me, Cricket's greenish brown eyes stared into the fountain water.

It was smooth as glass.

They'd turned off the fountain hours ago. It was still lit up in lights, though. The light was too strong.

I dipped my hand into the water.

Ripples.

Rings.

"You won your contest?" Cricket asked.

I sighed, heavy. "Nah."

"But I thought you had his granddaughter on your team?"

"Yeah, I think that messed us up."

He said, "I ain't sorry I tricked her."

"Poppa George is sick too. Real sick."

"Shoot, Bird. He'll get better. You'll see."

"You forgot your duffel," I told Cricket. He wasn't carrying it.

He shrugged. "I'm done with that, man, snatching stuff. I got other ways."

"That's cool. You're still wearing your Beast mask, though."

"Hey!" he said. "My buddy Hank gave me an idea. I may start foraging in the hills for wild ginseng."

That was that plant Tuyet and me found in the forest near Barrelhouse.

Cricket said, "Ginseng, the wild Appalachian kind, sells for a thousand bucks a pound!"

Figures.

I had a whole bush right at my hands and didn't even know. That was my kinda luck, I guessed.

"Yo, we lost the contest, but we found Maestro Island," I said.

Cricket's face was blank.

I went on, "I told you. Our VR game? We reached the island, but then . . . it got weird . . ."

He nodded. Finally, I looked him dead in the eyes.

"What?" he said.

"My neck," I said.

"What?"

"That wasn't no fish lips on my neck," I said. I rubbed the spot. "You put yours there. The swimming hole?"

"Oh, God!" he shouted.

"How long you been like that?" I asked.

"You callin' me queer now?" he asked.

"Yup!" I answered. "You as gay as a doorbell."

"What!"

I laughed. "I got a gay uncle in Jersey. He always says that."

"You call me gay, you the one with a gay uncle. Nobody in my family's like that. That night that happened, you felt a fish on your neck."

"*Yo* . . . ," I said.

"That was it." He laughed, tugging at his mask. "That ain't funny."

"Why you laughing, then?" I asked.

He stared back into the fountain. The water was still again. I imagined Cricket dunking his hand into it, Scooping it around. Splashing waves, scattering shapes.

Water shifted like that.

Liquid.

It could become anything.

Cricket said, "When I was ten, I remember thinking that other boys looked 'neat.' Different from girls. Back then, I wasn't attracted to other boys or nothing like that. I was too young. *But* I thought there was something neat about some of them."

"Look, man, I hear you, but I don't really feel that way about other dudes."

He squinted at me. "You don't *think* you do . . ."

I said, "I mean, my uncle who's gay? I'm not flashy like Uncle Melvin at *all*."

He kept on staring into the fountain and spat into it. Where his spit hit on the water sent out trickles of rings and rings and rings. Made me think of something.

"That game we played," I told him. "When we reached Maestro Island, there was this question dude asked."

"What question?"

I smirked. "He called it the most crucial one in the world."

"Well. What is it, then?"

I paused.

"Hey!" somebody shouted.

It came from behind, the darkness. I glanced over there. Elrod.

Zipping toward us like a wild dog in the moonlight.

"Hey! I see you, sucka!" Elrod screamed. He blew a whistle and screamed into his walkie-talkie: "I got the creeper! I got 'im!"

Cricket flipped down his mask, sprung up and took off into the night.

"Stop!" Elrod yelled. "You stop, right there!"

Sprinting in clunky shoes for once, Cricket stumbled in the dark. He hit the ground hard. Elrod was on top of him before Cricket could bounce back up.

I ran over to where they fought. Elrod sat on top of Cricket, choking him by the neck with his nightstick.

"Don't resist, boy!" Elrod shouted. "Quit resisting!"

"Yo! Elrod!" I shouted. "Stop! Stop it!"

I tried ripping Elrod's baton away, but he wouldn't let go. His eyes went cold. He was choking Cricket so hard, I thought he was gonna kill him.

I clocked Elrod on the side of his head with my fist. He yelled and elbowed me in my ribs. I fell backward.

In the dark, I could hear Cricket gurgle underneath his mask.

He couldn't breathe.

"Quit resisting!" Elrod screamed at him.

I felt for the nearest thing next to me that I could in the dark. And knocked Elrod upside his skull with it. He fell back onto the grass, clutching his head and rolling over a couple times.

Back to the ground, I dropped the smooth rock I'd snatched.

Just as Rich and that new security guard came running up from behind me, I knelt over Cricket. Snatched off his Beast mask. His freckled face was hard to make in the moonlight.

His eyes were shut. I didn't think he was breathing.

He looked *gone*.

I started to bawl.

.60

IT WAS ABOUT noon, Saturday, when they started.

People had been trickling in all morning. Now, there was a pretty good-sized crowd gathered outside the large window where I looked out.

White people. And Black and brown ones.

All kinds.

Felt like I'd seen all this before.

I watched some dude with a yellow megaphone start shouting into it. The early crowd that had come were respectful at first, like that vigil back in Bushwick. But now, they were all starting to get loud.

Whoever the dude with the megaphone was, he was sure getting them all amped up. When he turned his face, I saw it was Cricket's uncle Norm.

Pretty soon two cop cars rolled up on the group. The sheriff tried to get everybody settled down. The crowd began shouting at the cops.

In fact, I could hear Dalton Spratt screaming in the face

of one of the ARCC security guards. They were nose to nose, yelling, like he'd done with me.

Dalton had turned deep purple too.

The Beast.

"Who you think *you* are, boy?" I could hear him scream at that guard. Then, Dalton glanced at the guard's name tag. "*Larry?*" Dalton yelled at him. "God's sake! Oh, I heard 'bout you, you dumb *tater*! I heard yer biscuit ain't *done* in the middle, boy!"

If I hadn't felt so down, I woulda laughed.

Dr. Spoon and Shug were two of the first here. They brought a whole chocolate hillbilly posse with them. Some faces I recognized from their Affrilachian society. Mosta the others I didn't.

That dude Shelton with the truck drove a lot of people here. And so did that woman Paula from the book club. She even brought snacks for everybody in her van.

Then, Uncle Billy's Nieces and Nephews rolled up in their white cars, just like the one Wendell drove. A bunch of them tried to calm down both the angry crowd and the cops. I was sure Uncle Billy's didn't want anything more bad to happen.

How Cricket ended up was bad enough.

Elrod had told him to stop, the same as how we heard those BK cops told William Dexter that night. But I'd seen Elrod go after Cricket myself. How he attacked him, wanting him dead.

Cricket's life hadn't meant *nothing* to Elrod.

Now, a TV news crew from Charlotte showed up outside, recording everything. The Uncle Billy's folks started talking to the TV reporters. I knew the Nieces and Nephews would be trying to put a shiny impression on everything.

One news guy with a camera broke off from the rest and ran toward our window. He waved at me, like he wanted me to come out and speak to the crowd.

"I never seen hill people so *waspish*," Becca said.

She stood beside me, both of us staring out the window onto all the excitement on the lawn.

"It ain't all 'cause of Cricket," I told her. "They got no love for Uncle Billy's."

Becca glanced away. "I guess they don't," she said. "I'm sorry for treating you like trash when we first met. And for what I said about Lester."

"Okay," I said.

"You're nice. I shoulda known that, but to be honest, I don't think I wanted to."

Becca was dead serious.

"At first," she added.

I stared down the hall behind us. Becca's parents were arguing, super furious. They were screaming on Dr. Hunter.

"Of all the witless, imprudent muddles I've seen in my years," yelled Becca's mom, "*this* catastrophe takes the cake!"

"This is *very* bad pub, Geraldine," Becca's dad told Dr. Hunter. "All these backwoods hillbillies out there."

"And all those cameras!" Becca's mom put in. "From Charlotte!"

Becca's dad: "If we take a bath on this, Geraldine, believe you me, *you* will be the one comin' out dirty!"

He stuck his finger at Dr. Hunter's nose.

After that, Dr. Hunter'd had enough of them, I guessed, because she straight-up rolled around. Me and her met eyes for a second. Then, Hunter sighed and marched into an office.

She slammed the door behind her.

Drama.

Becca's parents, and a few other Uncle Billy's people in suits, tromped inside the room after her.

I picked up my Coke off the coffee table and took a sip.

Becca and me started to walk down the hospital hall. Before passing under them, I glanced up at the big words engraved across the gold archway above: WELCOME TO THE WILLIAM WHITT WING—HORSEWHIP HOLLOW MEMORIAL.

At the end of the hall, I could see my own daddy yapping on his phone. When me and Becca passed by the room with her parents and Dr. Hunter, we could still hear them shouting on the other side of the door.

I sipped more Coke.

"You gonna get fat again," Becca told me. "All that pop."

I was surprised to hear her suggest that I *wasn't* still overweight. Even though I'd lost about eight pounds since I'd been here, I still felt heavy on the inside.

Far ahead, I watched as my sister Shireen popped her

head out of the lounge. She stood beside Daddy, messing with her phone too, trying to get a clear signal, I bet.

Both her and Daddy frowned at their screens. Another door slammed back where Becca's parents argued.

"Your folks are *pissed*," I told Becca.

She nodded. "Like always." We continued down the hallway until she spoke some more. "When I'm older, I won't be *nothing* like them."

I nodded. "That's good." I tossed my half-full Coke into a bin.

"Our group lost 'cause of me," Becca said. "If I'd won a prize for cleaning Horsewhip's dirty ol' water, it would look bad for my family's business."

Was that the truth?

"I been thinking," I said. "Was our project as great as we thought it was? I mean, the Virtual Gears built a *hydrogen-powered* fan. Anybody can buy a water filter online. Or make one with some charcoal. I thought Hunter would *have* to give us that money because of you. I don't think we really deserved it."

"*Huh*," Becca said. "Well, you didn't win your treasure. And I embarrassed my folks. But they'll never take Maestro Island from us."

She grinned.

It felt like I was seeing Becca smile honestly for the very first time.

After that, she twirled around and strolled back toward her parents and all their drama.

At the end of the hall, Daddy was there waiting for me outside the hospital room. My sister still fooled with her phone.

When they'd heard what had happened at ARCC, they'd got Uncle Mel to rent them a car and drove all night to get here.

I sure was glad.

He told me they'd left Poppa George recuperating at home. Several of Ma's health aide friends were looking after him around the clock.

It would be good to see him.

Even though I'd let him down.

Daddy and I slapped hands before he said to me, "Let's rap, Jack." We stepped into the waiting room and sat side by side in hard wooden chairs. My ribs ached where Elrod had elbowed me.

I'd overheard Dr. Hunter say he'd been sent home from work until they discovered how it all went down.

How different would that have gone if Elrod had a gun?

In the hospital lounge, I reached into one of my pockets. I'd brought my tiny piece of coal with me. Hard and shiny. I fiddled with it between my fingers. I found it that day me and Cricket rode to Hawk's Nest Tunnel.

Black diamonds.

". . . According to our reporters on the scene of the small mountain township, demonstrations are growing by the hour. And threatening to grow violent . . ."

347

The news was on TV.

Daddy and me watched news reports from the protest just outside where we sat. One of the protesters on television waved a JUSTICE FOR ALCOTT WASHINGTON! sign. Another's said: DON'T DRINK THE WATER! Shug's fired-up face flashed on the screen. Her sign read: NOT AGAIN! TAKE BACK OUR HOLLER!

Daddy chuckled. "These country folks is *upset!*"

"Yeah. *Really,*" I said. I tucked my little coal into my pocket. "Daddy?"

"Yeah?"

"They had a contest at camp," I said. "I tried to win it for the money."

"How much?"

I shook my head. "Don't matter. I didn't get it. I wanted it for our rent back home, you know."

"Javari . . ."

"To help out," I said. "But I goofed. Sorry."

My father reached his arm around me and brought me closer. "What you sorry about, son? I should be apologizing to you, putting you through all this." Daddy leaned in toward me. "We ain't gotta move. No more eviction."

"Huh?"

"No eviction," Daddy said again. "I got me a promotion at the hardware store. I went in there and asked old man Rudy for a raise and told him all the reasons why I deserved one and he surprised me—he agreed!" Daddy laughed loud.

"You lyin'," I said.

348

"Nah," he answered. "Rudy just confirmed, just now. I am the new evening manager. Honest. I'm getting a nice raise and cash bonus that'll let us pay off what we owe the landlord."

It took me a while, but I smiled at all this. A whole load was lifted.

Daddy told me, "You inspired me to ask, Javari, inspired me to try for something better. To *be* better."

I straight-up did not know what to say.

"And I'm *thanking* you," he said. "Me and your grand-dad started chilling again. I go down to his room and we sit and listen to jazz, like you said. Smooth. Enjoy the music together."

"That's great, Daddy."

"We don't talk much, which is probably a good thing." Daddy snickered. "And if my old man gets too negative, I excuse myself. But, I discovered, if you sit there while his music plays, he won't speak. I might prefer him that way."

"Will Poppa George ever change?" I asked.

"It's hard to change old folks' ways, Jay. But you ain't gotta make their ways your own. Accept Poppa for who he is. You can love folks despite their faults."

"He *fights*," I said.

"My old man is a tough model."

"I'm glad we don't have to move," I admitted.

"Me too," Daddy said. "Me too. We'll see what the future brings. Rents steady climb."

My heart sank just a little. I think he could tell. Daddy palmed my head.

"Javari," he said. "We'll always be black diamonds."

I believed him. "Rare and powerful," I said. I showed him my piece of anthracite. "You know they call these black diamonds around here?"

"Really?" Daddy said. He grabbed it, spinning it around. "Makes sense. We tough too."

61

WE SLID BACK ACROSS the hall into Cricket's hospital room.

He was still lying there in bed with his skimpy hospital gown on and that funny brace around his neck. Cricket's mother, Miss Maddie, was propped in a chair beside him.

My moms sat on the opposite side. They were all chatting about something just before we came back into the room.

"Oh, is that so?" I heard Ma say to Miss Maddie. "What borough?"

"Bird!" Cricket spoke up. His voice was still cracked and sounded awful. "Where's my pop?"

"Oh, the machine was out," I lied.

"That stuff's no good," Daddy said. "Rots your teeth."

Miss Maddie chuckled. "If it wasn't for Co'-Cola, I wouldn't *drink*!"

"How you, Jay?" my mother asked.

I nodded my head. Nobody said nothing for a while.

"Jay!" Ma said. "You know Cricket's daddy stays in New York?"

"What?" I said.

I glanced at Cricket, who looked out the window, embarrassed. He'd told me his father was dead. Made me feel sorry for him.

"Yep," said Miss Maddie. "His pa's lived there since after Cricket was born. Don't know where, exact."

"Cricket should come visit," Ma said.

"Speakin' of home . . . Deniece, we need to get on the road," said Daddy.

"I'm hungry," said Shireen.

"Anybody else hungry?" Daddy asked.

"I would not say no to a good ol' coffee," Miss Maddie said.

"We'll bring you back a cup from the cafeteria," Ma told her.

Miss Maddie hopped up. "I'll come git it. Girl, I need to stretch these hams. Want anything, angel?"

Cricket tried to shake his head. Miss Maddie bent down to kiss it. Daddy opened the door. More shouting from Becca's parents drifted in.

"Ooo-whee!" Miss Maddie howled. "Them Whitts is madder than a pair a' wet hens. That won't be nothing compared to when we sue." She cackled.

My father led Ma and Shireen by the hand. I heard him say: "Niecey, Rudy called back. We finally got some good news, baby . . ."

The door shut.

Me and Cricket were alone. I plopped down in the chair where his mother had sat.

He grinned. "Your mama thanked me, Bird. Said she's grateful I changed her boy's 'unhealthy attitude.'"

I rolled my eyes.

He went on, "Your ma said I'm a good role model."

"She don't know you, Crick," I said.

Cricket laughed and then frowned like it hurt. His voice was scratchy and low. "Yeah," he admitted. "Your folks say you don't smile much. That's funny, 'cause when I think of you, you always smiling."

I grinned. "Me and my family gotta leave soon."

"Yeah."

From far away, we could hear some shouts and chants from outside. The violence on Cricket—who everybody around Horsewhip Holler suddenly seemed to love—had brought together a lot of different types of people.

They blamed Uncle Billy's for what happened, since it went down on their campus. I wondered if this might be the beginning of Horsewhip standing up to that company. Demanding that Uncle Billy's treat them right. If they didn't stand up for themselves, way out here in the hills, I didn't see who else really would.

"Yo," I said. "You were never gonna tell me about your father? Him living in New York?"

"Naw," Cricket said. His face grew dark. "My daddy didn't never want nothing to do with me. So, I just pretended he *was* dead."

"That's nothing to feel awkward about. I guess that's why you hung out with me. To find out more about where your daddy lived?"

"Maybe a little at first, Bird. But that changed . . ."

My insides felt funny.

He wheezed. "All these years"—Cricket's voice cracked—"I thought that if my grandpa hadn't died at Hawk's Nest, that maybe my own pa woulda stuck around. You know? I felt like that just broke my family. Washed out that glue that held us . . ."

We remembered.

Paintballs.

Nephews and Nieces.

Ridin' Miss Daisy.

Floods.

Hawk's Nest.

Ridin' the rails.

Synchronous fireflies.

Our fountain.

Barrelhouse.

"Man, I thought ol' Dalton was gonna knock the bottom out of you!" Cricket hollered. "He thought you was a real spud."

"Now he thinks I'm a congenital liar too, thanks to Tuyet."

"Con-gen-i-tal," Cricket repeated. "A feller who cain't help lying. 'Specially to hisself. That's you, all right."

I reached up and hid my eye.

"Quit it!" Cricket said. "I think it looks neat, your funky eye. Looks like you got it in a scrap. Like you're a tough guy. I reckon you *are* pretty hard. You really saved my skin."

We were quiet.

"We had fun," Cricket said.

"Yeah, we did," I agreed. "West Virginia. Wild, wonderful . . . *Wilderful!*"

Cricket laughed and coughed. "Bird," he started, all serious, "I don't believe you know what kinda bike you ride yet."

I knew what he meant. "Maybe not," I said.

"I knew back when I was ten."

"You're my friend, I know," I told him.

He grinned, looking like ol' Crick again. Like he could wrestle bears.

I stretched over and gave him the biggest bear hug. Before I quit, I also gave him a peck on his freckled-up cheek.

Cricket turned red.

He'd mapped out the most wild, wonderful summer. I held on to him for one last *wilderful* second. . . .

$1 + 1 = \infty$

Turns out, the answers to both me and Cricket's equation *and* the Maestro's most crucial question equaled the same dang thing.

Infinity.

AUTHOR'S NOTE

Ha-kaa! Ha-kaa!

Thank you, *everyone,* for answering the call and venturing into the wilderness within this book. Though fiction, *Holler of the Fireflies* captures glimmers of my own early life experiences.

The pluck of my actual childhood friend Tuyet also helps illuminate this story. The real Tuyet was a classmate during my elementary school years and a confidante. So many hours we spent burning up minutes on our parents' telephones!

Becca's "sewage swim" in chapter 45 was inspired by a real event during this same time of my life. While away at summer camp, some friends and I disobeyed our camp counselors' orders by going on a secret swim across a small lake in the woods. We felt like we had gotten away with something until the next afternoon, when we discovered our counselors had forbidden us from swimming in that lake because it was supposedly polluted with sewer water.

To this day, I'm not sure if they were pulling our leg or not.

The character of Cricket is partly inspired by another childhood friend I had for just one summer. When I was very, very young, back in Missouri, a boy named Scooter spent a summer with his grandparents, who lived in my neighborhood. Scooter and I became fast friends. We carried out "expeditions" and "camped" beneath a flying saucer in the playground while eating peanut butter and jelly sandwiches packed by my mother.

When that magical summer ended and Scooter returned home to his parents, I cried like a baby. After all these years, I have never forgotten him. Now, as a grown gay man, I sometimes wonder if Scooter was my first crush.

I was born and raised in the Midwest but have some family roots in Appalachia, a region of America that is too often forgotten. Much of *Holler* derives from the unconquerable spirit of the wild and wonderful people of West Virginia, as well as that of my own relations throughout Missouri, Tennessee, Kentucky and Virginia.

Back when my family first visited Appalachia, I was struck by its graceful green mountains, beautiful mists and lush hollows, much like Javari is in this novel. I also remember meeting African American relatives there who were so light in complexion that I mistakenly thought they were white.

One even had freckles.

Growing up, I was blessed that my family gifted me as much of the world as they could. My parents led us all over our country. I've often said that travel is vital food for a child, and I passionately believe these early family excursions—camping, road trips, airplane rides and cruising the Missouri and Mississippi rivers on our boat—fed my instincts as a storyteller and future writer.

Speaking of writing, I am forever thankful to friends, colleagues and new acquaintances for their encouragement and support in my creation of this novel. I am appreciative for feedback from Telinda "Lin" Forney, executive director of the Pigeon Community Multicultural Development Center in Waynesville, North Carolina; Dr. Cicero M. Fain III, PhD; Dr. William H. "Bill" Turner, author of *The Harlan Renaissance;* and his son, J. K. Turner.

A very special thanks to my editor, Nancy Siscoe at Knopf, for her expert notes, insights, understanding and patience. And also to my literary agent, Steven Malk of Writers House, for being so great at everything he does. Additionally, I thank the skillful team of professionals and creatives at Knopf and Penguin Random House for their commitment over the years.

I especially want to thank my best friend for decades, Etefia Umana Sr., to whom I have dedicated this novel. When we were teenagers—and I had not yet "come out" as gay—Etefia, who is heterosexual, had an intuition about me. He would often quip about my then-hidden queerness, encouraging me to just be myself, which I eventually did.

Etefia was truly affirming and supportive during an era when many people were still quite homophobic. Times have improved since those days, but I will always remember that

Etefia was ahead of *his* time when it came to acceptance and unconditional friendship.

He is more than a best friend; he is family.

One final story note: that fanny pack Javari's mother duct-taped together was a real thing. My own mother made the same for me when I was a teenager leaving on a solo trip to Europe for the first time. She was petrified I would get mugged and be left to perish on some Parisian sidewalk.

I made it back.

Love you, Mom.

Wildment!
David Barclay Moore
Los Angeles, 2022